Praise for *The Rush*

"Michelle Prak doesn't give you a minute to catch your breath on this Australian outback rollercoaster. Compelling and explosive: you won't be able to put this book down."

Hayley Scrivenor, author of *Dirt Town*

"An electrifying outback thriller that's unlike anything I've read—I couldn't put it down. *The Rush* will make you rethink your next road trip."

Mark Brandi, author of *Wimmera*

"This has to be the most terrifying book I've read in years! Michelle is a very assured writer, and her characters are so believable. I genuinely cared whether they lived or died, which is what made the book so deliciously tense."

Shelley Burr, author of *Wake*

"An utterly chilling read with an unexpected twist, this crime novel is hard to put down."

Vikki Petraitis, author of *The Unbelieved*

"*The Rush* flips the trope with sudden floods, then piles on the threats for its women heroes . . . Like a river in full flood, Michelle Prak's heart-pounding debut thriller sweeps the reader along through masterful twists all the way to its shattering ending."

Greg Woodland, author of *The Night Whistler*

"What a rollercoaster ride . . . I loved it! Michelle Prak shows outback Australia in all its dangerous glory, a place to which villains are drawn and where heroes are made."

Kelli Hawkins, author of *Other People's Houses*

"Taut, unpredictable, terrifying; the uniquely Australian weather and landscape are both joyful and become an unwitting accomplice. Michelle Prak weaves such a suspenseful story that you might never want to be alone or isolated again."

Neela Janakiramanan, author of *The Registrar*

"Great characters and a wicked plot. A haunting road trip through the outback with a terrifying finale. I loved this book."

Tim Ayliffe, author of *The Enemy Within*

THE RUSH

A NOVEL

MICHELLE PRAK

CROOKED
LANE

NEW YORK

Copyright © 2024 by Michelle Jean Prak

Published in the United States by Crooked Lane Books, an imprint of The Quick Brown Fox & Company LLC.

Crooked Lane Books and its logo are trademarks of The Quick Brown Fox & Company LLC.

Library of Congress Catalog-in-Publication data available upon request.

ISBN (hardcover): 978-1-63910-716-2
ISBN (ebook): 978-1-63910-717-9

Cover design by Luke Causby

Printed in the United States.
  .

www.crookedlanebooks.com

Crooked Lane Books
34 West 27th St., 10th Floor
New York, NY 10001

First Edition: May 2024

10 9 8 7 6 5 4 3 2 1

PROLOGUE

Tuesday, February 7
6 PM

"THAT SKY COULD be trouble. We better hustle."

Quinn Durand climbs into her four-wheel drive, and Bronte, panting, springs over to her. Quinn checks her phone. She's spent too much time at the farmhouse and now curses quietly. No reception; network's flaky already. She'd checked the storm updates regularly for the first few hours. When did she forget?

She starts the engine and heads to the gates, black poles in the distance. The horizon is an otherworldly purple, and rain clouds, woven tightly together, bring forth an early night. The sun would usually be blazing for another few hours, but it's being outgunned.

At the gates, Quinn turns left to head back to the Pindarry, gripping the steering wheel just like her mother coached her. "Both hands on the wheel, love. If you have an accident, it'll be hours before any help arrives." The dirt on either side of the road is orange, and beyond it there's scratchy saltbush squatting in orderly lines as far as the eye can see. The sunlight grows harsher each year, and there will come a time when even the tough scrub can't put up a fight. This prickly field will survive for now, though. By tonight, rain will bounce onto the hard earth like pebbles.

The water is welcome, yet it seems this region never gets the balance right. Earlier, radio reports predicted that roads would be swamped and towns cut off. Quinn's heart beats faster. She was eleven years old during the last flood, and her father was still alive. She remembers racing beneath the rain, giggling and shouting, shadowed by the family's dogs, their teeth snapping at each other in contagious excitement. Her mother laughed, spinning with her arms out like a movie star. Quinn had never seen a wider smile on her face. "Think of the rainwater tanks!" her mother cried.

That downpour continued for another day, and then another, and soon the dancing and smiling stopped. Her father and his team trudged around with scowling faces and dripping hats. "Nothing but water and dead animals," he said on the phone. They lost more than half their cattle to drowning and something Quinn found hard to pronounce back then—hypothermia. Crews of neighbors and volunteers banded together with bulldozers and excavators for the dreadful task of burying carcasses.

A decade later, and back into consecutive years of drought, that flood is a bleak memory. The local landowners crave rain once again, as it's essential to their livelihoods, yet it still unsettles Quinn.

The car cabin darkens and fat drops splat on the windscreen, early warnings of what's to come. The wipers smear dust across the glass, as messy as a child's finger painting. Bronte turns to her with anxious brown eyes. The dog has been with Quinn since she was a red-and-blond pup and travels everywhere with her.

"It's all right, girl."

There's still time to reach the Pindarry before the sun disappears.

Only this morning, she helped Matt and Andrea fill sandbags and stack them against walls, leaving an emergency pile near the pub's entrance for easy access while they were unsure where they might be needed. They have enough food if the storm leaves them isolated for a few days. They have enough for the next few weeks—that's always the way out here. Quinn doesn't know how she'll cope, being holed up with her employers and their toddler son, Ethan. They're nice people, calm and polite even during the pub's busiest times, yet it's their home and Quinn needs her alone time. That was another reason to spend most of the day at the old house. Bit by bit, she's been packing up the rooms, removing three generations of the Durand family. She's stopped consulting with her mother and brother, who no longer want to talk about what to keep and what to throw away. They're scattered across the continent now, each in a different home, starting new lives. They don't understand the comfort Quinn finds here—early evenings on the cement verandah, the feel of the February breeze on her neck.

Each time Quinn returns to the farm, she retrieves items to stow in her room at the pub. Today it was more photo albums, plus some of her father's tools, which Matt may like. And her father's rifle. She isn't sure what to do with that. Perhaps Ryan will want it. Her father taught them both how to use it many years ago. For now, it's zipped in a gun bag lying along the length of the boot.

Quinn knows the bends and dips of the road so well she jokes that she could drive it blindfolded. So when an alien mound appears on the shoulder up ahead, she slows and squints through the drizzle. It could be a dead roo, but there haven't been kangaroos in this district for a long time. There's nothing for them here. Is it a bag of rubbish?

Bronte whines and scrabbles across the seat nervously as the four-wheel drive decelerates. Quinn buzzes down her window, and flecks of rain fly into her face. The air is still warm. She slowly passes the hump, staring.

"Shit," she whispers.

It's a body, a bizarre and fragile sight, its head vulnerable on the ground.

She pulls over and switches off the engine, reaching for the worn Akubra that will give coverage from the rain.

She shoves Bronte away. "You stay here." If this is what it looks like, her red heeler shouldn't be sniffing around.

Rain peppers Quinn as she runs back to the body. As she nears, her steps slow, her eyes widen. She watches for movement, some sign of life. It's an adult, arms and legs motionless, unshielded from the barrage above. She gasps at the pale face, bruised and swelling. A male, heavyset, his eyes sealed shut. She lowers herself, crouching within arm's reach, finally seeing the chest rise and fall beneath a rain-sodden T-shirt.

"Hey, can you hear me?" Her voice sounds girlish to her own ears.

Bronte yaps from the car as Quinn scans the area. There's no vehicle, no skid marks, no broken glass. No other bodies. How did this man get here? It's like he's dropped from the sky. The Pindarry is another ninety kilometers west, and the nearest working property is seventy kilometers to the southwest. The nearest town is Minnarie, 202 kilometers south, and that's little more than a fuel stop and a dying store. Quinn and this man are the only two people for miles around.

Whoever this is, wherever he came from, he needs medical attention, urgently.

Then his arm flings up and a cold hand clutches Quinn's wrist.

She shrieks and tries to pull away, hears Bronte's faraway barking. Her heels dig into the ground, but the stranger's hand is a vise she can't break.

1

Hayley

Monday, February 6
9:30 AM

SOMEBODY HAS TO be first in the water, and Hayley is determined it will be her. She grins, not in excitement at the impending splash but in anticipation of forming bonds with the others. They'll remember this later, they'll remember spontaneous Hayley, beach lover and the heart of the group.

She kicks the thongs from her feet and dashes across the sand, clumsily at first over the deeper, fluffier mounds where she threatens to stumble, then more swiftly over the compressed layer, as hard as marble near the foamy waves. The sea comes in folds, a mostly predictable rhythm, and Hayley heaves her legs higher to brace for the chill. She isn't shy about letting out a squeal as her skin meets the ocean and she turns to catch the reactions of the others.

Scott stands back, as expected, arms crossed. She knows exactly what he's thinking. *Why is Hayley acting like this? Why put on a show?* Of the three of them, her boyfriend was the one she was most concerned about when she posed this idea, this romantic notion of meeting here at the beginning of their road trip.

"If we start at the beach, then it truly is a south-to-north journey," Hayley had explained. "What could be better? We'll go from sea to sea. It's much more fun than just leaving our house in the morning and heading straight into traffic."

Now Livia approaches, her face tucked into a smile. Livia wears no-nonsense boxy canvas shorts and a cream-colored T-shirt that might make other girls fade into the background. On Livia, the clothes reveal strong brown limbs that move with ease and Hayley can't tear her eyes away. There's nothing tentative or awkward about Livia—she's fluid. The morning sunlight gleams on her cropped hair, and her wraparound sunglasses are a new, protective climate-control series. As she enters the sea, Livia clutches her arms to her chest in a dramatic shiver, and the girls beam at each other, standing calf deep.

"Are you coming?" Hayley calls to Scott.

He pulls a face. Joost stands alongside him, the difference in their height comical. Scott isn't exactly short, but he'd never be described as a tall guy either. Joost—well, he'd be described as *that super-tall Dutch guy*. He whips out a hand and slaps Scott's arm as if to tag him in a game of chase, and Scott steps back and scowls. Joost hasn't noticed; he pumps his legs and sprints to the water. They all watch as his spindly limbs fling from side to side, carrying him over the first set of waves until he's waist deep. Then he draws his arms together into an arrowhead and plunges in.

"Show-off," Livia says in her Brazilian accent.

Hayley cackles loudly, clutching her stomach. Joost reappears, ginger hair plastered to his forehead, then dives beneath the water again.

Livia wades closer. "This is lovely."

Hayley wants to say *You're lovely too*. She holds back. One step at a time, she tells herself. She has a good feeling about Livia and doesn't want to fluster her newest friend.

There are fishers on the jetty a hundred meters away, holding rods. Indigo stick figures who may or may not be watching them. Wary seagulls glide overhead. Hayley's legs have adjusted to the coolness. She draws her feet along the ocean floor, relishing the grit on her soles. How perfect this is. It was right to bring them here.

When she looks at Scott, he's walking away, head down. He plonks himself where the sand meets the concrete wall, settling into a sliver of shade. Even this early, it's more than thirty degrees, and pasty Scott isn't used to being out in the sun. Hayley watches as he removes his spectacles and examines them. She won't leave the water to go check on him, won't let him spoil this.

Hayley and Scott scraped together the money for this trip, their first holiday since they started dating two years ago. Living in a share house together and about to face their third and final year of an accounting degree, Hayley had itched for an adventure. This drive from Adelaide to Darwin wasn't the most exotic choice; it was one of the cheapest. And Hayley hopes it will help assuage her guilt at not having seen much of her own country. She's tired of hearing international students' travel stories in class and not being a part of it. It took several dedicated months to convince Scott it was the perfect time for a road trip.

"When we graduate and get jobs, we'll only have four weeks' holiday a year," she'd said. "That's not much."

"Gee, thanks for the reminder," Scott said.

"C'mon, a road trip will be fun."

"We don't have the money."

"It's not expensive! We don't need hotels, we just need a tent."

"You're forgetting the biggest cost."

"What?"

"Fuel."

"We can get a few others to drive with us, share the cost."

Scott made the same tart expression he always did when Hayley suggested anything new. "I guess we could do that, but who are we going to invite? Everyone we know is either busy or I wouldn't want to be stuck in a car with them."

"Let's advertise on a travel website or forum or something."

"That's how you meet serial killers."

Hayley had slapped his arm. "Stop it! I'm being serious. I wanna do this."

"All right. There's a forum I've heard about . . ."

And so Scott eventually helped Hayley to plan, even arranged to borrow his grandfather's four-wheel drive and his sister's tent. They booked leave from their casual jobs— Hayley's in a doughnut store and Scott in supermarket night-fill. Hayley joined a backpackers' online forum and browsed the threads.

"We don't even have to advertise," she told Scott. "There's plenty of people here looking for a ride."

They found Livia first, meeting her in the lobby of her youth hostel on a sticky Adelaide evening in January. The corridor was crammed with vending machines selling choco-late and instant noodles, and young people strode past, all looking impossibly cosmopolitan, fit, and full of purpose. Hayley studied the bulletin board on one wall, with its fly-ers for bus companies, surfing lessons, and budget Kangaroo Island tours.

At twenty-four, Livia was the oldest of their bunch. In army-surplus pants, black boots, and a buzz cut, she looked to Hayley like she'd stepped out of a *Terminator* movie.

"What would you think if I cut off my hair like that?" Hayley asked Scott later. Her hair was a geometric bob, crafted to help her look like the online gamer chicks Scott admired, a difficult style to maintain.

"Don't shave your head," Scott warned. "You wouldn't be able to get away with it. You've got a completely different shape."

Livia had been in Sydney for an international climate summit for young people, a rolling event held on a different continent each year. Sydney was her third. She had booked a spot on an environmental activist ship out of Darwin for the end of February, where the plan was to disrupt illegal fishing.

"Wow, you're a world traveler," Hayley had said. "A real adventurer. Aren't you worried it'll be dangerous on the boat?"

"Dangerous? You mean, on the ocean?" Livia had directed her dark eyes to Hayley.

"I mean—the fishermen, won't they get angry at you? And what if there are pirates?"

Livia had smiled. "I don't doubt they'll be pissed off, but we can't stop because the bad guys might scare us, right?"

"How are you able to afford all this travel?" Scott asked, and Hayley kicked him under the table.

"I won a scholarship from a climate fund, and my parents help too."

"Amazing. Awesome," Hayley said, slurping her bubble tea.

Livia asked about the size of the car, whether they had experience changing a tire, and if they were bringing additional fuel.

"All good ideas," Hayley said to Scott later on, although none had crossed their minds.

"She's clever. She'd be good to take with us," he said.

It had taken more time to settle on Joost.

Most of the other applicants were female, and Scott refused to "travel with a bunch of girls." Yet when they examined the online profiles of the males, Hayley was uneasy with their smiles—too leering, too polished, or too fake. She said she didn't want to "travel with a sleaze." In Joost's online photo, he was clean-cut and beaming, taking a selfie with the canals of Amsterdam behind him.

"How about him?" Hayley had tapped at the screen.

Scott leaned closer to read the profile. "Dutch. Most of them speak English, right?"

"I think so."

"I guess he could be okay."

Joost had jumped up and pulled the chair out for Hayley when they met at a city café. He poured water for everyone while she stared at his Apple watch. He had a quick smile and a vitality that made Hayley sit to attention as he described how his parents were funding his gap year from an engineering degree back in the Netherlands. He gave the right answers to all of their questions, and there was nothing they could fault.

"I'm not sure I like him," Scott had said when they were alone again.

"Are you kidding? What's the problem?"

"Don't you think he's a bit of a dick?"

"No way—he was so polite. He was lovely! If we don't choose someone soon, we'll never go."

So Scott relented, and Joost joined the gang.

Hayley watches as Joost returns from his swim, jerking his head left and right to dislodge water from his prominent ears.

She turns toward Scott, who's sitting in the distance with his hands flopped over his knees, surprised that he's not staring at his phone. He'll find this holiday challenging because it means less screen time and more socializing, more time spent in nature. He's going to miss his online buddies, his gaming console. Scott spends most days staring into his laptop, and it's not because he's devoted to his studies. This trip will be good for him. He'll get some sun on his skin. It will be good for both of them, Hayley thinks. They might actually begin talking to each other again.

"We should go," she says.

"I agree. This beach is nice, but we have a schedule," Livia says.

"First stop, Port Augusta!"

"How far is that?"

"Almost four hours."

"Four hours. This country is so big."

"Isn't Brazil big too?"

"Sure—but I don't drive around Brazil."

There's thrashing behind them, and as Hayley turns to look, she's assaulted by a wall of icy water. Joost laughs with a surprisingly high-pitched staccato, clutching his pale belly. Hayley giggles to show she can take a joke, blinking the salt from her eyes.

"You are not swimming?" Joost asks.

"I just wanted to dip my feet," Hayley says. Her vision blurs, though rubbing her eyes will only make it worse.

"This ocean is beautiful. You Aussies are very lucky."

"Thank you." Hayley beams as if she's had a hand in the water quality.

Joost bends, grinning, fingertips drumming the water, poised to unleash another splash.

Livia glares. "Don't you dare."

There are patches of pink on Joost's cheeks, and although he's just nineteen, his reddish hair seems to be receding. He grins ruefully, straightens, and lumbers back to the sand. Hayley can't imagine he fares well in real heat. She watches the way his cotton clothes suck at his skin, then remembers her towel is in the boot of the car, folded at the bottom of her backpack. That's okay. Nothing can spoil this moment.

She walks onto the baked sand, pauses with arms raised high, and turns like she's on a slow carousel, the sun fuzzy on the other side of her eyelids.

CHAPTER

2

Andrea

Tuesday, February 7
3 PM

ANDREA STANDS OUTSIDE the Pindarry and waves. It's a routine that can make her feel foolish, as if she's imitating royalty on a palace balcony, but it's not easy to get tourists to come out this far. She wants to make sure they tell family and friends about the "charming and friendly outback pub" they visited.

"Bye! *Bye!*"

Ethan bounds along the verandah, mimicking her farewell, but the three-year-old is studying the wooden boards more than watching the departing guests, focused on his next two-footed leap. Andrea smiles as she watches him, his feet strapped into green sneakers, elbows tucked by his side, mouth puckered between chubby cheeks.

The two rental vehicles fade away in swirls of dust, and she shifts the damp curls from the back of her neck and studies the sky. It's hard to believe rain is on the way. Overhead, it's still blinding bright, and the only clouds seem to be experimental brushstrokes whisked across a canvas. Hopefully, Quinn won't take too long at the farm and get caught in the weather. Andrea looks down, ruminating over the sandbags positioned either side of the double front door and stacked in piles at the far end of the verandah. Surely they won't get that much rainfall? Still, the verandah is only a step above the dirt car park in front of them, so it pays to be careful.

"Okay, matey, let's go inside," Andrea says.

Ethan keeps bouncing and moves toward her, the only acknowledgment that he's heard his mother. She waits at the door, her eyes adjusting to the cool shadows.

The front bar is a long, rectangular space, with wooden tables and bench seats set beneath windows that overlook the shady verandah. It's a rare day when all the tables are full apart from regional horse race meetings, outback car rallies, or organized tours. Then, they can meet people from all over the world. Matt said it would be the best part of managing this place. These days, Andrea knows that no matter where people come from, they still take the same time dithering over the menu and they still leave the same mess behind. During busy periods, she and Matt often hire young travelers for two-week stints. Quinn is their only full-time employee, and the three of them capably share the workload of the isolated pub.

Matt is collecting plates from the furthest booth, balancing them in the crook of one arm. He's wearing his uniform of denim jeans, scuffed brown boots, and checked shirt with the sleeves rolled up—he'd never buy a short-sleeved shirt. He heaps clinking cutlery on top and reaches for an empty coffee mug.

"I'll get those," Andrea says.

"Thanks, love." They weave around each other, well practiced at this dance.

Her husband retreats to the kitchen through a door on the other side of the bar.

"Want to help Mummy?" Andrea asks Ethan. He shakes his head. "I don't blame ya." She laughs, watching him scramble to a table where he's left an arrangement of toy animals.

Andrea piles coffee cups, then pulls a washcloth from her back pocket and swishes it across the tabletop before moving behind the bar. They installed a shiny new coffee machine when they took on the pub lease, Andrea's idea, and it has paid off. Now they sell safety-conscious travelers more lattes than lager. Andrea scrubs the cups and, once they're shining, places them in a stack.

Matt appears in the doorway, freckled arms hanging by his sides, and Andrea knows he's wondering about other chores to be carried out.

"Whatever happens, we've got plenty of supplies," he says.

"Yep," she says.

"The cars are tucked away."

"Uh-huh."

"The outdoor bins are tied up. The sheds are closed. We're sandbagged up the Yazoo. What else needs doing, love?"

"What about that last bloke?" Andrea isn't keen on being confined with strangers during the coming storm. That is, if the pub does get cut off. It might not even happen. Andrea's new to this remote part of South Australia and listens to the experts; still, she wonders if all this preparation might be for nothing.

"Shit. I forgot about him!"

"He'll wanna get ahead of the weather."

"I reckon you're right." Matt moves close and gives her a peck on the forehead. He ruffles Ethan's fine hair, then strides out of the door to the guest rooms.

"The huts" are six transportable units with just enough room for a double bed to be wedged inside, offering a comfortable enough last-minute bed for visitors, especially the kind who spend unplanned hours at the bar and can't drive any farther. Like the middle-aged bloke from Sydney who arrived yesterday. He seemed nice, although he did share long and boring stories.

"C'mon, darling, let's go out the back," Andrea tells Ethan. Even though he's heavy and has been walking for years, she scoops him onto a hip and ferries him through the kitchen. It's a large area with a walk-in cool room, benchtops lining green walls, and a tall table in the center. One door leads to an outdoor bay with two upright freezers and an aging power generator. Then it's a short corridor and one step down into the family's living quarters.

This rear half of the stone-and-brick building has two bedrooms of equal size and one bathroom. There's a square living area in between, with no windows. Andrea likes the setup because it helps them escape the harsh sun. Some nights, when Ethan's in bed, she and Matt squeeze onto the soft couch with Quinn at one end, put their feet up on the coffee table, and watch movies together. Matt always falls asleep halfway through the movie, leaving Andrea and Quinn to discuss the plot quietly. Andrea wasn't sure about a live-in employee, but Quinn is more a family member now, a niece, and she's grateful for the company.

Ethan is squirming for freedom. Andrea sets him down and watches him race plastic animals over the furniture. There's still kitchen cleaning to do, but she sinks onto an armchair, legs outstretched. Beyond Ethan's happy humming, there's not a sound. It's too hot and oppressive for any birds to be singing, and there's nobody drinking in the bar. There's no drone of traffic, no planes flying overhead. There are no friends knocking on the door or phoning to arrange a playdate. Andrea relished the peace at first, but lately it seems thicker, more constricting, slowing everything down. It's a growing void, and she's beginning to feel untethered.

Matt loves the solitude, the tranquil expanse that surrounds them, the separation from their nearest neighbors. Funnily enough, he has become louder out here. It's as if he's found himself again, lost some earlier inhibitions. He greets visitors loudly, laughs and tells boisterous jokes from behind the bar, clomps around the house with Ethan on his back. He even snores more loudly. Andrea has done the opposite: retreated inside herself, become more contemplative, more hesitant. Sometimes, when their little crew is alone at the pub, Matt's voice startles her.

She rises and walks into her bedroom, stands in front of the tall mirror propped in a corner. She's wearing denim shorts, sneakers with socks, and a baggy red top. Her friends back in Adelaide would shudder at this outfit, although they haven't seen her in months—in some cases, years—and aren't likely to anytime soon. She steps closer, threading her fingers through her hair, checking the strands of gray creeping through. She'll need to dye it again soon, a tedious task she doesn't look forward to. Out here, she's her own hairdresser.

She turns side-on, places her hands over her midriff. It won't be long before the baby bump might be apparent to Matt. Being pregnant with Ethan was incredible—the persistent wriggling and pushing inside of her. It was a thrilling time and everything she and Matt wanted. But a second child? She hasn't told anyone, not even her husband. The choices are daunting. She isn't ready for this. Not a newborn, not at the Pindarry.

Hayley

Monday, February 6
12:30 PM

HAYLEY'S FEET ARE propped on the dashboard. She feels rebellious and carefree, and she's never felt either of those things before. The sun bounces on the windscreen, and she adjusts her pink sunglasses, gleefully purchased for this trip. When she put them on, Scott raised his eyebrows but stayed silent.

He nods at her shoes now. "Do you mind?"

"What?" Hayley says.

"This isn't our car, remember."

"I'm not doing any damage."

"Hales, it makes me uncomfortable. What if I have to brake suddenly?"

She pokes her tongue at Scott and brings her feet back to the floor. It's true, they borrowed this four-wheel drive, but it's old and they can't do much to ruin it. This type of diesel vehicle will be outlawed soon, and Scott's grandfather hasn't been able to sell it. He said they may as well take it for one last trip.

Hayley felt like an impostor when she first climbed in. What did she know about four-wheel drives and outback touring? The tires are massive; there's a bull bar on the front and a roof rack overhead. The seats are worn soft, and the leather around the gear stick is cracked. There's a brown stain over her door; maybe someone splashed coffee there. Coffee may be the odor Hayley is picking up; then again, the smell could be Joost in the back. She hopes not. Hayley doesn't want to see any flaws in her new travel buddies, yet there was a whiff of something from him when they rendezvoused this morning.

In the car park at the beach, before they truly started out, Scott took ages adjusting the driver's seat and the mirrors, nudging them centimeter by centimeter. Now his lips are pressed and his shoulders are taut. While the car is well suited to their journey and Scott said he was keen to do most of the driving, Hayley can feel his tension. He doesn't drive often, and certainly not a bulky vehicle like this. Their usual transport is the metro train that ushers them from their suburban share house to the uni campus.

Hayley touches Scott's thigh softly. "You all good?"

"Yeah, I'm fine," Scott says. He twitches his leg, and Hayley removes her hand.

She studies her nails for a moment, newly manicured, such a rare treat. Was she right to choose Neon Blue Shimmer, or should she have gone with Cherise Pink? Either way, she tries not to fuss with them too much, worried they might break. She stares at the old radio in the console, counts its corners, including the inner and outer edges. One, two, three, four . . . five, six, seven, eight. Clockwise and counterclockwise. Then again to double-check.

When she recognizes what she's doing, she moves her gaze to the flat landscape outside. They pass a patch of charred ground—fields burned by recent summer fires. Occasionally, there are crumbling houses, sometimes with a rusted-out vehicle sagging beside them. Even more rarely, clusters of trees hug the verge, several with blackened bark. Hayley wishes she knew what the trees are called. A white pipeline accompanies them now, and she can't recall where it began or how long it has been beside them. Where does it come from and where is it going? She strokes her smooth nails and hopes Livia and Joost don't ask. Painted black letters on the pipeline flash by: THERE IS NO PLANET B.

"How long until we reach Port Augusta?" Livia asks.

Hayley consults her timetable. "Approximately fifty minutes."

For weeks, Hayley has been plotting their route, maintaining a colorful chart on her travel app, adding and subtracting attractions to visit, estimating travel times and stopovers, using Livia's Darwin deadline as the end point. The 2,800-kilometer-long Stuart Highway is the spine of their trip, the road that bisects Australia. There will be occasional forays along minor roads to see sights like the Dingo Fence, vast salt lakes, and ancient rock formations. And there's a charming outback pub called the Pindarry Hotel Hayley's keen to visit, near some hot springs. She's saved short descriptions of each spot and has read them over and over again. She thinks about the photos she'll take, the trove of experiences to showcase on her Instagram account, the hashtags she'll finally be able to use. How jealous the other third-year accounting students will be.

"Can we listen to something else?" Scott nods at the Bluetooth speaker nestled between them, currently piping Hayley's playlist.

"You don't like Marshmello?" she says.

"I'm tired of it, that's all."

"Of course, sorry, I didn't mean to hog the music . . ." Hayley hunches over her screen, flicks through her sound library, and finds one of Scott's lists. A Pop Smoke song fills the car.

Scott bops his head. "That's more like it."

"Hell yeah," Joost agrees.

Livia presses earbuds into her ears, and Hayley wonders if she was tired of Marshmello too. What does the Brazilian listen to? Perhaps artists that Hayley hasn't even heard of. She makes a mental note to ask later.

Hayley opens the camera on her phone and points the screen out the window as blurred yellow fields rush by.

"What are you doing?" Scott says.

"Taking photos."

"There's nothing there."

"Don't be silly; there's scenery. Plenty of it."

Scott nods at the road ahead. "Take a picture of that."

Hayley looks up in time to see a bloodied kangaroo carcass, a pair of black crows soaring away from their prize.

"Scott!" she complains. "Don't be horrible."

"Oh, that's sad," Livia says.

"Got hit by a car." Scott is expressionless.

"There are heaps of kangaroos, right?" Livia says. "I heard they're in, like, plague proportions?"

Unsure of the answer, Hayley is grateful when Joost jumps in.

"That's right. They are a pest. The government culls them."

"I hope they do it in a humane way," Livia says.

"How would that be?"

"You know—quickly. With precision. No poisoning or traps, no suffering."

Joost looks at Scott. "Have you ever hunted kangaroos?"

"No." Scott frowns. "Why would I?"

"I thought it was a hobby out here."

Hayley shakes her head. "There's no way we would do that."

"A few years ago, I went duck shooting with my grand-dad," Scott says coolly.

Hayley stares at her boyfriend. "Please tell me you're joking! You've never mentioned it before."

"It's never come up."

"Duck shooting, roo shooting, it's all cruel."

"It might be like a safari," Joost says. "A very interesting, unique experience."

"That's messed up." Livia sounds stern. "It's inhumane, hunting innocent animals for sport."

"But if they have to be killed anyway? They are ruining the environment; you know that yourself."

Hayley counts the corners of the radio again, willing the conversation to take a different direction.

As if he's read her thoughts, Scott says, "I'm gonna check the wheel alignment when we get to Port Augusta."

"Why? You checked everything before we left."

"It . . . doesn't feel right." Scott nods toward the steering wheel as if the problem is obvious to everyone.

Joost shifts in his seat, and his knees prod Hayley's back. "Sorry," he says.

"I'm fine," she says.

He turns to Scott. "If there is something wrong with the alignment, what could we do? Are you going to fix it?"

"Not sure," Scott says, "but I'd rather know before we drive a thousand k's into the outback and the car breaks down, leaving us stranded. Wouldn't you?"

"Would we get our money back?" Joost chuckles.

Hayley makes a laughing noise, even though it isn't funny. They've pooled money for fuel, and while she's in charge of the funds, this isn't a moneymaking exercise. All her intentions are for a perfect, glorious trip through the center of Australia with new friends. They're in this together, even if she and Scott organized the transport and itinerary. After all, they'll be sharing a small cabin over the next twelve days. Already Hayley regards them as a team, the squad of friends she's been missing since high school.

Livia taps at her window. "Hey. Hills."

Hayley turns to look.

"The Flinders Ranges!" Hayley is pleased to recognize them. "Stunning, aren't they?"

The ranges rise nobly from the plains, forming a fortress-like line. To Hayley, they are peaceful, mysterious, keepers of centuries-old secrets. The crevices between the ranges are bathed in purple shadow, providing cooling nooks for animals. Or for creatures from fairy tales.

"I thought they would be bigger," Joost says.

"That's just the *start* of them." Hayley says. "They're hundreds of kilometers long. My parents took me when I was eight or nine. You'd be surprised at how green it looks in there—almost a different country to where we are now. There's these winding roads . . . it's so scenic."

"If you say so. They are not exactly the Alps."

"They're bloody amazing, aren't they, Scott? There's also Devil's Peak; it has a spooky ridge that juts out. It's awesome."

"Yeah, it's okay." Scott doesn't turn his head to look.

"Let's drive closer," suggests Joost.

"That's not our route."

"They are *right there!*"

"This is Australia, mate, not Holland. It'll take ages to go *right there.*"

"How long?"

"It'll add two hours, at least—one hour in, one hour back out."

"Bugger!" Joost says, and they laugh at his Australianism.

"I know it sucks, but we can't stop and see everything," Hayley says. "We gotta stick to the plan, right? Stay on the highway, get to Darwin on time."

"Absolutely!" Livia says. "I have a boat to catch, remember, guys?"

The boys seem to relax when they hear Livia's Brazilian lilt. Livia could tell them the engine was on fire and they'd nod and smile.

Hayley checks her phone. She read they might lose network coverage when they got farther north but couldn't quite believe it. How could black spots exist with the technology they have now? She opens her weather app and turns in her seat to face the others.

"Hey, that rain they forecast—it might arrive earlier than we thought."

"It never really rains in Australia, though, right?" Joost says.

"Not like Europe, I guess."

"And it's summer." He pronounces it *shummer*.

"Remember a little thing called climate change?" Livia arches her eyebrows.

Joost makes a show of checking the time on his watch. "It only took you three hours to mention it. I thought you would bring it up sooner."

Livia waves her hands around. "What other topic is there?"

"Don't you get bored by it?"

"I'm a climate activist. What do you think?"

The Dutchman snorts.

"It's our future, literally!" Livia insists. "Everyone needs to fight for our planet. It's the only thing that truly matters."

"Hey, everything is working out fine," Joost says. "We are just a teeny bit warmer . . . and everyone likes warm weather, am I right?"

"It's not just warmer weather. In some parts of the planet it's actually colder; that's why they call it *climate change*. It affects animals, insects, plants, crops, everything, the whole ecosystem. Most people don't get it because it's coming in increments."

"Yeah," Hayley pitches in, "you might feel we're doing okay—but what about our children and grandchildren and great-grandchildren?"

"We will not be around to hear our grandchildren complaining," Joost says. "Whatever happens to them will happen."

Hayley gasps. "That's a terrible thing to say. I'm always thinking about the droughts and bushfires and seas rising and what it means for people in the future. It freaks me out. I know I should be doing more about it, more than just recycling and using metal straws—"

"Ignore him. He's teasing, aren't you, Joost?" Livia stares out of her window.

"The Dutch reclaimed plenty of land from the sea," he says. "I am sure future generations will work something out too."

"Maybe you Dutch can help the Pacific nations that are sinking into the ocean," Scott says.

"Yeah, why not. They keep asking you Aussie neighbors for help, and they are still waiting, because your politicians are racist."

"Joost, why don't you shut the—"

"Please!" Hayley interrupts. "Don't argue. I want us to have a nice time together. This trip is so cool. Isn't it cool? Look around. There's hardly anyone else on the road, and we're camping out under the stars tonight. I'm looking forward to this."

Everyone falls silent as Pop Smoke's next track fills the cabin, the thumping bass notes incongruous with the calm bushland outside. They pass a WATER RESTRICTIONS IN FORCE sign. Hayley watches the rise and fall of the Flinders Ranges through Scott's window, her fingers tapping her thighs in their usual sequence, a calming undulation.

4

Livia

Monday, February 6
1 PM

THE PETROL STATION sits beneath a vast iron verandah over a concrete forecourt. It's a square white building with tinted windows you can barely see through, the customers shifting silhouettes behind the glass. Camera hanging from her neck, Livia walks past the air pumps and two battered lavatory doors to the back of the building, swatting the persistent flies circling her face. The verandah and concrete finishes, and her boots crunch over stones the color of dirty snow.

Livia is used to high temperatures in Brazil. This is different, more intense, the sun a relentless heat lamp on her head. And, if she's honest, she spends more time indoors when she's at home. Her parents like it that way, safe and secure in the temperature-controlled family apartment on the tenth floor, each day unfolding with comforting routine. Even her university course is entirely virtual. That's one of the reasons she loves to travel—to move in the real world while trying to convince herself she can help save it.

She stops at a waist-high wire fence. There's a wall of prickly bushes on the other side, growing in the most vibrant red dirt she has ever seen, a line of bull ants charting a determined course over it. She takes out her phone. It's close to midnight in Curitiba, and while her parents will be asleep, her younger sister Camila might not. It takes just a second for her call to be answered.

"Why are you still up?"

"Oh, olá to you too!" Camila says.

"What are you doing?"

"Nothing much, sitting on the balcony, listening to music."

Livia pictures the scene: Camila with her bare feet resting on the table, surrounded by skyscrapers and glittering windows, earbuds in.

"Where are you?" her sister asks.

"A tiny place called Port Augusta."

"Sounds like somewhere in America. Are you sure you're in the right country?"

"Ha! I'm sure. How did it go yesterday?"

Livia has helped plant hundreds of trees in Curitiba. Initially, her family teased her about her idealism, thinking it would be a short-lived interest. Nowadays they're all active in local environmental groups, helping to fundraise and lobby business and civic leaders and enlist other greening volunteers. While Livia travels, her parents and Camila continue the work, sending her regular updates. Yesterday they hosted a seed-raising workshop.

"It went really well," Camila says. "About a dozen people turned up."

"Mmm," Livia grunts. What's *wrong* with people? The turnout should have been better.

They catch up on Camila's basketball and Livia's route for the next few days, before she reluctantly ends the call. "Be good," she says.

"You too. Be careful!" Camila says.

Livia turns so the Flinders Ranges are over her shoulder, taking several selfies with her camera held high. She opens her mouth in a *wow!* smile and turns her head to her best side, then returns the phone to her pocket. She'll post to Instagram when she's back in the car—it's time for more professional photos now. She pulls up her Canon and starts snapping the hills. There's so much horizon, so much space and air, it's difficult to comprehend—no matter how confining that sizzling air may be. Behind the lens, she takes a centering breath. Maybe, if she comes back to Australia, she'll camp in the Flinders Ranges, perhaps even bring Camila along with her. The area is more tree covered than expected, although sections appear fire scorched when she zooms the camera in. There must be all sorts of wildlife in the hills— wallabies, kangaroos, white cockatoos, maybe eagles—and Livia wonders how they're faring. One type of rock wallaby was recently declared extinct, and the thought brings a familiar glumness to her. Species die and she's powerless. But after each climate summit, like the one in Sydney, she's reenergized—meeting committed people like her from all over the world helps her hope.

Livia runs a hand over her short hair. It's incredibly hot, too hot. Time to get back to shade.

Joost is cleaning the windscreen, stretching one sticklike arm far over the glass and back again. Livia's pleased to see him pitch in. She assumed he'd be more indolent, waiting for the others to do the work. Maybe it's his accent with its arrogant, entitled inflection that's hard to hear beyond. She reminds herself to be less judgmental.

Scott and Hayley emerge from the shop. He shoves his wallet into the pocket of his shorts, and Hayley balances an armful of snacks. Hayley is cute, Livia thinks, short and soft bellied, wearing quirky pink sunglasses. Her hair is an unflattering bob, and if Livia were a close friend, she'd suggest Hayley grow it out. She moves slowly and speaks gently but at the same time isn't shy about speaking up and trying to keep everyone happy. Livia likes that. Scott's fringe flops into his eyes, and his thick waist shows all the signs of a uni student who spends days and nights in a chair. The pair mutter to each other, neither of them smiling.

"Everything okay?" Livia asks. "Did you check the . . . wheel alignment?"

"Yeah, yeah, it's looks okay," Scott says.

"I think he should take a break from driving," Hayley says. "It's too much for one person."

"I'm all right."

Hayley looks wounded. "You can't do all the driving, Scott. It's hard to concentrate for so many hours."

He glares ahead, seems to think for a moment. "Fine. I'll drive to the next stop, and then somebody else can take over. Will that make you happy?"

"You said you'd do that when we got to Port Augusta! We're here now—it's time for a swap."

Scott makes a growling noise, wrenches open the driver's side door, and gets behind the steering wheel, ending the argument. Joost is working on the back window now, his T-shirt showing circles of sweat at the underarms.

There's a roar of approaching engines. The girls turn to look, and Joost pauses as six motorcycles cruise in, lining up at the next set of petrol bowsers.

Hayley yanks open her door and lets the snacks spill inside. "C'mon," she urges Livia.

Livia climbs into the hot interior and reaches for her drink bottle as Scott starts the engine and the whoosh of the air conditioner begins. Finished with his cleaning duties, Joost trots toward the bathroom.

When the motorbikes are switched off, their riders amble around in thick protective clothing. How cloying it must be underneath. Just looking at them makes Livia feel stifled. One rider grabs another in a headlock, and it seems to be affectionate wrestling until a punch is thrown. Their friends yell and wrangle them apart.

"Oh god, they're fighting." Hayley slides down in her seat. "What should we do? Do we do anything? Will the staff come out?"

The two men are eventually pulled apart by their mates, thrashing and swearing until one storms off. As he passes the four-wheel drive, Livia stares at the disks in his earlobes. He regards her with unsettling blue eyes, and she fixes her gaze elsewhere. She hears him laugh.

"They make me nervous," Hayley says.

"Don't worry about 'em," Scott says. He removes his glasses, cleans them delicately with a cloth from the glove box. "They're just mucking around."

"They were *fighting*! You saw it."

"They make me nervous too," Livia says.

"I hope they're not traveling north with us," Hayley says. "Can you imagine being in the same campground?"

Scott sighs. "They're just a bunch of mates on a road trip. There's nothing to get in a flap about."

"It's a woman thing," Livia says.

"What does *that* mean?"

"We're aware of our surroundings, all the time. We have to be."

"Don't they have a right to be here? You want them to stay home just because they make you nervous? I thought girls wanted equality—that doesn't sound like equality to me."

"Of course they can go wherever they like. I'm just saying they've triggered our radar, right?" Livia looks at Hayley.

Hayley nods. "Yeah, exactly. They worry me—that's the only way I can explain it."

"Whatever." Scott groans. "Where's Joost? Why's he taking so long?"

"Maybe he's buying deodorant," Hayley murmurs. She turns to Livia. "Do you usually travel alone?"

Livia shakes her head. "I'm usually with a group at a summit or a march. I only take my own side trips afterwards, and even then, I'm never *alone*—I connect with nice people. Like you." The pair grin at each other.

"I really admire what you do," Hayley says. "I went to climate marches in the first year of uni, but I've never been as involved as you. I'm so slack."

"There's plenty of things you can do besides marching. You've seen my blog, right?"

"Yeah, I love it."

"I wrote a Save the Planet series—you should read it. It lists ten simple changes you can make in one week."

Hayley nods. "For sure! I'll bookmark it."

They watch a few of the riders walk into the store while others tend to their motorbikes.

"I like the idea of volunteering overseas, helping villagers find water or working at a nature reserve," Hayley muses. "Maybe after graduation. I haven't even been out of the country yet."

"Never?" Livia has heard Australians like to travel.

Hayley shakes her head. "The furthest I've been is Canberra, and that was a school trip. We went to Parliament House. God, it was boring."

"Where would you like to go?"

"Everywhere! Even Brazil one day. Maybe I could visit you?"

"Absolutely," Livia says, although she's doubtful she'll stay in touch with Hayley after this Stuart Highway trip. It doesn't seem they have much in common.

"Here he is at last," Scott announces loudly.

Joost jogs into view, smile blazing, bony elbows pumping. When he climbs in, his sweaty head almost butts into Livia, and she leans away.

"All right!" he says. "What are we waiting for?"

CHAPTER

5

Hayley

Monday, February 6
1:30 PM

WHEN THEY REACH the 110 kilometer zone north of Port Augusta, the purr of the motorbikes steals up on them. Hayley checks her side mirror. The bikers are trailing like a line of ants. Their engines throb until, one by one, they overtake the car. She sits in discomfort over several minutes, wishing the process were swifter. Why do they travel in packs? The final rider blows a kiss.

"I used to have a motorbike," Joost says.

"I thought you Dutchies rode push-bikes everywhere," Scott says.

"Very funny."

"How do you pedal when you're wearing clogs?"

Hayley monitors the bikes ahead of them. Is this it now—they have to travel behind these blokes? It's horrible timing. Eventually, though, the bikers leave the four-wheel drive in their wake, becoming dots in the gray-road distance.

"Good riddance," she murmurs as the last one vanishes.

"What's your problem?" Scott says.

"I'd just feel better if they're not around."

"Stop being so dramatic."

Hayley grabs a packet of chips, even though she told herself she wouldn't open them for at least another hour.

"Dramatic is fun," Livia pipes up from the back seat. Hayley experiences a burble of happiness because Livia seems to be on her side.

Joost rummages through a small paper bag, holds up a green apple. "Bite, anyone?" They all shake their heads. He begins eating, crunching loud and fast, each bite echoing in Hayley's ears. "How long until Minnarie?" he asks.

"Why? Do you need the toilet already, mate?" Scott says.

"My parents messaged me. They want to know."

"That's nice," Hayley says. "Are your parents worried about you?"

"Of course they are worried. I am trawling the bottom of the world. Surrounded by desert."

"You make it sound miserable," Scott says.

"You can tell your parents we've got another two hours of driving," Hayley says.

Once a railway town, Minnarie's now a sandy resting point for north–south travelers, promising a few stores, one fuel stop, and one of the outback's last public telephones. Hayley's seen countless Instagram photos taken there. There's a camping ground north of the town, the first overnight stopover she's planned for the trip. Her belly tingles at the prospect of being in a tent with Scott, their own little hideaway, threading her arms around him as the night takes hold, the two of them in the wilderness and out of the city together for the first time. Maybe he'll shrug off his crankiness? They might even have sex, as long as Hayley is sure nobody can hear them. She'd be mortified to know others were listening in.

Not that they've been making much noise lately. Any sex has been swift, perfunctory, sometimes too rushed and forceful, probably because Scott is sulking. He wants to do things in bed that Hayley doesn't want to do anymore. Hands around her neck, his palm slapping her backside. She's watched enough X-rated content to know he's mimicking what he sees online. At first it was thrilling, then it began to feel mean, like she was a compliant object and they weren't in it together. What would Scott think if she spanked *him*? The idea seems laughable, but why? Why are women the ones who are humiliated? Hayley eventually put a stop to it, drawing Scott's hands away from her neck, coaxing him into her preferred, benign positions. Now, though, Scott doesn't look her in the eye on the rare occasions they make love. They often go to bed at different times; he stays up late in the lounge on his laptop. She suspects he's watching more porn and tries not to think about it. This road trip, their close proximity, it will freshen their relationship, she's sure of it. Everyone knows girls mature faster than boys. Scott needs time to catch up.

Hayley offers the open bag of chips to the others in the car, but nobody takes one. She crams a few more into her mouth, relishing the salt and the oil, before tucking the bag into the seat pocket. Counts the corners of the radio again—one, two, three, four; checking her previous calculations. When she looks outside, a still, greenish body of water emerges on their left. A dead lagoon, she imagines, and then she sees movement and bounces in her seat.

"Look, look, look! An emu!"

She presses her finger to the window. The bird steps over brackish stubble, raising its wiry legs in jerky movements.

"Wow." Livia claps. "That's the first emu I've seen in the wild. Incredible."

"It is *weird*. Ugly," Joost says.

"How can you say that? It's elegant, and they've got such big, beautiful eyes."

"Look how awkward it is. It can hardly run. It is amazing the species survived."

"I wish I could have taken a picture," Livia says.

"We're not stopping," Scott says.

"I didn't ask you to. I'm just saying . . . I wasn't ready."

"Show me your camera?" Joost asks.

Livia pulls a black bag onto her lap, switches it on, and they lean in together as she taps through recent images.

"How many megapixels?" he asks.

"Thirty-two point five," Livia says.

"Do you have different lenses?"

"At home, yeah. I only bring this one when I'm traveling."

"Why don't you just use your phone? They take good photos."

"Sure, phone cameras are okay, but my Canon blows them away."

Hayley wonders if there's an attraction there. Will they hook up during this trip? She dismisses the thought. While Joost might be interested, Livia probably has high standards. Joost holds a certain appeal, yet he's more boy than man, too keen to impress, and Livia would want someone more worldly, like her. Perhaps with a body more muscular, defined like hers. Besides, he smells weird, and it's become worse since the Port Augusta fuel stop. It's not just the sweat of body odor; there's a sweeter layer too, like rotting fruit. Maybe it's his sneakers. Hayley wonders about a polite way to tell him.

She turns the radio on.

"What are you doing?" Scott says.

"I wanna hear the weather."

"Check your phone."

"It's not as detailed."

The drone of an ABC broadcast fills the cabin. There's a news headline about the coming election, then a report about Cyclone Benedict building off the northern coast.

"Do they mean Darwin?" Livia asks.

"Don't worry, it'll be long gone by the time we get there," Scott says.

The weather warning for South Australia includes "possible flash flooding" in the north of the state.

Hayley widens her eyes. "What about that? We're heading right into it."

"It's in the general area. It's nothing like a cyclone," Scott says. "And anyway, they said *possible* flooding. I bet it doesn't happen and, if it does, we won't see more than a few puddles." He turns the radio off.

Hayley watches him for a moment. The seat belt stretched over his flabby stomach, his eyes narrowing behind his glasses. Hopefully, he's right, but what does he know about the weather? He rarely goes outside.

"It would be wonderful if it rained," Livia says. "It looks so dry. How much water do they usually get here, Hayley, do you know?"

"Um, I'm not sure." Hayley's fingers begin tapping as she thinks about her travel plan. There aren't any contingencies for bad weather, and she prays nobody will question her on it. They might have to stay in a motel, and she and Scott have only budgeted for tent sites. "Possible flooding" could mess with everything.

Joost moves, ramming her seat once more. "Really? Are we going to keep talking about the weather? What are we, like, fifty years old?"

"What do you wanna talk about, then, Joost?" Livia asks.

"How about girls? Hot Australian girls and where to meet them."

Livia snorts. "Oh, grow up."

"How about it, Scott—where are all the beautiful girls?"

Hayley stares at her boyfriend, waits for his response.

Scott pauses, his face composed.

"You're not gonna meet any chicks out here," he says. "You should've stayed in Sydney or Adelaide, if that's what you're after, mate. You should've done a nightclub tour, not an outback tour."

"There must be country girls around here. Lovely, *lonely* country girls."

Hayley titters nervously.

Livia sighs. "Let's change the topic."

"Why?" Joost asks.

"Because I've got a feeling it's gonna get gross."

"Nothing about me is gross. It's all beautiful, baby."

"Ha!" Livia picks up her camera and studies the landscape through the lens.

The conversation stalls.

Ten minutes pass. The rocking of the vehicle lulls Hayley, and when she glances at Scott, his eyes are hooded.

"Hey." She taps his arm. "You all right?"

Scott straightens. "Of course."

"Guys—we should swap drivers," Livia says. "I'm serious."

"Nah, I'll be fine, I swear."

"I am happy to take a turn," Joost offers.

"Thanks a lot, Hales." Scott slowly shakes his head.

"It's not a criticism—you've been driving for hours," she says. "Come on, have a break, let's chillax in the back. Please?"

Scott is silent. He's going to ignore them all. But then he checks the mirrors and they pull over, roadside gravel erupting beneath them.

"All right, who's gonna take over?" he says, falling back against his seat, one hand still gripping the park brake.

"Me." Joost unclicks his seat belt.

"Have you driven in Australia before?" Hayley asks. "Do you have an international license?"

"You asked me when we met, remember?"

The four leave the car, moving around the vehicle to find their new positions. Hayley is startled by the hot air, and flies attack her immediately. She uses both hands to bat them away.

As Hayley and Livia pass each other, Hayley can't help observing Livia's well-defined backside in her canvas shorts. She despises herself for turning to look, yet knows she would do it again, every time. She gets behind the driver's seat and tugs down her skirt to cover her thighs. Joost rolls back, forcing her to swing her knees sideways to avoid being squashed. He adjusts the rearview mirror, plugs his phone into the power socket and checks the screen.

"No mobile service," he says. "Ridiculous."

"Welcome to Australia." Scott enunciates each word.

They move onto the road. Joost's shoulders crowd Hayley's field of vision, and the windows seem smaller back here. The chips are still in the front passenger side, where Livia is sitting, and she wishes she'd grabbed them.

"All the global technology at your disposal, and still no phone coverage out here?" Joost says.

"It's a big continent, mate," Scott says. "Bigger than Holland."

"Netherlands."

"Whatever. Australia is a hundred and eighty times bigger."

"Oh, someone has done their studies."

"You only have to put up a few towers to cover your country—it's completely different here. Our regional centers are further apart."

"Exactly. In the Netherlands, each town is only a *short* drive away. So Australia *needs* the coverage more than us. If you are lost in the bush, you are on your own; police are too far away to help. People get stranded and die in the outback, correct? The outback is so big to search, you might as well be lost on Mars."

Scott folds his arms across his paunch. "Mate, people only get into trouble if their cars break down. And if they don't have enough water with them."

"Still, you Aussies cannot get your act together with the phone towers."

"We've brought heaps of water!" Hayley sings out. "We're all organized, everyone. There's no need to fret."

"Most of the people who die, die because they leave their cars," Scott continues. "And because they're stupid bloody tourists without a clue."

"Or if they step on a venomous snake."

"A lot of countries have deadly snakes," Livia says. "Australia has more to offer—the most remarkable animals you could dream of. Beautiful beaches, which aren't as crowded as they are at home—"

"Killer sharks," Joost says.

Livia looks at him, scratches her ear. "If you're so down on Australia, why did you come here?"

"I am not down on it."

"You keep criticizing it."

"I am only pointing out how dangerous it can be. Life on the edge . . ."

"So maybe you should have stayed in Europe and visited some safe cathedrals and museums. Gone to see Big Ben or the Eiffel Tower. Or some other phallic monuments."

Hayley chuckles, puts a hand over her mouth.

"No, you misunderstand me. The danger is an attraction. It makes this place much more interesting than"—Joost waves a hand toward the broad, flat expanse outside the window—"just staring at this."

"Can we change the topic?" Hayley pleads. What Joost says about phone coverage is true. For her, though, it's a bonus. She and Scott will be cut off from digital distractions and able to focus on each other. Without uni assignments, without Reddit, without his online gaming buddies, she'll have more of his attention. She sits angled toward him now, willing him to turn and look so she can make a kissy face.

But Scott doesn't turn, and after a few minutes, his legs fall wide and he lays his head on the headrest. His eyes shut.

Hayley stares at the back of Livia's neck, the shorn hair cut in a neat line, like an army cadet's. Joost begins humming to Pop Smoke, which is still playing through the speaker, one hand on the steering wheel, one arm propped against the window. Hayley doesn't like how relaxed he is, nor how long he lets his eyes shift from the road to linger on Livia. Hayley grabs his seat and leans over, smells his fetid scent.

"Have you driven long distances before?" she asks.

"Sure."

"Like, at a hundred kilometres per hour?"

"Yes."

"On this side of the road? What side do you drive on back home?"

"Why are you asking so many questions? This feels like a job interview."

"Just checking."

Joost gives a lazy smile. "Relax, Hayley. We all had to trust Scott driving. Now you have to trust me."

Hayley leans back, both hands clutching the chest strap of her seat belt, and stares at the scrub rushing past. When she pulls her gaze inside again, Joost winks at her in the rear-view mirror.

6

Andrea

Tuesday, February 7
5 PM

WHEN ANDREA OPENS her eyes, she's confused. What time is it? What day? Blinking into wakefulness, she slowly sits up. She's on the couch in the back room, and her neck is stiff and sore. The last thing she remembers is reading to Ethan.

The pregnancy is making her tired; what else is ahead? With Ethan, she was nauseous in the second and third months, the sort of queasiness that comes from a nagging hunger, and no matter how often she ate, it wouldn't go away. Will it be the same with her second child? There's been no sickness so far. That will be more difficult to manage when she already has a toddler, not to mention a hotel to run.

Andrea rubs her face, gets to her feet, and navigates around the pile of picture books on the rug. They've amassed a large collection; it seems books are being delivered to their post box in Minnarie every other week. It's her one indulgence, and she understands she's trying to make up for Ethan missing out on library visits and playgroups—things he would have in the city. It's an expensive habit, but Matt hasn't raised any concerns. He must be aware of why she's doing it too.

Andrea takes the corridor to the pub kitchen and continues into the front dining area.

"Hello, sleepyhead," Matt says.

He's at one of the window tables, a laptop open in front of him, Ethan perched opposite with his jar of colored pencils and a scattering of paper. It's dimmer than usual at this time of day. Steely clouds linger across the sun, and Matt has switched on the overhead lights. The change in atmosphere makes Andrea uneasy. It's like she's slept for days rather than minutes, like she's missed something.

"Thought I'd catch up on the invoices." Matt takes care of all the pub paperwork and enjoys poring over the figures, making sure everything is in balance.

"Quinn not back?"

"No." Matt shakes his head.

"I'm getting worried now."

"We'll see her for dinner, love. She's usually back by then."

Andrea nods, slips next to Ethan, and places her hand on a sheet of paper for him to trace. It's one of their recent favorite games, and Andrea giggles as the pencil tickles her skin.

"Mummy!" Ethan warns her to be still.

Matt taps at his keyboard, his index fingers moving at a ponderous pace. Andrea admires his long eyelashes as he's reading the numbers, the same eyelashes as their son's. She wonders about the baby she's carrying. Will it be another boy, or a girl? What will they look like?

From far away comes a rumble, and for a moment Andrea thinks it's the promised thunder. The family turns to look outside, where a thin road carries travelers from the main drag toward the Pindarry. The rumble becomes engine noise.

"Who's this, then?" Matt asks.

Andrea grimaces. "Oh, please don't say somebody's arriving now."

Matt rises from his seat and pushes through the front door—half wood, half glass—with Andrea and Ethan close behind him. Andrea perches on an outdoor bench with a view of the empty car park lined on two sides by hardy ghost gums. The air is clammy. A violet stripe on the horizon signals the expected weather change. The buzz of engines grows louder, bringing angry dust with it, and Ethan clings to her knee.

"Looks like a few bike riders," Matt says, squinting. "Wonder if they're staying?"

"I hope not," Andrea says.

"I'll look after them, love. Doesn't look like there's many. You could stay at the back with Ethan."

She musters a small smile, grateful for her husband's sensitivity.

*　*　*

Years before she met Matt, Andrea was working in a regional pub in the Riverland. As she was barely out of her teens, it was her first job away from Adelaide, back in the days before she learned to be busy and brusque, the days when it seemed every customer was harmless. One of the regular patrons was a biker, a man in his forties with a wiry beard rambling over a pointed chin. He often sat at the bar alone, reserving most of his conversation for Andrea. While the other staff members teased her about it, Andrea thought his attention was simply friendliness with a tinge of loneliness.

One Thursday night after her shift, the biker was waiting for her outside the hotel. He emerged from the shadows of a brick wall, making her jump.

"Sorry, it's only me," he said.

When she recognized him in the moonlight, Andrea gave an embarrassed laugh, as if it were rude to be startled.

"You scared me." She held a hand to her beating chest and veered around him, heading for her usual route through the car park and onto the next street. From there, it was a short walk to the rental she shared with two other young women. She hadn't saved enough money to buy a car, and besides, the town was so small it was easy to get around.

"What's the hurry?" The biker fell in beside her. Thudding rock music emanated from the pub, yellow light glowing on the other side of the opaque windows.

"I'm tired. I've got to get home and collapse."

"I'll give you a lift. I've got a spare helmet."

She shook her head. "Nah, that's all right."

"C'mon, don't be shy." His tone was warm. "You can trust me. How long have we known each other, Andrea?"

"Not sure."

"I thought you said you were tired. You don't wanna walk all the way home, not after you've been on your feet all night."

"Thanks, really, it's not far."

A hand seized her elbow and spun her around.

"Come on," the biker pleaded. Andrea smelled bourbon on his breath. He was a head taller than her, and his hand slid from her elbow to her wrist, tightening his hold. They were alone in the car park.

"*Let go!*" Andrea leaned back, using her weight to try to free herself.

Waves of alcohol and heat rose off him. He pulled her into a crushing hug and bent in for a kiss.

"*No!*" She angled her face away, couldn't believe what was happening.

There was shouting nearby, the biker loosened his grip, and then Dallas, the bar manager, was there.

"*What the fuck* are you doing?" Dallas yelled.

Andrea staggered away, and the biker stood with arms limp, oddly frozen.

"Get out of here!" Dallas ordered. Andrea would never forget her boss's blazing eyes, her expletives, the way she kicked at the man's legs.

"Calm down, ya silly bitch," he grunted, dodging her.

As he moved off, Dallas scooped an empty beer bottle from a crate and hurled it, glass shattering near the man's boots. She reached for another, and Andrea clamped a hand on her shoulder to calm her.

"Stop. It's okay, he's going," she said.

"That's not enough," Dallas huffed. "He needs to know not to come back."

As the man started his bike engine, he called out, "Sluts!" and gave them the finger.

Andrea never saw him again, except in occasional nightmares. She tried not to think about what might have happened if Dallas hadn't rescued her, but most of all, she was shaken by the change in the biker. She'd thought he was a nice guy, lonely. It was the first time she had met someone who could morph from friendly to violent. How had she not detected a threat in him earlier?

She worked with Dallas for another year, trying to put the experience behind her while also adjusting her instincts, her radar for danger. Dallas moved to Western Australia, and they kept in touch with texts for a few months before the messages stopped as they both got on with their lives. Sometimes Andrea wonders if Dallas is still working in bars. Does she have a family? Is she happy? Is she still fierce?

Andrea still gets rattled by bikers, but she refuses to let one sickening evening condemn her to hiding.

*   *   *

Now she gives Matt's hand a squeeze. "I'll be okay to help."

Matt kisses the top of her head. "Thanks, love," he says. "We need all the guests we can get."

The motorbikes approach the pub, leaving the road and taking the turnoff to the wide dirt car park. They curve around each other smoothly like ice skaters, six altogether, and stop beneath the spindly mulga trees that form the nearest patch of shade. When the bikes are switched off, the land seems eerily quiet. A soft breeze stirs, collecting the dust created by fat tires.

"I'll tidy our things away," Andrea says.

"Righto." Matt nods and steps off the verandah to greet the new arrivals.

Andrea urges Ethan indoors with her. She scoops up the laptop, pencils, and paper and stuffs them into a drawer behind the bar. The invoices will have to wait for later. The bikers are likely to want a meal, and the fryer will need to heat up. If Quinn were here to help, the strangers could be on their way sooner. Surely they know about the heavy rain forecast? Who would want to be on a bike in weather like that?

She hoists Ethan into his high chair. It's almost too tight for him, and they don't use the tray table anymore. Instead, she scrapes the chair close to a corner of the bar and makes sure he has toys within reach. "Okay, buddy, sit here and be good, hey?"

She checks her appearance in a mirror on the wall, yanks her top away from her chest so her breasts aren't too defined. Her pulse quickens at the sound of male voices approaching. There's a prickling over her skin, and she tells herself not to overthink. It's probably a group of city slickers, exploring local gorges and tracks, just middle-aged mates on an annual pilgrimage away from wives and kids, not bikies. They won't be any trouble; the worst part might be pretending to laugh at dad jokes. Without guests, the pub won't make a living, and this group could mean a fair amount of money. Yet Andrea knows the nearest police officer is hundreds of kilometers away.

The door opens and men stride in, bike helmets cradled under arms. One of them has gaping holes in both of his earlobes formed by the black disks that were popular a few years ago. He seems younger than the others, who appear to be in their fifties, with graying hair and creased faces. Several men have faded tattoos on their arms, but Andrea can't see any symbols or patches belonging to motorcycle gangs.

"Gentlemen, hello," she calls out.

"Hello, gorgeous," one of them says. "You're a sight for sore eyes!"

Here we go.

The rider with holes in his earlobes surveys the place. "This is bloody paradise." The pub's air conditioning has chilled the room, the counters are polished, and bottles of beer look frosty behind the fridge glass.

A stocky man with salt-and-pepper hair balances his helmet on a barstool. There's a brightly colored woven band around one wrist. He bends to Ethan. "Hello, little fella. My name's Dom. What's yours?"

"He's Ethan." Andrea puts a hand on her son's back, feeling him squirm under Dom's gaze. Ethan pushes his feet at the bar, threatening to topple the high chair, so she plucks him out.

Dom holds his hands up. "Sorry, just being friendly. Nothing to be scared of."

"He's just a bit shy," she says.

"Shy? Working in a pub? He ought to get a different job." Dom cackles, revealing beige teeth.

Andrea balances her son on her hip. "Come on, Ethan, Mummy will take you out back, and you can watch *Ringo Dingo*. How does that sound?" She carries him to the living area and sets him up in a corner of the couch with a tablet on his lap, swiping to select his favorite cartoon playlist. She doesn't like leaving him alone with an animated babysitter, but right now it seems sensible.

Walking away, she checks over her shoulder. Ethan is already spellbound by the screen.

Within moments, Andrea is busy pouring drinks with Matt and the din of the bikers fills the bar as they discuss the weather.

"We wanna be in Coober Pedy before the storm," Dom says.

"Good idea. You don't wanna be on the road," Matt says. "Could get hairy."

"Do you reckon it'll be that bad? The rain?"

"Hard to tell. Sometimes the bureau is right, sometimes they're wrong."

"All part of the fun."

"Where have you come from?" Andrea asks.

"Adelaide, most of us," Dom says. "A few from Gawler. We're heading to a mate's funeral."

"I'm sorry to hear that."

"Aw, he's given us a good excuse to get together. This is our first big ride in years. The members are not as young and tough as we used to be."

A few of them order bacon and egg rolls, and she's relieved to retreat from their gaze and begin cooking. There's hoarse laughter from the bar, some of it from Matt. Her husband does enjoy this life. It's easier for him—he grew up in remote southwest Queensland, and he's used to wide spaces and people few and far between. When he does meet new people, he strikes up eager and inquiring conversation, scouring for information, for tales from the road. Andrea is more reserved, having been raised among brick houses that shared tin fences, where people pretended not to hear the neighbors argue. Over the years—ever since meeting Matt—Andrea has slowly weaned herself off the suburban retail centers, the cement footpaths and Stobie poles, moving with him to out-of-the-way towns around the country. They followed pub jobs and a sense they were making progress, growing older and wiser—even if they didn't have formal qualifications, even if their bank balance was low.

Shortly after they married at one of their favorite pubs, they settled in Roma, Queensland, the biggest town they had ever lived in together. Andrea wanted to try a different lifestyle, so Matt got a job in the cattle saleyards, and she worked happily in a shoe store. Ethan was born there, and they stayed for almost two years. Andrea had thought they'd put down roots and was thinking of an online university course.

Then Matt grew irritated with the routine. Nothing made him content: he complained about his saleyard colleagues and began to drink every night, slumping in front of the television. He hated the petty politics and wanted to get back into the cheer and bustle of hospitality. When this gig was advertised, Matt's eyes were so bright that Andrea could not say no.

Now here they are, managers of an iconic pub in remote South Australia. The Pindarry is more than a hundred years old, with rooms and sheds added over the years, anchored by the picturesque verandah. It's often featured in outback tourism blogs and Instagram posts. They've even been listed in a *New York* magazine's "Top 10 Outback Secrets." The dirt surroundings make it impossible to keep dust out, although previous managers placed large rocks around the building to help. There's no point trying to grow grass here, but cotton bush and native myrtle soften the scene. The few native trees on the property are alive only because their roots are so deep, and they regularly shed bark, as if disrobing in the heat.

Andrea still gets mesmerized by the dazzling sunrises and sunsets, and by the fact that there's not another building in sight.

This might be where she gives birth to their second child.

She feels a spark whenever she remembers the baby. It's easy to get caught up in routine and forget the pregnancy when she's working ten-hour days. Matt will be overjoyed, yet for now, she protects her secret, ruminating over the possible next steps. Should they keep the baby? Matt's content with their new life and little family, where he wakes every morning and nobody is giving him orders. He's master of this parcel of Australia, and Andrea doesn't want to upset that. Still, there's no denying a baby will change things, make them even more challenging. She's unsure about caring for a newborn out here. As a first-time mother in Roma, she had other new mums close by, a playgroup where they relearned all the children's songs they'd forgotten. There was a kinder-gym, a medical center. Out here? None of that. But it's the lack of a nearby doctor that makes her fret the most.

Andrea moves fast, juggling frying pans on the stovetop, blowing a stray curl from her eyes. They won't return to Roma, that's a given, so she's been searching for other options. Her parents are still in Adelaide and would love to spend more time with Ethan, but it's difficult to picture moving in with them, even for a short period after the baby is born. And what would happen at the Pindarry? They can't afford more staff. Every idea she comes up with presents problems she can't see around.

"How ya going?" Matt sticks his head through the kitchen doorway.

"Good timing," Andrea says, handing him two plates.

"They look delicious, love."

Andrea smiles. Matt always says that, no matter what she's prepared.

She peeks into the bar. One of the men heads for the toilet door in the corner, another to the exit. Matt delivers the plates and pours another beer. Andrea hopes the bikers won't be over the driving limit. What if they ask to stay? The last thing she wants is for them to settle in for the night. If the coming storm is as bad as predicted, if it floods roads, they could be confined here for days, and she doesn't want to think about what their continual company might be like.

Out in the yard, a bike engine starts up. It revs once, twice, three times, like a lion growling a warning. People's heads turn, and Dom, the older rider, stands and looks through the glass of the pub door.

"Stupid bastard," he says, pushing through the door.

"Everything all right?" Matt calls after him.

"I'll go check," Andrea says.

From the verandah, she sees a motorbike doing slow loops around the yard, its wide tires stirring up an auburn haze. The rider with the holes in his earlobes is perched behind the handlebars. He's not wearing his helmet, and scrappy hair hangs down his neck. He hunches over something tucked on the seat in front of him, and Andrea thinks he must have brought his dog.

Her stomach plummets when she realizes it's Ethan.

Her son is supposed to be inside, safely watching his screen. Instead he's atop a powerful engine with a stranger's arms around him.

Andrea leaps onto the dirt and waves and yells. "Stop! Right now!"

The rider hunches down farther, speaking into Ethan's ear. The bike sticks to its arc, and Andrea sprints to interrupt it, as if she has the power to stop a charging bull.

"Hey, watch out, love!" Dom bellows.

The bike heads in her direction, wobbles for a second, and then swerves around her. Every part of Andrea wants to throw herself at it and rip Ethan away, but she doesn't know how to without hurting her son and herself.

"*Matt!*" she screams. Where is her husband?

Like a traffic cop at a busy intersection, Dom steps in, raises his hands to halt the bike. It jerks to a stop, and Andrea reaches Ethan before the engine has been switched off. She lifts her son away, eyes scanning him for injury, then presses his head to her chest.

"What do you think you're doing?" she spits at the rider.

"He's okay. We were just having fun." He grins. His startling blue eyes are bright with mischief.

"You can't just grab somebody else's kid!"

"Calm down. I take mine on my bike all the time—"

"This is *my kid*."

Matt arrives, taking in the tense faces. "What's going on?"

"Where were you?" Andrea screeches. All her fury is now transferred to Matt: his easy manner, the amiable welcome he has given this mob of lowlifes.

"Sorry about that," Dom says. "Rosey can get out of hand."

"Rosey?" Andrea snarls.

"Yeah. Forget about him. Your boy's okay, right?"

"Just *leave us alone!*"

"Hey," Matt says. "Will someone tell me what's going on?"

"He had him *on the bike*." Andrea stab-points at Rosey. "They were doing doughnuts." Balancing Ethan on her hip, she rushes indoors. Murmuring and low laughter follows her, and tears prick at her eyes. There's nothing funny about this, and she's not overreacting. She pictures Ethan falling from the bike, a wheel running over his head, and more tears threaten as she reaches the privacy of her bedroom. What if Rosey had gone down the track a bit, out of sight? Anything could have happened.

"You okay, baby?" she says. Ethan's arms are hot around her neck, and he doesn't make a sound.

She kicks the bedroom door shut, lowers them both onto the mattress. She can sense Ethan's fear and confusion, keeps him on her lap, brushes back his soft hair and steadies her own breathing.

"Well," she whispers. "That was a bit exciting, wasn't it?"

Ethan stares at the floor.

"You went on a big motorbike. How did that happen?"

Silence.

"Did you finish watching *Ringo Dingo*?"

Ethan nods.

"Okay. You got bored? And you came to look for Mummy?"

He nods again, teeth nibbling his bottom lip.

She rubs his back. "That's okay. It's hard when Mummy and Daddy are busy. I'm sorry I didn't see you . . . You can't follow strange people, Ethan. It's not safe."

It's not the first time she's tried to teach Ethan this lesson, and now Andrea wonders how much a three-year-old can absorb. He sees strangers every day, he watches his parents greet them eagerly, he sees people striking up quick friendships. Still, his nature is cautious, somewhat withdrawn, and Andrea has nurtured that, relied on it. So what happened today? Ethan doesn't have the ability to explain.

Andrea holds back a sob. She's not having a baby out here. She's not. It's impossible to monitor one child, so what hope does she have with a newborn distracting her?

Matt eases open the door and crouches by them, one hand on Ethan's plump thigh, the other on Andrea's back.

"Is he all right?"

"I think so." Andrea doesn't look at her husband. She wants to cry now he's here, wants to be held and tell Matt how terrifying it was, but that will only unsettle Ethan again. And she resents that Matt didn't intervene sooner.

"The guy, Rosey, he feels bad about what he did," Matt says. "I told him off, and he's apologized."

Andrea shakes her head at the mention of the man's name, so pretty, so incongruous with the feral bloke he seems to be.

"What kind of person puts somebody else's kid onto their bike?" There's a tremor in her voice. "He could've fallen off. He could've . . . you know. Ethan didn't have a helmet on."

"That fella, he's an idiot, plain and simple. There was no malice."

"I don't care what his motivations were. I want them all out of here, now! Tell them it's time to leave."

"They are going—after one last drink."

"You can refuse them."

Matt makes a pained face. "Let's see how we go, hey? I know they're keen to be on their way before the rain gets here."

"I'm serious, Matt. I don't want them here a second longer."

"Honey, I can't just turf them out. They're customers."

"This is our venue, we can do what we want."

"I don't want to create any trouble—do you?" Matt leans closer and looks into her eyes. "Let's keep it all calm, keep it friendly, and they'll be gone soon. We don't want to stir up any bad feeling."

Andrea turns away, blinking at the wall, her body trembling. She can't stop seeing Ethan on the motorbike, caught between the biker's arms, both of them circling her. Can't stop reliving being unable to grab him. How can Matt be so placid? Doesn't he understand Ethan's vulnerability, the dangers they face every day?

"Matt, those men are not sleeping here tonight. If they start to ask, shut them down, tell them no. They need to go before the downpour gets here."

"Of course. Absolutely."

"And I'm not going back to the bar. I'll stay with Ethan until they've gone."

"Fair enough. Do you want me to get you anything?"

Ethan wriggles; he's had enough of his mother's lap. Andrea lets him slip off. He clambers across the mattress toward a toy dinosaur on the bedside table.

A male voice disrupts the family discussion.

"Hello? Anyone there?"

Andrea's heart skitters. Do these men have no boundaries?

Matt jumps up, his frame filling the bedroom doorway. "This is our private area," he says firmly. "Nobody is allowed back here."

"Sorry, mate."

Andrea recognizes Dom's voice.

"The fellas are getting restless—just thought I'd check on how the last beer is coming along. You don't want us to serve ourselves, do ya? Because that's a slippery slope." There's a chuckle.

"Nope." Matt shakes his head. "We don't want you to serve yourselves. Don't touch anything, I'll be there in a sec." He turns back to Andrea. "You all right?"

She nods. "Yes, you go back. They need to be on their way!"

She makes sure to say the words loudly so Dom can hear.

7

Livia

Monday, February 6
4 PM

IT TAKES LESS than ten minutes for Livia to erect her one-person tent. The most difficult part is getting the pegs into the parched, packed dirt. The earth doesn't want to let anything in. But once the pegs are set, she adeptly slips the poles into place and tugs the light material up so that the roof pops into position.

She resists saying *Voilà!* Hayley and Scott are still grappling with their abode.

"Livia, you're done already," Hayley observes. She waits with hands on plump hips as Scott scuttles between the corners of their tent, stretching it over the dirt. He's ordered her not to touch anything until he's worked out how it should lie.

"I've had plenty of practice," Livia says. "Come, take a look."

She holds the tent flap up and Hayley gets on her hands and knees, crawls inside the low dome and makes admiring noises.

"So cute. It's tiny!"

"It's all I need," Livia says. Her stomach lurches; she's hungry. They need to finish setting up so they can turn their attention to dinner. "Want any help?"

"I've got it under control," Scott says.

"I don't mind. The more hands the better."

She joins them on the ground, straightening out corners and connecting poles that will create the frame. Scott huffs and issues unnecessary instructions until the purple-and-yellow tent is finally standing. Joost helps too, squatting down to hammer in the final pegs. He looks like a praying mantis on the ground, his shoulder blades poking from beneath his T-shirt. It's a big tent, Livia thinks as she stands back, much larger than two people need. It is garish in this environment; perhaps it will make the Aussies feel safer. The young couple hasn't spent much time out of the city, and this may be the most traveling they've ever done together.

Hayley circumnavigates the tent, taking photos on her phone.

She grins. "Home sweet home."

*   *   *

They drove into Minnarie an hour earlier, passing more WATER RESTRICTIONS IN FORCE signs at the town entrance. Only a few dozen streets radiated from the main thoroughfare. Livia noted the houses with their wilting front gardens and sun-ravaged awnings, roofs topped with satellite dishes and enormous air conditioner units. There were no people outside, no children on bicycles; this was a hideaway world where everyone sheltered in temperature-controlled homes behind drawn curtains, leaving their withering gardens to struggle beneath the punishing sunlight. Most of the stores in the main street appeared closed—defeated—including a bakery and a butcher's, their windows dark and dust covered.

They were surprised at the subdued interior of the food store. Almost all the lights were turned off, and there was no music playing. It saved on power bills, Livia supposed, and also made the shop seem cooler. The four wandered among near-empty shelves while a middle-aged woman with a greasy ponytail watched from behind the counter. Hayley browsed a rotating rack of meager souvenirs, spinning it around and around, searching for the perfect fridge magnet or key ring. All of the postcards had curled corners. Scott grumbled about how expensive everything was compared to prices in the city, standing with arms folded, refusing to explore, standing inside only because it was cool. Livia grabbed a six-pack of water from a low shelf. She'd have preferred to keep refilling her canteen, but there'd be few pit stops with taps over the next few days.

"Good idea," Joost said, kneeling to do the same. At the counter, he selected a packet of kangaroo meat jerky. "Will you try some with me?"

Livia wrinkled her nose. "No, thanks, it's probably as tough as nails."

"Where is your sense of adventure?"

"Maybe I'll try—you go first."

After paying, Joost tore open the packet, broke off a piece of jerky, and chewed thoughtfully. "Not bad. Salty." He removed another strip of the dried meat and held it out to Livia. "Open wide."

"You are *not* feeding me." Livia ducked away and took the food from his fingers. Joost watched as she nibbled. "Glad I tried it, but I don't think I'll ever eat it again."

Hayley finally purchased a key ring, a tiny boomerang with dot painting, and Livia wondered if any Indigenous Australians had been involved in its manufacture. Had it been made in Australia at all? Hayley also stocked up on sweets, and, as a group, they chose an easy, sausage-in-bread dinner option.

The campsite was five minutes north of Minnarie, essentially a cleared area with solar-powered lights, metal picnic benches, and a cavernous unisex toilet block. There were a few caravans and four-wheel drives, no tents. They drove in a slow circle before settling on a patch of dirt near twisted mulga, where no caravans could venture. Not that February was a busy time of year for camping. It was still too hot this far north, and most Australians were focused on getting back to school or work after the holidays. Except for uni students like Hayley and Scott, who weren't due back in class until March.

An elderly couple dressed in pale cotton and wide-brimmed hats were packing up a caravan nearby when the four arrived. Livia smiled and waved as they climbed from the car, and the man tottered over on bony legs.

"What a bunch of fine young people!" he announced. His nose was scarred and pockmarked, perhaps from skin cancer, his eyebrows and lashes so light they were almost invisible. "How's it going?"

"Good, very good," Joost said, assuming captaincy of the group.

"We're on the way out." The old man had a broad Australian accent. "We were supposed to wait for some friends here, but we've changed our minds. You kids heard the weather warnings?"

"Yes. We have. Do you think—" Joost began.

"We've been keeping track," Scott said, wrenching captaincy back.

"Good-o," the old man said. "It's going to be interesting if we do get all that rain."

"It won't be too bad, will it?" Hayley asked.

The man spread out his hands. "Might be enough to wash away some dust . . . might be enough to wash away the roads!" He laughed, and they all joined in.

"Are you heading home?"

"Yep, the missus and I have had enough dramas on the road over the years. She wants to be tucked up safely, and I don't blame her."

"What drama?" Livia asked. She enjoyed hearing older people's stories.

"Bushfires, for starters. The border fires two years ago, do you remember them? Just terrible." He shook his head. "We were stuck in the car, towing the van, surrounded by fire and smoke, couldn't see a thing, the world was just orange and red. And then"—his tone became subdued, and Livia leaned in—"it got dark, so dark.

"I thought it was the end for us," he said. "There were crackling flames everywhere. It's hard to imagine. With all the doors and windows shut, it was suffocating—hot as an oven. I could barely breathe. The wife still has nightmares."

"It will give me nightmares just thinking about it," Livia said. "What did you do?"

"We lay down real low, across the seats, kept a blanket over ourselves. Even when we were boiling hot, we stayed under—that's what the authorities say you should do. And we waited it out. We were very lucky, we survived, and I can't say the same for dozens of other people. And then there was the time we were stuck on the Nullarbor."

"The Nullarbor, I've heard of that," Livia said.

"Big area between South Australia and Western Australia." He spread his arms wide to illustrate. "A long, long highway, almost completely straight! Well, police closed it because of fires on either side. They wouldn't let anyone pass—hundreds of people had nowhere to go and nothing to do but to stay holed up outside the local roadhouse. There weren't any hotels or motels, nothing."

"One highway?" Joost said. "No other roads?"

"Yep, from here to the west."

"And if it was cut off, nobody could move?"

"Yep," the man replied, and Joost shook his head disdainfully.

"How long were you there?" Livia asked.

"It was nearly a week—longest week of my life," the man said. "There were arguments and crying and carrying on, especially from families with kiddies. A helicopter dropped supplies, and the roadhouse owners had to ration the food and water. And the toilet paper."

"How awful," Hayley said. "I bet people were angry and upset."

Scott rolled his eyes. "No, Hayley, they would've been ecstatic."

The old man turned to his wife, whose face was creased in concern. "Well, we better move on. Take care, look out for each other. Drive safe and don't camp here too long."

They watched him hurry back to the caravan.

Joost snickered. "As if we would stay here more than one night."

Hayley's face fell. "I'm sorry . . . this was the best camping site I could find."

"Of course," Livia jumped in. "This is what backpacking is all about."

"Come on, let's get our tent." Scott took her hand, and they walked away.

"That was a bit harsh," Livia told Joost.

"You must agree"—he waved a hand around—"this is like a third-world country."

"You obviously haven't been to a third-world country."

Joost opened his mouth and closed it again.

"Is this your first trip away from home?" she guessed.

"Not at all. I have been to Germany and Belgium."

Only just over the border from his home country. "On your own? Or as a kid?"

"With my parents, yes."

"So this is your first solo adventure."

"Yes." He nodded. "The first adventure, you could say."

*　*　*

Now the sun is lower in the sky, and it's a cooler twenty-eight degrees. Petite brown birds flit through nearby trees, perhaps thornbills. Livia isn't sure. They hop as if the branches are too hot to settle on. Flies buzz around her face trying to get purchase and she waves them away, glad of her tent cover for the night. Joost will sleep in a swag, an oversized sleeping bag in khaki green. He wants the "full Aussie experience" and bought it online for this trip. All he had to do to set himself up was roll it out. Livia sees he's positioned it closer to her tent than to Hayley and Scott's.

All the other vehicles have gone. The old man and his wife weren't the only ones leaving.

"Guys, is it strange nobody else is here?" Livia asks.

"I think it's awesome," Scott says. "We have the whole place to ourselves."

Livia swipes at more flies. She thinks of the old man's travel stories. More like war stories. But they're not heading into a catastrophic bushfire, it's just rain, the fallout of a cyclone that might not even reach Australia's northern tip. Rain can't match the ferocity of flames, and she's curious to see how a deluge might bring the landscape to life.

Hayley tucks her phone into her pocket. "I'm starving. Let's get dinner ready early." She grabs the loaf of bread and sausages, and the four move to the picnic area—a corrugated-iron roof shading two tables atop a concrete slab. "Will you guys start the fire, please?"

The camp barbecue is an oil drum on the ground with three enormous logs bordering it, acting as seats. Scott and Joost stand around the drum, pondering the ashes inside, while Livia and Hayley head for the nearest table.

"Women in the kitchen, men by the fire, am I right?" Livia smiles.

"We're pathetic, aren't we?" Hayley says. "Such traditional roles."

"Is it like this at home—back at your house with Scott?"

"Oh, no, nothing like this. We share with another student and take turns cooking. Scott cooks a lot, actually. But I've got to admit—I do most of the cleaning."

"How long have you been together?"

"Almost two years."

"Wow, that's a long time. You're so young."

"We met in first year of uni."

"You're practically married."

"Ha! We did talk about it in the early days—getting married."

"Really? Whoa, that's moving fast."

"We don't talk about it anymore; we're focused on finishing uni first. We must seem old-fashioned to you?"

Livia pauses. She thinks marriage is a patriarchal institution with no benefits for her whatsoever, but Hayley doesn't need to hear that. "Not at all. If you love someone and you want to stay together, that's only natural."

"That's so true."

The two women settle onto bench seats. The baked metal is warm beneath Livia's thighs. Joost is exploring nearby scrub, collecting kindling, while Scott has gone to the car, perhaps for matches.

"How about you, Livia, do you have a partner?"

"Well, no long-term relationships, nothing like you and Scott, but . . ."

"Go on." Hayley grins, baring teeth so bright that Livia wonders if they've been professionally whitened. Perhaps Hayley did it ahead of this holiday.

"I often meet people, and depending on how long we're in the same country, we might hang out for a while. Share accommodation, that kind of thing."

Hayley's grin grows wider. "Have you hooked up with someone while you've been in Oz?"

Livia wonders how much to share. She normally keeps romances to herself, but it feels important to bond with Hayley. "Don't tell the others." Livia lowers her voice. "I recently spent four days with this gorgeous guy from Portugal."

"Ooh, was he at the Sydney climate event too?"

"Yes, he's gone home already."

"Do you have a photo?"

Livia swipes through her camera roll, then holds up her phone screen.

"Oh my god, he's hot." Hayley's eyes bulge at the image of a dark-haired man in a tight T-shirt.

"We've been messaging every day, but honestly, we'll probably never see each other in real life again."

Hayley pulls a sad face. "That sucks."

"I'm fine with it," Livia says, and she is.

Hayley leans closer. "How about Joost? What do you think of him?"

Livia gives a theatrical shiver, and Hayley giggles.

"Joost is okay looking," Livia concedes. "I'm sure he appeals to some people." She looks over to where Scott and Joost have started the fire and are staring into the early flames. Joost stands tall, shoulders wide, his unblemished skin shining in the heat.

"He's very confident. Some girls love that," Hayley says. "But I'm still working him out . . ."

"I know what you mean."

"Do you think he has somebody back home?"

"Maybe."

Livia studies the pair some more. Scott prods the fire with a stick as Joost watches. They're speaking to each other, although she can't hear what they're saying, and Scott laughs. Livia turns her attention to the tabletop, reading the black-marker dates and initials left by previous visitors. She traces a signature with one finger. "The man with the caravan—he seemed worried about the weather."

"He's old. It's his job to be worried."

"Still, everyone else has gone—"

A bird lands on the next table, its feathers in shades of brown and eggshell, perfect for blending in with the environment. Its eyes are dark marbles.

"Hello, cutie," Livia whispers. "Hayley, what type of bird is this?"

"Not sure."

"Is it a wattlebird? Wait, no, it's smaller—some kind of sparrow?"

"I'm sorry, I'm a big dumbo when it comes to remembering bird names." Hayley's cheeks grow pink.

"No big deal," Livia says. "I didn't know any birds back home until I downloaded an app that explains them all, including whether they're native or introduced. You could do that."

"Yeah. Maybe."

"I have a theory—if we know more animal names, we can be more connected to them, more invested. I'm very big on protecting native species too."

"I guess you've blogged about that?"

"Ha-ha, I absolutely have!"

When the fire is settled, Scott arranges the sausages on a wire grill over the flames. The other three rest nearby, sipping warm water from bottles. Livia uses the sleeve of her T-shirt to mop her face, glad of her short hair. Joost's skin is glowing from the heat of the coals, or perhaps he's already sunburned. He sits with pale legs stretched over the dirt, and his hunched back looks elastic.

"When is the sun going down?" he groans.

"Not for ages." Hayley uses a paper plate to fan her face.

Scott tends the sausages, turning them regularly with tongs, glowering at the smoke and perhaps also at being given this task.

Hayley claps her hands together. "Let's play a game."

"Oh, here we go," Scott says.

"Shush, you! I wanna have fun."

"All right, what's the game?" Livia asks.

"Two truths and a lie."

"I think I know this one."

"Explain, please," says Joost.

Hayley grins, the gleeful party host. "We all take turns. Everyone shares three things about themselves—two things are true, one is a lie. And we have to guess what's what."

"I don't think we should do that," Scott says.

"Why not?"

"Sounds like torture."

"Don't be a pussy, man," Joost says.

"Fuck you."

Hayley stops flapping the plate and glares at her boyfriend. "Can't we just have fun?"

"Settle down," he grunts.

"No." She gets to her feet. "Why do you have to spoil everything?"

"I just don't feel like playing that game, okay?"

Hayley steps over her log and tramps away, arms swinging, sneakers crushing twigs. The others gape at her retreating back.

Livia turns to Scott. "That was mean. All Hayley wants is for us to have a good time."

Scott studies the flames for a moment, then stands and hands Livia the tongs. "I'll go talk to her. Don't let the snags burn."

He moves, unhurried, after Hayley.

Livia stares at the tongs in her hand. She loathes cooking, wonders why Scott gave her the task and not Joost. She kneels in front of the barbecue, feeling the blaze on her cheeks, turning the sausages. The heat of the flames keeps the bugs away, and she's glad of that, but increasingly uncomfortable about the situation unfolding. Scott constantly scolds Hayley, who's now having a tantrum. Will there be more quarrels on the way to Darwin? Maybe she should've chosen her traveling party more carefully.

Joost shuffles along his log to be nearer to her. "This is not exactly a resort, is it?"

She shrugs. "It's what I expected."

He nods in the direction of the other two. "Day one, and they are already arguing. Why are they even together?"

"They're out of their comfort zone. I'm sure they're not normally like this."

"This is why I don't travel with a girlfriend."

She looks at him. "You have a girlfriend?"

"Not at the moment. I had plenty in the past."

"Oh, congratulations."

"Look at me." Joost runs his hands down his slim sides. "Nobody could resist."

"Ha." Livia gives a wan smile, reluctant to spar with Joost. She hasn't entirely worked him out yet, and alone with him at the campfire, she wonders about that lack of knowledge. What is he—eighteen, maybe nineteen years old? His cheeks have a young, fleshy quality, and his short nose is piggish. He may even be in his twenties. He's studying engineering, although she isn't sure she heard that right. He's unashamedly inspecting her, maybe inviting conversation, but instead Livia surveys the scrub around them. Hayley and Scott are nowhere to be seen, yet they couldn't have gone far.

The sky softens into a darker blue with a sprinkle of early stars.

Joost slaps his palms together, and the sudden crack makes Livia flinch.

"Caught one!" He opens his palms to reveal a dead mosquito.

CHAPTER

8

Hayley

Monday, February 6
5 PM

Hayley feels small and foolish, with an overwhelming need to hide her face from the others. She moves far enough away from the campfire to be invisible, sticks scratching at her ankles, coming to a stop beside a pair of gnarled trees. Tears fill her eyes. What are the others saying about her? How long should she brood here?

When Scott appears, she turns her back to him even though her heart leaps.

He moves to her side, rustling through the brush. "All right, Hales, I've come to apologize," he says. "I was being a dick, okay?"

"You were," she agrees. "Why are you being so *weird*? We're meant to have a good time on this trip."

Scott holds his arms out, and Hayley steps into the hug, closing her eyes, enjoying his solid chest and pudgy stomach. He's her Scott, and he's apologizing. He doesn't want to hurt her. This is a misunderstanding.

All too soon, he pulls away.

"What's going on?" she says. "We've been looking forward to this for so long; now I feel like I dragged you out here, and that's not true."

"Yeah, I know."

"Are you bored already? Do you wish we'd stayed home instead? Do you miss your laptop?"

"No. I don't miss any of that."

"Then what's wrong?"

"I just need to get my head sorted. I've got a lot on my mind."

"Like what?"

"What if the car breaks down? What about this bloody storm people keep talking about? We could get bogged, even wreck my granddad's car. There's no roadside assistance to come rescue us, not without waiting for hours."

"You're fixating on things that may never happen, Scott. What's the point of that?" Hayley studies his eyes, dark disks behind his spectacles, wishing he were easier to read. "Have I done something wrong? Are you annoyed with me?"

"No." He pauses. "You haven't done anything wrong. I'll try harder to relax and enjoy the trip, all right?"

Hayley steps closer, and they kiss. She frowns in concentration, as if her kiss might inject happiness into Scott. He remains stiff, but at least he's trying.

She takes his hand, and they head back to the campfire. They can hear Livia and Joost talking.

"You don't like Joost, do you?" Hayley whispers.

"Not especially," Scott says.

"Why?"

"Not sure."

"Is it because he stinks?"

Scott chuckles quietly.

* * *

After dinner, the four sit around the barbecue coals. Hayley and Livia perch on one log, Scott on another; Joost has found a forgotten camp chair and sits high above them all. Livia retrieved a cask of red wine from the car—one of her contributions to the trip—and everyone sips from a travel cup. It's dark and much cooler now, so cool that Hayley considers fetching her hoodie. But she doesn't want to leave the cozy circle, doesn't want to miss a second. Scott has moved the car closer, plugged in his phone and powered up the portable speaker. He chose Hayley's Aussie playlist, with Sarah Blasko and Thelma Plum, a peace offering. Sitting around a campfire, the Milky Way overhead—this is the type of holiday scene she has dreamed of.

"Tell me again why we're drinking this?" Hayley grimaces. She prefers premixed cans of vodka, direct from the fridge.

"Red wine transports the best," Livia explains. "White wine or beer, not so much—they taste disgusting when they're warm. And spirits are out of my budget."

"*This* is kinda disgusting," Hayley says.

"Warm beer is fine. I drink it all the time," Joost says.

"Says the European," Scott mumbles.

"What is the Dutch word for wine?" Hayley asks.

"*Wijn*," he says.

It seems only slightly different from *wine* in English, and she can't quite identify Joost's intonation. Everyone tries mimicking him, "*Vein? Vine?*"

"*Wijn*," he repeats.

"How about the word for beer?" Livia says.

"*Bier.*"

"That's so funny," Hayley gasps. She laughs so hard she has to grip the log to stop from slipping. Livia is laughing too, tears pooling in her eyes.

"How about campfire? What's the Dutch word for that?" Livia asks.

Joost studies their faces, lips pressed, enjoying the moment. "*Kampvuur.*"

The girls howl with laughter, and Scott snickers into his cup.

"I think I'm gonna wet myself," Hayley says.

"Obviously, many Dutch words sound different to English," Joost says.

The laughter subsides, and Hayley draws in a long breath, relishing the open air, so different from the suburbs. What's that scent? Wattle or wildflowers? Cicadas chirrup. She sips more wine and decides it's not so bad. There's a comfortable warmth in her chest and cheeks, and she catches Joost looking at her, eyes glinting with a friendliness that's new. He's recognizing how fun she can be, perhaps even attractive. Hayley knows she can be a slow burn for some people.

"More?" Livia holds up the cask.

"Yeah, sure," Hayley says.

"Take it easy, I don't want you puking in the tent tonight," Scott warns.

"I'll be fine."

Scott's nursed the same drink for a while now, and it's a good thing he's taking his driving seriously. In contrast, Joost holds out his cup for a refill. Livia pours Hayley's first, then, as she turns away from Scott, Hayley sees him study Livia's backside. *There it is!* she thinks. It was bound to happen— she herself has done it. She makes a snort-giggle noise, and Scott pulls his gaze back, stares piously into his cup.

"So, we go to the hot springs tomorrow?" Joost says. "Bathers . . . or au naturel?"

"What?" Hayley says.

"He means skinny-dipping." Livia pulls a face.

"Oh, no way! I'll be wearing bathers," Hayley squeals.

"Fine," Joost says. "I was not sure what was expected."

Hayley gulps her wine. The idea of being naked with everyone is way more than she's comfortable with, and she can't imagine Scott taking his kit off either.

"And then one more night in South Australia?" Livia says. She seems to know when to change the subject.

Hayley nods. "Yes, another campsite. Smaller than this one, I think."

"When we cross into the Northern Territory, will I have to show my passport?" Joost asks, and they all laugh because they can tell he's not serious.

"What time do we need to leave tomorrow?" Livia asks.

"Eight. Not horribly early," Hayley says.

"Cool. It must be time for spooky campfire stories, then."

"Oh, please, no," Hayley says, although the idea is appealing.

Joost grins. "Aren't you spooked enough already?"

"What do you mean?" Livia says.

"We're in the Australian outback—this is where the real scary stuff happens. Backpacker murders."

"Oh, come on, that's not fair! It doesn't happen often," Hayley says, with so much gusto that wine slops onto her wrist. She sucks at her skin.

"Two words: *Wolf Creek*."

"That's just an old movie."

"Based on real events." Joost angles his head like a serious professor.

Livia stares into the fire. "I've never seen it, and I never will."

"It is a brilliant film. A classic."

"It's a horror movie, right? With lots of blood and violence? No, thanks, I'm not interested."

"Actually, it's not just horror, it's much more than that." Scott extends his leg in front of him. "The tension in the story is outstanding. The production is brilliant."

Hayley looks at Scott in surprise. "I didn't know you liked *Wolf Creek*."

Her boyfriend shrugs. "I might've watched it a few times."

"Absolutely," Joost says. "It is raw. Like . . . primal. The filmmakers are honest; they do not hide things; it is not like one of those big scary American movies with all beautiful people in a mansion dying one by one. The producers treat the audience like grown-ups. One of the best parts is the scene in the shed when the girl wakes up, and she is tied—"

"Please!" Hayley cries. "I don't want to be reminded of the gory details. It's an awful movie. Livia, don't watch it— you're doing the right thing."

A gust of wind arrives, stirring up trees and bending the flames.

"Ooh, that was weird." Livia gazes around.

"Here's the cool change!" Hayley chortles, then mashes her lips shut. She's being overly loud, drinking too fast, her mind growing woolly.

"Are you girls cold? I could grab a rug," Joost offers.

"Thank you." Hayley beams. "That would be *amazing*. There's a blanket just inside our tent. I didn't know if we'd need it . . ."

"I'm fine, thanks," Livia says.

Joost leaps up and dashes to the colorful tent while Scott stares at Hayley with an expression she can't decipher. Fire-light glints over his spectacles. Is he amused? Jealous?

When Joost returns, he drapes the checkered blanket around her, and she snuggles in.

"Wow, thank you, Joost."

"No *worrrrrries*." He stretches the phrase, Aussie style, and she giggles.

As Joost sits, Hayley checks over her shoulder, sensing something. But there's nothing there. The solar lights mounted on the picnic shelter cast a glow for several meters and the lights of the toilet block shine farther away, all the bulbs surrounded by flying insects. Otherwise, the campsite is shrouded in darkness. The ring of bushland hems them in; the prickly wattle and saltbush watch them. With more

campers and caravans, it would be a bustling, well-lit destination, and Hayley imagines friends sharing meals, children
running and laughing. Right now it's like they're the final
guests before the park permanently shuts down.

"How will you go in your swag if it rains, Joost?" she asks.

"I will be fine," Joost says. His cup of wine is almost hidden between his large hands.

"I guess it depends on how much rain we get," Livia says.
"If it buckets down, you won't get any sleep."

"I could share your tent." His eyes flash at Livia.

"Uh, no, thanks."

"Please?" Joost squeezes his shoulders closer together. "I
will not take up too much room."

"Seriously, though—we should have a plan," Hayley says.

"If it rains really hard, Joost can shift into the car," Livia
suggests.

"Good idea. Scott, you should give the car keys to Joost,
just in case."

"Nope."

Hayley is embarrassed. Joost just laughs. "Do you not
trust me?"

"What if we need the car keys?"

"Why would you?"

"Dunno," Scott says, not meeting Joost's eyes. "Still, you
shouldn't be taking care of them. I promised my grandfather
I'd look after the car."

The group settles on a solution—Scott will leave the car
keys on top of a front tire. They're the only campers left, so
there's no danger the keys will be taken by somebody else.

The breeze grows stronger, dry leaves scatter, and Hayley's head is reeling from the wine. She swigs what's left and
stands.

"Coming, Scott?" She holds out her hand to him.

*   *   *

Hayley stiffens in the sleeping bag, confused by the noise that's woken her. Is it a million crashing pebbles? She lifts her head and remembers they're in a tent in Minnarie, far from home. It is exhilarating and discomfiting all at once. Raindrops bounce off the canvas, and the ceiling ripples. It's muggy in the tent.

Her mouth is dry; she shouldn't have drunk so much wine. She gulps from her water bottle, then inches back down into her sleeping bag. Sleeping out here isn't so bad, she tells herself, although the side she's lying on aches despite the sleeping mat beneath her. She thinks back to when her parents bought her a *Finding Nemo* tent and set it up in the back garden. It was thrilling, staring at the bright nylon above, listening to the crickets—until the neighborhood grew quieter, the temperature dropped, and Hayley became scared. She crawled out of the tent to discover her parents drinking wine on the patio, the sun still in the sky. They laughed when she said she wanted to sleep in her bedroom after all. Now she's managed a few hours' sleep, it's proof she's not that nervous kid anymore, and the rain is a thousand tiny hands applauding her.

Hayley checks the time on her phone. It's just after one AM. There's no internet reception, and she tries not to feel disappointed at not browsing her friends' social media profiles.

There's enough moonlight to make out Scott's face, centimeters away, his hair a fringed shawl hanging over closed eyes. When they crawled into the tent earlier, she began kissing him, pressing herself close and making it clear she wanted sex. After only a few kisses, though, he pushed her away, saying he was tired. It's important he has plenty of sleep if he's doing most of the driving again tomorrow.

Hayley rolls onto her other side for a more comfortable position, and her mind is melting into bizarre dreams when a voice reaches her ears. It's male, speaking in a strange language. Joost. She wonders what's wrong, then remembers he's sleeping open to the sky. He'll be soaked and looking to climb into Scott's grandfather's car.

There's more griping. Her fingers tap from pinkie to thumb and back again, rising and falling like playing a piano.

She wonders about Joost having the car keys now. Was that a good idea? If he wanted to, he could drive away before they even had a chance to struggle out of their sleeping bags, and they would be stranded here. While they did vet him, in truth they've only known him for one full day. He could be anyone.

Wide awake now, Hayley props herself on an elbow and thinks about waking Scott. It would make him cranky, and he's already been annoyed by her fretting.

A car door slams and Hayley tenses, pausing her breathing to hear the engine start. There's only silence. Joost must be settling down inside. Of course he is. Why would he race away into the outback on his own?

She relaxes her jaw, counts the seconds between her breaths. Tells herself *Everything is okay, everyone is safe, everything is normal.*

Her thoughts turn to her itinerary instead. There's the outback springs soon, which should be fun—like soaking in a hot tub. Later, they'll eat at the Pindarry, and she might even drink a freezing-cold beer. Isn't that what you're supposed to do at a genuine Aussie pub? Hayley doesn't drink beer, but in this heat it might taste wonderful, and it has to be better than cask wine. Then there's the famous Dingo Fence. Livia and Joost don't have anything like it where they're from. If only the weather doesn't mess too much with her plans. Who wants to sit in hot springs when rain is falling on your head?

Once they reach Alice Springs, there'll be mobile phone reception. Hayley plans to upload photos to her social media accounts. They'll be the most remarkable posts she has ever shared.

The patter of rain is soothing, and her body relaxes. She rolls over one more time and gently touches Scott's back.

"Sleep tight," she whispers.

Andrea

Tuesday, February 7
6 PM

T HE SOUND OF engines splits the air, and Ethan looks up, startled.

"It's okay, the motorbikes are leaving," Andrea tells him.

They're on the floor of the compact living room, large wooden puzzle pieces spread around them. Andrea gets up and goes to Quinn's room, where the window overlooks a section of car park. Hiding behind the curtains, face pinched, she waits to see them leave.

"Drive safe," Matt calls out.

"Pfft, drive safe," Andrea mutters. Her husband, so cheery and polite to those hoons—boys on bikes who should have grown up by now.

"If we get into any trouble, we might be back!" one rider cackles.

Bikes rev again, and Andrea wraps her arms around herself. The engines crescendo, and several riders appear at the window's edges. Bit by bit, they roar away. Andrea returns to the lounge and offers her hand to Ethan. "Let's go play outside." He refuses her hand and trots down the corridor toward the verandah. They pass by the bar, where Matt is collecting empty beer glasses.

"They've gone," he says cheerily. "We've got the place to ourselves, love."

Andrea doesn't smile back. She's not ready.

At the front steps, she scans the sky. A band of clouds is shifting closer, like a lid being pulled over a box. Soon they will be shut inside a storm. The hotel sandwich boards that usually sit at the car park entry have been packed away—the OPEN signs, the menu, the brightly colored beer and coffee advertisements. Potted plants have been stowed inside, below the windowsills, and the outdoor chairs and parasols are stacked neatly in one of the sheds. The Pindarry is on a slight slope, and the modern addition at the back sits on a higher cement foundation. They've lined the original section with sandbags piled three high along the pub's frontage and side walls. It seems premature, even ridiculous, in this parched land. Further afield, she imagines the scrub to be shivering, anticipating the long drink to come. Water restrictions have been in place ever since they took over this business and they've been painstakingly careful with how much water they use, including two-minute showers, and even then they capture the runoff in buckets to use as mop water for the floors. It's hard to imagine rain pouring freely from the sky.

Matt joins her, hands in pockets.

"We should have been watching Ethan," Andrea says, her tone tense.

"It's hard when we're busy, love."

"We need to do better."

Ethan bounds onto the dirt, finds a long stick and begins towing it over the ground.

"See, he's okay." Matt nods at their son. "He's probably forgotten all about it."

"Well, I haven't forgotten. And I'm not okay."

"Don't be angry, love. We'll get to bunker down together during the storm . . . We'll have a rest. It'll be like a mini holiday. What do you reckon?"

"A weird holiday."

"Weird, yes." Matt nods. "And without work to do. No visitors to look after. That's the definition of a holiday, right? We can take it easy. Cook a few nice meals. Watch some of those movies that have been piling up."

She narrows her eyes. "I s'pose."

The light changes around them. "Shit, look at the sky," Matt says.

Swatches of thicker clouds have arrived, the sun leaking around their edges, forming a chessboard-like contrast. There's a shiver over her arms. "Wow, I've never seen it look like that before. Have you?"

"No. Pretty mind-blowing, right?"

Matt stands behind her, knits his hands around her waist, and rests his square chin on her shoulder. This would be a nice time to tell him she's pregnant, yet Andrea keeps her lips firmly together. The incident with Ethan still has her twitchy. She needs time to regroup.

The rain begins as a gentle tapping at first, so quiet she could be imagining it.

Matt gives a whoop.

"What, Daddy?" Ethan asks.

"Can you hear that?" Matt squats down beside Ethan on the dirt. The boy touches his own face; he's felt a few drops on his cheek. Andrea leaves the shelter of the verandah and tilts her face skyward. There's an uncomfortable swirling in her gut, a mix of excitement and trepidation, and she wishes they could predict what's going to happen tonight. She has never stayed at a place that's been sandbagged.

"Mummy, Mummy!" Ethan jumps up and down. Raindrops fall faster and fatter until they're thrumming onto the ground without pause. Matt grabs her hand, the trio twirl around, and she shrieks with laughter as water sluices from the shed roofs and begins to turn the car park into a gleaming plateau.

"It's beautiful!"

"Can you believe this?" Matt says.

After a while, Andrea tugs her family toward the verandah. "Come on, we'll get cold."

They retreat beneath the tin roof, watching the rain like it's the most captivating movie they've ever seen.

"Everything is going to be so . . . clean," Andrea says.

"This is bloody brilliant."

"The farmers will be happy, right? It's a good time of year for this?"

"It's always a good time for this. As long as it doesn't get, you know, too much."

They glance at each other. Matt's referring to the floods years earlier, before their arrival. Nature can be at extremes in this part of Australia, and it's cruel for those trying to make a living from the land. Andrea knows it ruined Quinn's family farm and killed a lot of their livestock. Quinn's father died a year or so later. Andrea has never asked for the full story. The time has never felt right.

"I hope Quinn's not far away," Andrea says. "What do you think's keeping her?"

"Sometimes she stays into evening," Matt reminds her. "She'll be fine."

The Durand property has been for sale ever since Quinn started working at the Pindarry. Quinn claims she's packing it up, but it's slow going and Andrea privately questions whether it's turned into an unhealthy hobby. Quinn's mother, Trish, has returned further south, to the Clare Valley where she grew up, while Ryan, Quinn's older brother, works in

Canberra's public service. He could not have chosen a more different life, throwing himself into a bureaucratic role in the nation's capital. And they're still waiting for a buyer for the farm. For decades people have grazed cattle in this region, and punishing drought has made it tougher and more costly. It isn't suitable for crops, so Andrea suspects the only buyers will be an international conglomerate with deep pockets and long-term plans to own more of Australia. It's too bad for Quinn, who was raised here and is determined to stay in the region.

"Tonight is different," Andrea says. "Quinn knew about the forecast. I thought she'd be back by now."

"She's a clever girl," Matt says. "I bet we'll see her headlights any minute now."

"Fingers crossed."

"Let's get Ethan ready for bed."

The family walks inside, and Andrea flicks on the verandah lights for Quinn. It looks like a different world already. There are no cars, no guests. Nothing moves except for the rippling sheets of rain. A smile breaks over her face. Matt is right: this is the perfect time for them to bunker down for a make-believe holiday.

The pub telephone rings, startling her.

Matt reaches it first. "Pindarry," he answers.

Andrea watches him. His face is serious; he's looking at the floor more than at her.

"Righto," he says eventually. "I'll come out now."

"Where are you going?"

"It's Greg. His place is flooded."

"What, already?" Andrea squeaks.

Greg is one of the few remaining pastoralists in the region. He's an aging widower who occasionally drinks at their front bar, staying overnight in a hut and leaving bleary-faced the next morning. Greg lives with his adult son Ian, who is often away working in a Northern Territory mine.

Their property is eighty-two kilometers northeast, in a valley that's less dry than most.

"Is Ian there?"

"No, that's why Greg needs a hand."

"Was he ready for this? Did he do any sandbagging?"

"Yes, but he's already sprung a leak. I'll find out more when I get there."

"You can't leave me and Ethan."

"I won't be long. You'll be fine here; we've got everything ready. You won't even know I'm gone."

"What if you get stuck on the roads?"

"It's only just begun raining."

Andrea snorts. "Enough to mess up Greg, apparently."

Matt takes her hands, looks into her eyes. His own eyes are calming, his smile lopsided.

"I'll be as quick as I can. We need to be good neighbors, yeah? We'd want Greg to do the same for us. Besides, Quinn will be back in a minute. I might even pass her."

"What if we get visitors?"

"Now? I reckon those bikers were the last lot we'll see in a long time."

Andrea compresses her lips. It doesn't seem fair. Of course Matt wants to do the right thing, but she's still not happy with him for leaving now that evening is falling. Whenever he goes on errands, there's always been Quinn or a seasonal worker to stay with her.

She watches her husband gather a coat, torch, head lamp, and thermos. Then he kisses the top of her head.

"Be careful," she says. "Please."

"Call me if anything goes wrong, I'll turn right around."

It's only after Matt's left and Andrea's reading a bedtime story to Ethan that she remembers something important—why didn't her husband take one of the satellite phones? His mobile phone might not be enough if the weather is as disruptive as it promises to be, and Greg's property is out of the CB radio range.

Don't torture yourself. She and Ethan will just start the mock holiday without Matt, that's all. He'll be back before they know it.

CHAPTER

10

Livia

Tuesday, February 7
6:30 AM

IT'S TEMPTING TO stay curled up on her sleeping bag, but her bladder is screaming to be emptied. Livia slides her feet into her boots and grabs the small duffel bag that has traveled with her around the world. Drizzle falls as she crawls out of the tent, the sun is feeble in an overcast sky, and the leaves of the nearby saltbushes are glistening. Compared to the heat and the flies of yesterday, she's woken to a new world.

She races to the bathroom block, skirting the wide brown puddles that have formed. There's no movement from Hayley and Scott's circus tent, and Livia isn't surprised to see Joost's khaki swag rolled up and stuffed beneath the four-wheel drive. He must be sheltering in the car.

When she's settled on a toilet seat, Livia takes her phone from her bag, forgetting there's no mobile reception. Pity. It would be good to read a weather update and check her social media messages. Her family keeps her updated with regular stories from home, including photos of their greening projects. She might also have some messages from her gorgeous Portuguese friend.

The place smells like damp cement and dirt. Rain drums on the roof, and she thinks of all the animals getting a much-needed drink. Every time she's in a new land, Livia experiences a mix of emotions. She's thrilled to be an explorer yet uncomfortable about the carbon footprint her travels create. She's grateful for her parents' patronage, yet there's guilt for accepting their money while she embarks on far-flung volunteer work. She's very privileged to be in this position, but is she fooling herself? Is this making any difference to the future of the planet? Maybe Australia should be her last trip; maybe it's time to focus on projects closer to home. There's a lot to be achieved there.

Livia washes her hands in a cool steel basin, where water spurts from the tap with a chugging sound, struggling to flow. A shiny square is glued to the wall, and although it's meant to be a mirror, all she can see is her fuzzy outline. What will the facilities be like on the Darwin boat? Cramped, for sure, and she won't have much more than a bunk to herself.

She bends over the sink to taste the running water—metallic yet clean; she's tasted worse—and has a few more slurps. Taking a washcloth from her duffel bag, she scrubs her face, head, and neck. Adds soap and removes her tank top to clean her armpits.

A shape moves at the corner of her vision, and she jumps. Joost is meters away, silently watching her.

"You scared me!" Livia gasps, snatching up her top to cover her chest.

"Oops," he says. He's in the same clothes as yesterday and shoes without socks.

"What are you doing standing there?" Livia asks.

"I need the bathroom."

"So go! Don't hang around watching me."

Joost grins and shakes his head, as if it's Livia who has done something perplexing. She tracks him entering a toilet in the row behind her. As the door shuts with a clang, she pulls her tank top back on, grabs her things, and races out into the rain, scowling. How long was Joost there? Was it an accident, or was he perving? He should have said good-morning as soon as he saw her. Did he see her breasts? Livia isn't a prude, but she is in charge of who looks at her body and seethes at the thought of Joost's eyes roaming over her. That wasn't cool.

Livia walks into a puddle and waggles her boot angrily, then reaches her tent and scrambles inside. Crouching, she removes her clothes and replaces them with a fresh set. Although the rain has arrived, it's balmy too, so she's back in shorts and a T-shirt.

With her camera in a small backpack, she leaves the tent. There is no sign of Joost. Good. She intends to explore on her own. And she is still disgusted with him.

Hayley and Scott haven't emerged, probably lulled by the hypnotic rain. The group needs to leave Minnarie by eight AM to stay on schedule, so she trusts they have set their phone alarm. Really, they should be up already and making the most of this rejuvenating morning.

Livia heads for a line of skinny mulga and then past them, searching for wildlife. At this early hour—and with the rain disturbing them—there may be a lot of animals moving about. She has photographed plenty of birds in South Australia; now it's time to capture a lizard or two. Maybe a furry marsupial, something more exotic to share online. Recently, her Instagram has featured scenes from the summit—people she met, speakers onstage—and her engagement rate has dipped. She needs a few appealing animals to bring her audience back.

She steps carefully over sun-bleached sticks, lying like cracked and discarded bones. Sometimes her boots snap twigs, and she hopes the streaming rain will mask the sound so animals don't flee. She thinks about the Indigenous owners of the land, wise caretakers walking barefoot. There's so much to learn from them. She needs to source more books about Australia's precolonial history when she returns home to Brazil. Moving farther into the bush, she regularly looks over her shoulder to memorize the route back.

Something blurs in front of her eyes, and she stops. She almost walked through a cobweb strung between two trees. It's partially broken, its delicate strands buffeted by the weather, and Livia widens her eyes in wonder. There's a spider within the threads, eight incredibly long and thin legs splayed out, the width of her palm, with a golden body. It's not a species Livia knows, and it's lucky she didn't blunder in and wreck its home. Slowly, she removes her camera from the bag, covering it with one hand to shield it from raindrops, then adjusts the focus and starts shooting. She'll show photos to the Aussies back at camp; they might know what spider it is.

Livia sighs in satisfaction, steps away from the web, and moves on.

A large bird swoops overhead, and she tracks it across the pewter sky, too slow to lift her camera and take a photograph. When she looks down, her head spins. If she hadn't rushed away from Joost, there would have been time to grab something to eat. She squints around, scouting the landscape for the direction she came in, for something familiar. She stands on tiptoe, as if that will help her spot the campsite over the trees and bushes. It doesn't help. Everything looks the same: the faded leaves with water dripping from them, the spiky cane grass.

Livia's heart skips as stories of lost travelers flash through her mind. People wandering the outback desert, the sun beating down on their heads, eventually dying of thirst. It's easy to go off course in this landscape. It's been ten or fifteen minutes, so how far could she have gone? Not much more than a kilometer, she thinks. She returns her camera to its cover, pushes it deep into her pack, and zips it all closed. This isn't a problem. She will take a few steps and see something familiar; she might even hear the others talking, preparing breakfast. She could call out but doesn't want to embarrass herself unnecessarily, at least not yet.

Retracing her steps, she arrives at a long and deep furrow in the earth that wasn't there before. She admonishes herself. She could have stumbled into it and injured an ankle. Then she realizes—she can't recall any significant landmarks. Out here in the unfamiliar bush, especially on this blustery morning, everything blends together. The giant spider is nowhere to be seen. She stops, tells herself to think and listen.

"Hey!" someone calls.

It's Joost. Livia is drunk with relief. She didn't think it possible to be so happy to hear his voice.

"Are you there somewhere, or are you lost?"

"Both!" Livia laughs and begins to walk in the direction of his voice.

Joost is by a tree, snapping a twig between long fingers. He has changed and is now wearing dark cotton pants, a T-shirt, and a gray beanie.

"I wondered if you were okay." He grins.

"I'm a bit disoriented," she admits.

"That's okay; you are a girl and not expected to be good with directions."

Livia reaches his side and glares at him. "Why do you have to act like an asshole?"

"Sorry, it was a joke, all right?"

"More like an insult." She still can't see the clearing, not even the roof of the picnic shelter or toilet block. "Where's the camp?"

"Not far."

"Shall we head back?"

"What is your hurry?"

Joost drops to his knees, starts raking the ground.

Livia frowns. "What are you doing?"

He rises, hands cupped, grinning. "Look." He makes a gap, and she sees a tiny lizard trapped there.

"A gecko," she says. "Poor little thing is scared."

"It is fine."

"Let him go."

Joost crouches, and they watch the gecko slither free. When he stands, he's laughing, holding a twitching tail between two fingers.

"Why did you do that?" she barks.

"Relax, the tail grows back."

"It's still painful! You put him through unnecessary stress."

Joost studies the tail a moment longer before tossing it away. Livia feels ill.

"Which way's camp?" she says, not looking at him.

"I am sorry. I heard about geckos' tails; I have never seen it in real life. That was a one-time thing. I would never do it again."

Livia grunts.

"Do not be angry. Here."

Joost puts a hand into a pants pocket, removes a rectangular tin.

"Oh god, you haven't got a lizard in there, have you?" Livia demands.

"Of course not. Come look."

He hunches over the tin to shelter it from the rain. Livia reluctantly moves closer, sees rolled-up joints packed tightly together.

"What are you doing?" Livia moves back. "It's not even seven AM."

"Oh, listen, missy, we are on a holiday here, right? So relax."

"I am relaxed."

"You are acting very—how should I say it?—uptight."

Livia doesn't tell Joost he makes her feel that way.

"Where did you get that?" she asks. "Why didn't you share with everyone last night?"

Joost tilts his head. "I do not want to waste this on just anybody."

"Well, thanks but no thanks." The rain falls harder, and Livia hopes her expensive camera is safe. Droplets trickle down her neck, and her wet clothing is uncomfortable. "I want to head back to camp and pack. I haven't taken my tent down yet, and we need to leave before eight to stay on schedule."

"Jesus, you act like a schoolteacher."

"Easy for you to say. You only have to roll up a swag."

"True. I planned ahead."

"Are you going to point me in the right direction or not?"

Joost lifts an index finger and starts turning around slowly, pointing and grinning.

"Oh, forget it, I'll find my own way!" Livia is stunned to find herself on the verge of tears, a simmering mixture of frustration and tension that makes her cup her hands over her eyes.

"Don't worry, I have got you." Joost slings an arm around her shoulder.

Instantly, Livia is transported back to those nights in dance clubs and bars, fending off drunken guys brimming with booze and bravado. Except there she was surrounded by a crowd, including protective pals and club security staff. Joost's arm easily envelops her, weighty, his scent musty, and she tries to shrug him off.

"Joost! Don't touch me!"

He tugs her closer. "Let me help you. I am being a gentleman. Stop being so . . ." He mumbles something indecipherable. It must be Dutch.

Livia wriggles, and they lurch sideways. One foot twists, and she extends a leg backward to stop from falling over. Joost laughs and releases her. Instantly, Livia trots away, no longer caring about trampling over nests or lizards or even about going in the right direction. Her only thought is to put space between them.

"Hey, come on. I was only playing. Don't go!"

Livia stumbles forward, dodging trees and thorny bushes.

"Seriously!" Joost shouts after her.

She checks over her shoulder. He's following a few meters away, knees bending with exaggeration, as if she's a frightened animal that might startle and disappear.

He points. "Camp is that way."

"How do I know you're not lying?"

"I am not a monster."

"You better not be playing around."

Livia still can't see the Minnarie campsite and has no confidence about finding it on her own, so she moves in the direction Joost pointed. The rain falls more urgently, coursing over her, the landscape hounding her back to her tent.

She moves on, Joost closely behind.

11

Hayley

Tuesday, February 7
9:30 AM

"WELL, THIS IS going to mess with our itinerary."
It's been an hour since they left Minnarie after a breakfast of muesli bars and coffee. Scott's driving, this time with Livia in the front passenger seat. The Brazilian asked to sit there. Hayley was curious why but didn't want to appear like a noncosmopolitan Australian who was paranoid about who sat next to her boyfriend. So now she's in the back seat with Joost, who has his head rested back, face slack with sleep, knees spread wide and hands lying on his thighs. A beanie covers his eyes.

Since they packed up and shoved everything into the four-wheel drive, the sky has grown darker and is sending down sheets. Scott has slowed to around eighty kilometers per hour while increasing the speed of the windscreen wipers, yet it remains difficult to see far ahead. The bitumen melds with the hazy sky.

"This rain can't last much longer, can it?" Livia asks.

"Dunno," Scott says.

"Please be careful, don't run over any animals. It's so hard to see."

"I don't plan to kill any animals, no."

Hayley's fingers move on her lap in their habitual ripple. She doesn't like not being able to see clearly out the windows; it's like being in an endless car wash. Claustrophobia nibbles at her.

"Do you think we should have kept to the highway?" she asks. Not far from Minnarie, they turned off onto a secondary road, which promised to be a more direct route to the hot springs. It's narrower and its edges are not as well maintained.

Scott shoots her a look in the mirror. "The whole point of this road trip was to do more exploring, remember? Are you saying you don't want to go to the springs now?"

"No, I do want to go."

"Well, what, then?"

She pouts. "I dunno . . . it seems wrong, going to sit in some spa during a storm."

Scott sniggers. "Do you reckon we'll be electrocuted?"

"Actually, I agree with Hayley," Livia says. "I'm not bothered if we miss out on the springs. We could go straight to the pub—the Pindarry Hotel, isn't it? It doesn't seem smart to be driving around in this weather."

Hayley beams, grateful for Livia's sisterly support. "Yes! I'm so looking forward to the Pindarry. We can order hot food and—"

"We have to go to the springs," Joost interrupts.

Hayley's startled. Joost stays motionless, face half-hidden. She didn't know he was listening.

"We don't *have to*," she says.

"I did not come all the way to Australia to drink in dusty pubs. I can drink beer at home."

"It's not any ordinary pub; it's been around since the early days. It's famous. It's the only pub for miles around—"

"We made a detailed driving plan, and we all agreed to it," Scott says. "I don't reckon we should chop and change things now."

"Yes," Joost says. "That would not be smart. The springs first, the pub second."

Livia is quiet, and Hayley sinks back, defeated. "I guess you're right, we agreed to a plan."

Joost stretches his arms extravagantly, his fingertips grazing her shoulder. Pulling his beanie awry, he looks around. "Can we go faster?"

"Mate, there's close to zero visibility," Scott says, jaw clenched.

"The road is straight. How difficult can it be?"

"We could drive into oncoming traffic," Hayley points out.

Joost snorts. "When is the last time we saw another car?"

"Go back to sleep, mate," Scott tells him. "Leave the driving to me."

Joost gives a mock salute.

Then, as if someone has flipped a switch, the torrent falls harder. The roadside vegetation is almost invisible. Hayley has an urge to duck her head, to shrink inside herself. There's the *click-click-click* of the car indicator. "What's happening?"

"I'm pulling over," Scott says. "I can't see a thing. It's ridiculous."

"It is ridiculous, all right." Joost's voice is so soft only Hayley hears him.

The car slows, and Scott steers to the side of the road. He switches off the engine. The windscreen wipers freeze mid-wipe, and for a moment everyone in the car seems to freeze too.

"How long will we stay here, guys?" Livia asks.

"Dunno." Scott slips off his seat belt and alters his position, pulling one knee up.

"It'll get better. The clouds will pass," Hayley says.

Joost rubs his face and stretches again. "Okay, family, what now?"

"We wait," Hayley says primly.

Scott buzzes down his window, sticks his head outside for a second, then quickly closes it, raking his fringe back in place. He removes his glasses and dries them on his T-shirt.

"I am roasting in here," Joost says.

Hayley silently agrees. The air in the car has become oppressive, and the windows have fully fogged.

Joost pushes his door open, and everyone turns at the change in sound.

"I am going to cool down." He slams the door behind him.

Hayley, Scott, and Livia look at each other.

"Shall we drive away?" Scott asks, and Hayley giggles.

Joost moves to the front of the car, turning the rest of them into his audience. Hayley sees a fuzzy shape on the other side of the windscreen, and her mouth falls open as he begins hopping around, punching the air in an awkward dance.

"What is happening right now?" Livia raises an eyebrow.

Joost varies his rhythm and grooves closer to the ground, clearly enjoying himself. He tears off his T-shirt and whips it around his head like someone at Schoolies Week.

"Quick, hand him some soap!"

Hayley is pleased when the others laugh.

"You know what?" Scott says. "That actually looks like fun."

He drops his glasses onto the dashboard, opens his door, and disappears before Hayley can comprehend what he's said. In seconds, he's joined Joost. They high-five each other, then Scott takes off his top too. Even through the water on the glass, his flabby shape contrasts with Joost's stretched torso as he struts and bobs. Hayley squeals and covers her face with her hands.

"What's got into them?" she asks, delighted.

"Scott looks . . . happy," Livia observes.

Hayley clutches the seat in front of her, craning to watch the pair. "Yeah, he does."

At last Scott's putting in an effort to get along with Joost, to have fun like she asked. He's never done anything so spontaneous before, and he never dances. A year ago, when they went to pubs and clubs, Scott always stood on the edge of the dance floor, and if she ever tried to get him to join her, he would twist away, mortifying them both.

"I wonder how long they'll keep this up."

Livia stares out of her side window.

"Are you all right?" Hayley asks.

"I'm fine."

Hayley feels bad. Livia must be anxious about the weather and getting to Darwin on time.

"Do you have travel insurance? I mean, if you miss your boat?"

"If I miss the boat, I miss the boat." Livia gives a tiny shrug. "There are no refunds—it's not that kind of trip."

"Shit. Sorry."

"It's not your fault. I helped plan our dates; I knew what I was doing. Anyway, I'll still make it, don't you think? The rain won't slow us down that much, though maybe we won't see absolutely everything we planned to see."

"That's right, we can be flexible," Hayley says. "Hey, when you're in Darwin, you might get to see some crocs— that would make an incredible photo for your blog."

Livia turns in her seat. "Have you seen crocodiles before?"

"No. Actually, I haven't been to the Northern Territory."

"Then it will be the first time for both of us."

"True! And hopefully this crappy weather will be over by then. I'm so sorry about this."

"Hey, it's not like you can control it."

"Are you having a good time? I hope you don't regret joining us."

"It's fine, honestly," Livia says, and now Hayley hears impatience in her voice.

The barrage becomes lighter, and she looks at the road. The guys have disappeared. "Where did they go?"

Livia removes her seat belt and reaches for the ignition.

"What are you doing?" Hayley says.

"Turning the wipers on so we can see."

The dashboard lights up, and the wipers lurch to life. Water whooshes from the glass, but there's no sign of Scott and Joost.

"Where have they gone?" Hayley asks again.

"It's Joost. I bet he's playing a joke—they're hiding, try-ing to scare us."

This is odd, Hayley thinks. It's hard to conceive that Scott is hiding, playing along with Joost like a pair of kids. She gets onto her knees and looks through the back window. The glass is steamy, and the invisibility unsettles her. "Can you see them?"

"No."

"What should we do?"

"Let's wait. They'll soon get bored."

"Maybe we should get out and look?"

"I'm not leaving this car," Livia says firmly.

"We could—"

THUD! THUD!

"Aah!"

Scott and Joost, one at each passenger window, are slap-ping their palms onto the glass and braying with laughter.

Hayley clutches her chest. "Oh my god, I nearly had a heart attack."

"I told you," Livia says. "This would be Joost's idea."

Hayley squishes her face closer to Scott's. "You're a maniac!" His dark eyes ogle her, and she laughs along with him. She'll tell her friends this story when they get back home.

There's a clunk from inside the cabin. Livia has jammed down her door lock, securing the entire car.

"Why did you do that?"

"They can play games, we can play games too," the Brazilian says.

"What?"

"Let's see how they like being made to stay out there for a while."

Hayley bounces on her seat. "Ha-ha, I love it." She ignores a pang of unease, the kind she'd get if she called in sick to work when she wasn't sick at all.

Scott's the first to try to get in. He moves to the driver's door and pulls the handle. Hayley hears his muffled "Hey!" and laces her fingers together, hoping he'll appreciate the joke.

"Okay, guys," he calls, "sorry we freaked you out. Open the doors, please."

Livia doesn't move.

Joost tries the other side, then sinks out of view.

"Hayley." Scott returns to her window. "That's enough now. I wanna get back in." His wet T-shirt is draped around his neck, and his hair is slick. He's not grinning anymore.

She looks at Livia. "Can we let them back in? Scott's soaking wet."

Livia shakes her head. "Just a minute longer."

"Why?"

"I wanna show Joost I can play tricks too."

"What do you mean?"

"Just—can you be quiet for *one second*?" Livia raises her voice.

Hayley gasps. It's true—Livia thinks she's better than her. She's speaking as if Hayley is a child.

"I'm sorry . . ." Livia turns around, but Hayley isn't listening. She flicks her lock, unlocking all the other doors, letting the rain and Scott and Joost inside.

12

Andrea

Tuesday, February 7
7 PM

"F UCK!"
As the power goes out, Andrea curses because she isn't better prepared.

She has tucked Ethan into bed. Too restless to stay still, she roamed the Pindarry under the sound of the frenetic rain, creeping from the living quarters to the bar and back like an intruder. She checked her phone every ten minutes, anxious about text messages or missed calls from Matt. She wanted updates from Greg's place, how bad it was and how long Matt would be there, and then the building lights flickered and died.

She stands motionless and waits for the generator to come on. Twenty seconds pass, and she's worried. This is the second time the pub's lost power since they took over, and last time the generator came on automatically after just a few seconds. She moves through the ghostly kitchen to the side exit, gasping when she opens the door and spray flies in her face.

The old generator rests on concrete on the far side of the upright freezers. As she approaches, the weakening sunlight reveals water on the ground, and she groans in dismay. The generator needs to be kept dry—how did they forget to cover it? She thought they were fully prepared, and now she grinds her teeth, feeling like a foolish city slicker. Keeping a wary distance, she examines the machine, peering at dials, kneeling to check its damp footings. A gecko scurries past, lightning quick, startling her. She could try to switch the generator on manually, except she isn't sure it's safe to touch it at all. Is it possible to be electrocuted? The rain and wind tears at her while she stands in indecision.

"Fuck!" she swears again. She kicks the generator and stomps indoors.

For the second time, she checks on Ethan, his dinosaur-print sheets tucked around him. She smooths the bedding, glad he's asleep so he's not rattled by the blackout. She's unnerved herself, which makes her more annoyed Matt has been called away from them.

Back at the front bar, the stillness of the pub is a stark contrast to the bluster outside. The battery-powered emergency lanterns are stowed on a shelf beneath the bar, wedged behind packs of coffee and sugar. She switches one on and places it on the counter, releasing unnerving silhouettes around the room.

How long has it been since Matt left? It's probably time to phone him; it would be comforting to know he's arrived safely. She'll suggest Greg come stay with them tonight, and they can clean up his farm tomorrow. Why should she and Ethan be left here on their own? But on looking at her phone, she sees that important symbols are missing from the screen. Whatever has knocked out the electricity has also knocked out the phone lines.

"No!" She wants to throw the phone to the floor. Instead, she stares sulkily into a dark corner of the ceiling until she remembers. She kneels and pulls open a deep drawer housing power cords, a mini first-aid kit, high-vis vests, and other emergency items. Her hands seize the red metal box, as welcome as a surprise gift. It's one of their satellite phones. She can call Matt.

"Let's fire this up, shall we?"

She extends the stubby antenna, fiddles with the power button at the side, and watches the tiny screen blink to life. Matt has shown her how to use this phone, though this is her first time alone. She punches in her husband's mobile number and holds the phone to her ear. It is lumpish and unwieldly. There's no response, no dial or ring tone. She studies the phone, wondering if she dialed correctly, and tries a second time. This time there's a sound through the receiver, and it's the *whir, whir, WHIR!* that indicates a problem with the phone line. She grits her teeth. Matt's phone must be out of action too. Andrea tries Quinn's number next, just in case, and the result is the same. Now they are truly cut off. She hasn't heard from Quinn for hours. Did the girl decide to stay at her farm overnight? She's never done that before; maybe the weather has deterred her from the roads.

Andrea has been to the Durand farm once, back when they hired Quinn and she was preparing to move into their second bedroom. Andrea offered to help her shift some items because she wanted to be a good employer, the thoughtful boss who was part of Quinn's life. She was keen to get to know Quinn if they were going to live and work together every day.

The farmhouse could be reached via a long, stony driveway lined with towering river red gums that looked like the next breeze could blow them over. As Quinn's car rumbled toward the house, they passed a vast hole in a dip in the adjacent paddock, its surface crisscrossed with gaping cracks. Andrea realized it was an empty dam, a sight as sad as a dead animal.

She recalls the three-bedroom vanilla stone building with its wraparound verandah, set on a cleared piece of land looking over the rest of the property. There were two storage sheds nearby, with tin walls of varying shades and ages, next to newish water tanks. Andrea tried to imagine the Durand family living there, cattle meandering in the far distance, farmhands and trucks moving about. Their beloved Bronte tearing around the yard, a child in each bedroom. Two parents working from dawn to dusk, sitting sagged around the kitchen table each night, exhausted and hoping for rain. Until it rained too much.

Andrea followed Quinn onto the verandah, taking in the empty plant pots lining the walls, dead sentries. She stood on the metal grid by the doorway and thought of all the boots that had been wiped there over the years. How did Quinn endure coming to this shrine, the only family member still doing it?

Maybe that was why she maintained the routine.

"You wouldn't believe the funny things I'm finding," Quinn told her as they roamed the musty rooms.

Andrea smiled. "Like what, hon?"

"Our old baby toys," Quinn said. "School certificates. Awards that *every* kid gets. Christmas cards I drew. Tiny red gum boots I used to wear."

"Parents do that," Andrea said. "They get sentimental."

Quinn's Akubra was stuck firmly on her head, tendrils of her honey-colored hair escaping down her neck. She seemed to be hiding under the brim.

"When will the place be completely empty, do you think?" Andrea asked.

Quinn kept her eyes trained on the floorboards. "Dunno. There's no hurry, right?"

"No updates from the land agent, then?"

"Nope."

Andrea wanted to ask what would happen if there were no suitable offers for the farm but couldn't do it. The options were bleak, and it was unfair to prod Quinn, who was undoubtedly already anxious about the future. The Durands had already sold off parcels of land over the years and might have to lower the asking price. While Andrea has no idea if they are in debt, she does know farmers often borrow money to stay afloat and the Durands may need every cent they can get. And although Quinn's brother is earning a salary in Canberra, it's unlikely to make a dent in what the family owes the bank. Her father's departure only made things more difficult for them.

So far Quinn appears reluctant to leave the district. She studied an online science degree for a year, then deferred, claiming to be unsure about her career direction. She wouldn't be the first young person to drift into a life of hospitality work—it's what Andrea did.

Andrea places the satellite phone back into its box, listening to the intensity of rainfall outside. The weather bureau said it would be intermittent over the next twenty-four hours, but she's sure they've already had more than was predicted. She picks up the lantern and begins checking that the pub windows are closed, as if the storm might try to break in. In the kitchen, she opens a fridge, removes a container, and begins spooning cold macaroni into her mouth, leaning on a bench. Hopefully the power won't be out for long, because they can't afford to lose food. Luckily, pregnancy is making her hungry, even though she ate a large dinner with Ethan earlier. When she's done snacking, she moves through the living room to Quinn's bedroom.

She holds the lantern high and inspects the place. A phone charger cord trails from beneath the bed. A cushion rests against the pillows, embroidered with a red wattle pattern, perhaps sewn by Quinn's mother or grandmother. Bronte's plush bed sits in a corner, a chew toy left in the center.

There's a chest of drawers where Quinn has stacked photo albums and frames. It's unsentimental storage—they aren't for display, except for one photo that faces the room. It's Bronte as a chubby puppy, looking more cream than red, her jaw widened in a yawn, her ears flopping and not yet perky. Andrea picks up the frame and studies it with a smile. Quinn adopted the heeler as a pup from a neighboring farm when the owners were selling up and leaving the land. Quinn had wanted to take in all four of the neighbor's working dogs, but of course Trish wouldn't allow that number. Andrea wonders if she and Matt should buy a puppy for Ethan, then reminds herself she's not making firm plans for the Pindarry right now.

She reaches across the bed to check the window. It's unlocked, in fact slightly ajar, and the windowsill is wet. Andrea pulls it shut.

There's no real sense of Quinn in this room, and it could belong to almost anyone. Andrea wanders to the open wardrobe, where a stack of cardboard boxes takes up most of the space. She peeks into the top one and discovers green-and-white ceramic mugs. Maybe Quinn hopes to use them in her own home one day. She must feel so alone in the world. Why couldn't her mother stay on in the region? Andrea can't imagine leaving her child to pack up the family home and fend for themself like this.

She's fitting the lid back onto the box when the grumble of a motorbike engine returns.

CHAPTER

13

Livia

Tuesday, February 7
3 PM

"How deep do you think it is?"

"Not as deep as it looks."

"How can you be sure?"

"You said you are driving across with me, right? So trust me."

Livia darts a look at Joost. She's surprised at the nervous knot in her chest and wants to lighten the situation. "I guess I should trust you—you're Dutch, you guys know all about water levels and dikes and whatever, right?"

Joost chuckles. "Something like that."

"Don't play any games, okay?"

"What do you mean?"

"You know exactly what I mean. No mucking around."

"Promise." He places a hand over his heart, long fingers splayed. "This is serious business."

The engine is turned off, and the windscreen wipers are busy redistributing ripples across the glass, revealing a sky stained purple. They'd been searching for the turnoff to the hot springs when they met this washed-out section of road. They have no idea how deep it is. When they parked, they all searched for long sticks in the scrub. It felt like fun. After removing shoes and socks, they waded partly into the stream and used the sticks to gauge the depth. Joost walked the farthest, water lapping at his calves, still far from the middle of the pool.

"It is not so deep," he told them, throwing his stick away.

"Seems deep to me!" Hayley said.

"We can't be sure," Scott said. "We need to be more accurate."

"What do you want to do, get your measuring ruler out of the car?"

Scott curled his lip. The boys' relationship was back to normal, Livia thought.

"Everyone knows you're not supposed to drive into a flooded road," Hayley said darkly.

"What is the definition of flooded?"

"That." Scott pointed at the road.

"Are you kidding? It is a tiny bit of rain. You Aussies are not used to it, that is the problem."

"Mate, you're talking like an expert, but you don't know a thing."

"I know that water is spooking you."

Livia paced in front of the four-wheel drive, shoulders bent against the sheets of rain. "Can we stop arguing?"

"Let's just turn around," Hayley said. "We can get onto the highway again."

"No. It would be a huge waste of time," Joost said.

It took another half hour to agree on their next steps. Joost and Livia were keen to drive through, confident they could traverse "the puddle," as Joost called it. Livia was uncomfortable siding against the Aussies yet had a feeling the car would make it through. She couldn't bear the thought of turning around to spend more hours stuck with people she was becoming increasingly frustrated with.

Joost raised a hand. "I will do the driving."

"Why should it be you?" Scott frowned.

Hayley tugged at Scott's arm. "Oh, for god's sake, let him do it."

Livia was uncomfortable with the shine in Joost's eyes. What if he drove recklessly, stranded them all here? He needed supervision.

"Joost shouldn't take all the risk," she said. "I'll hop in too."

"Always the volunteer." Joost smiled.

"Great!" Hayley said. "We'll wait here to help if you get into any trouble."

"Two people will weigh the car down more," Scott muttered.

"Gee, thanks," Livia said. "I'm not that heavy."

"Let's take some stuff out of the car," Hayley said.

"That is not necessary," Joost said.

Hayley insisted.

Now Livia steps from the four-wheel drive, eyelids batting in the wet, and dashes over to Hayley and Scott. The tents and two bulky backpacks lie at their feet, Livia's tent the oldest and most worn. Scott's glasses hang inside his T-shirt collar, and Hayley is taking photos with her phone, not smiling. The couple look like sodden, solemn refugees, so Livia pulls a funny face, trying to make this lighthearted. Her right foot slides through a puddle, and Hayley has to reach out to steady her as she teeters.

"Thanks," Livia gasps. Then, "Are you guys mad at me?"

"Why would I be mad?" Hayley flashes a weak smile.

"We're driving your car through water; you both think this is a foolish idea."

"Nah, we took a vote . . ."

"I'm not mad, but if you ruin the car, I will be," Scott says.

"Are you coming?" Joost calls through his window.

"One second!" Livia yells.

Scott jerks his head at Hayley. "C'mon, let's wait over there."

Hayley chews her lip. "I've changed my mind—it's too risky. We should wait for the water to go down."

Scott slaps his forehead and groans.

"We've already wasted so much time," Livia says. "I'm sure it looks worse than it is."

"Could we think about it for a while longer?" Hayley says.

"The longer this takes, the deeper it gets!" Scott says.

"We should all stick with the car. It's the rules."

"It's only going a few meters! We'll be watching the whole time, for fuck's sake."

Livia touches Hayley's arm; the skin is cold. "We're going to make it across. It'll be so shallow we'll laugh. Then we'll stop, throw our stuff back in, you guys jump inside, and we can *all* keep going."

She gives one more arm squeeze, then rushes back to the car before Hayley can change her mind. She climbs in beside Joost, whose mouth and eyes are wide open, mimicking someone at the top of an amusement park ride. His enormous knees are only just tucked beneath the steering wheel.

"Come on, girl!" he whoops.

"Don't call me that."

Livia yanks at her seat belt, thinks for a second, then leaves it dangling by her side. She buzzes her window down, and the rain flies in.

"What are you doing?" Joost says.

"I might need to jump out."

He laughs. Revs the engine. He still wears his woolen beanie. It hides his scant hair and emphasizes the sinewy contours of his face, his scooped nose.

"Don't fool around," Livia says. "Drive carefully, okay? We can do this, then we'll repack everything and keep going."

"I love it when you order me around." Joost laughs some more.

Livia looks at him. "I'm serious. Be careful."

Joost releases the hand brake and is still grinning as the four-wheel drive inches forward. Livia's heart flutters. She focuses on the water ahead of them, shining like a silk ribbon, wavering under the pelting rain. Joost eases them closer, and the water is gradually displaced until suddenly it sprays into plumes either side of the car.

"Careful!" Livia barks.

"I got this," Joost says.

Livia turns and stares through the mucky back window, sees the outlines of Hayley and Scott behind them, forlorn and holding hands. Hayley must have sought the comfort. The poor kid—the threads of her careful holiday plan are fraying. Livia wouldn't swap places; she couldn't stay and wait, be so passive. Yet she wishes one of them were in the car with her rather than Joost. Why wasn't Scott game enough to drive? He's so cranky and keen to dominate the group, yet when there's a chance to lead them out of trouble, he backs away.

Livia swings back in time to see water rushing at the car's bull bar and lapping in waves at the doors. It must be close to a meter deep—she could reach down and touch it like she's on a river cruise. This is not the sunny outback adventure she expected. After three days in Sydney listening to devastating tales of Australian drought, she anticipated dehydrated land, scorching days, and sunburnt skin. Not this deluge, this awkward swamp.

There's a loud crack, and Livia twitches in her seat. "What was that? Did something break?"

"Relax, it was thunder," Joost says.

"Relax . . . *it was thunder*," she repeats. "One more thing I didn't prepare for."

Livia wanted Joost to drive slowly, and now she wants him to speed up. Her eyes close as she tries to swallow the fear, the creeping certainty that if they don't move fast enough, the flood will suck them down.

The vehicle sways, and Livia throws out her arms as if she can steady it. How deep is the water now? Perhaps more than a meter. Could the car overturn? Could they be swept away? Is she capable of escaping through the window? Her eyes snap open, and she bends to remove her boots.

"Nearly there," Joost says. "Do not panic now, girl."

They push forward, water spraying on all sides. The wheels spin without a true grip and Joost places his forearms on the steering wheel as if propelling the car himself. Then they begin to rise higher. Livia watches out her window. She isn't imagining it; the water is falling away. A smile creeps over her face as the bull bar noses up and, seconds later, the tires are free and wet ground is visible below.

She raises a triumphant hand and offers it to Joost, who slaps it midair. It stings. "We did it!" For the first time, she meets his wild smile with her own.

He lets out a long "*Woooot!*" and blasts the horn five times.

She buzzes her window up, already thinking of the hot springs ahead. It doesn't matter that it's raining; she's going to jump in. It's a once-in-a-lifetime opportunity, after all. What a contrast it will be to feel the searing water on her body, cool rain on her head. Then, the Pindarry Hotel. Livia will change into different clothes, perhaps the one cotton dress she packed, and she'll put her boots somewhere to dry out. She's ecstatic, can't wait to see Hayley's relief when she rejoins them. She twists in her seat, and although Hayley and Scott are farther away now, they are clearly waving and clapping. Livia turns to Joost.

"Oh god, I'm so relieved."

He grins. "You were freaking out."

"Can you blame me?"

The four-wheel drive rolls on, the road flat, no immediate puddles ahead.

"When are you stopping?" Livia asks. "Are you going to do a U-turn?"

"In a minute."

"What do you mean?"

"I will stop when it is safe."

Livia reviews their surroundings. Joost could be right; they need a safe spot to turn around, one without saturated ground and lurking ditches.

After a moment, she points. "There's not much water here. It should be okay."

Joost keeps driving.

"What are you doing?" she asks. "We're going too far. There's no need."

"I want to teach them a lesson." Joost's voice is soft.

She stares at him. His tongue is poking between his teeth. "A lesson? Not cool. You promised you wouldn't play games, Joost. C'mon, let's go get the others."

He stays quiet.

"You think this is funny? I don't think Hayley and Scott will appreciate it. This is *their car*. We've left them outside in the rain!"

"We will just drive a bit further."

Thunder cracks again, like the sky is being prized open. Livia crosses her arms. "Fuck this. I am having nothing to do with whatever you're up to. This is all your idea, so don't blame me when things blow up."

"They will not blow up."

"Scott is going to freak out!"

"Oh, I am *so* scared of Scott freaking out."

Livia is astonished by the wicked delight in Joost's eyes. "We need to stick together; we don't have time to play around. In case you've forgotten, we're in the middle of a storm!"

"Hardly a storm."

"Well . . . the worst is still on its way. I'd like to be at the Pindarry before dark."

"Nobody forced the Aussies to leave the car," he says. "They could have come with us."

"Well, they weren't super keen, and they're waiting for us now," Livia says. "They've learned their lesson—Scott was wrong about how deep the water was. You were right, we made it. Can't you be happy with that?"

She looks behind them. Somewhere back there, Hayley and Scott are standing and wondering why the car has disappeared. They pick up speed, and Livia tenses. The tires hiss over the road, the earth on either side shiny wet clay.

"C'mon, Joost." Livia tries to sound untroubled. "Enough is enough. Turn around, please."

The Dutchman does not respond, and she thumps the dashboard in frustration.

"Turn! Around!" she roars.

Joost sighs, long and slow, a patient parent. It makes Livia want to scream.

She could try pleading, though she doesn't think it would work. If anything, he would enjoy it. She could slap his arm, try to break him out of this nonsense and show him how serious this is, but she's loath to touch him or invite a return slap. Maybe the steering wheel could be wrenched away, except any movement might make the car slide across this road, and something tells her Joost is not as terrified of crashing as she is.

"Guess what?" he says.

"I'm not playing guessing games."

He checks the rearview mirror, then looks at her. "We are not going back. Surprise!"

Livia presses her heels hard to the floor of the car, her whole body stiff.

"Stop it, Joost. The time for joking is over."

The four-wheel drive becomes faster still, and Joost relaxes into his seat.

"I am tired of the Aussies," he says. "Those two are boring. Hayley is always whining and asking questions. She is so needy. And Scott is like a tired, slow, old man."

Livia clutches her door handle.

"But you—I like you," he says.

14

Hayley

Tuesday, February 7
3:15 PM

"D O YOU THINK the car will make it?" Hayley asks. She grips Scott's hand with both of hers in an attempt to stymie her shivering. It would be nice if he put a reassuring arm around her, but he's rigid, more concerned about his grandfather's car than his girlfriend, her shaking body and fractured nerves.

"Bloody hope so," he says.

"I'm surprised Livia wants to try this."

"Me too."

"I had the feeling she wanted to stay away from Joost."

"Huh. It doesn't look that way now."

Everything is gray—the sky, the road, the bush, her mood—and the temperature has plummeted since the morning. Hayley's draped her hoodie over her head for shelter, the warmest piece she packed for the road trip, though it's quickly become another piece of sopping clothing.

"I know we're supposed to be grateful for rain," she says, "but this sucks."

Scott stares ahead. "Joost better know what he's doing. He has to drive slow and steady. We can't have too much water splashing underneath the car—it'll wreck the engine."

"There's water everywhere." Hayley gestures with one hand. "How can he avoid it?"

Scott doesn't respond. She wants to ask why he didn't drive if he knows so much about it; however, he's already simmering, and she doesn't want to start an argument.

They watch the car roll forward. The tires disappear first, then arcs of brown water spray from either side like fire hydrants. Livia turns to look through the back window. Hayley shouldn't be surprised by how brave the other girl is, given she'll be on an activist boat in the Timor Sea soon. This is a walk in the park in comparison.

"I can't look." Hayley shuts her eyes for a second, and Scott drops her hand. He takes a few steps and she follows, trying not to feel hurt about the space he's putting between them. They stare hungrily as the car reaches the water's midway point. It may be the deepest section, the most dangerous, and any moment now Hayley expects the water to envelop the bottom half of the car and for it to become stuck. Then what? Livia and Joost climb out? All four of them have to wait in the rain for someone to come and rescue them? What if the level keeps rising and the car is swept away like a paper boat?

The vehicle moves on. "They're gonna make it," she says.

Scott regards her with the beginnings of a smile. The car continues, the water falls away, and then Livia and Joost are safely on the other side.

"They did it." Scott claps loudly.

"I'm so *happy!*" Hayley jumps and waves at the others. "I bet that's the worst puddle we'll see. It'll be easy-peasy from here on!"

Scott isn't listening. He's watching Joost and Livia's progress, the car still lumbering.

Hayley stops jumping. "Where are they going?"

"I guess they're finding a spot to park," Scott says. "It's muddy at the side of the road, and they could still get bogged if they're not careful."

Hayley stands by Scott, moving from foot to foot to generate heat. "I am so over this rain."

She takes in her backpack and tent on the ground. *Not yet*, she thinks. *Wait until the car stops and Joost and Livia come back to help.* Maybe it was silly to remove all this stuff— their belongings are drenched—yet there's a chance everything can dry tonight if they can get a room at the Pindarry. She didn't think of booking accommodations, because the plan was to camp every night. How many rooms does the hotel have, and are they already booked out? How many other people are traveling in this weather? She removes her hoodie, wrings it out, and tucks it beneath her pack. The hotel might have a dryer for guests.

"What the hell is going on . . ." Scott mutters.

Hayley looks up, sees the beam of distant lights, then quickly loses them in the mist. The car has disappeared. "Where did they go?"

"Maybe they turned a corner. Though I didn't think there were any . . ."

"Why are they driving so far?"

"Look, I don't have any answers, okay?" He glares. "C'mon."

They walk to the floodwaters' edge and stop, staring as if waiting for a rare bird to emerge. They watch and wait, shuffle nervously, and Hayley does not want to be the first one to give voice to their fears.

Scott fumbles for his phone. "Fuck," he says as he checks the screen. "Still no reception."

Hayley's fingers flutter across her thighs. "I know what's happening."

"You do?"

"Joost is playing another joke."

"That arsehole. This isn't funny. That's *my* car."

"Or . . . do you think something went wrong? Did the car break down?"

"Why do you ask so many questions!" Scott raises his voice.

Hayley turns away, struggling to banish panic and tears. Like her, Scott is agitated, and there's no point prodding him for answers. She scans the road behind them. No vehicles are coming. She looks forward again, tells her fingers to be still.

"Okay," she says, "okay, okay, okay. This is what we'll do. We'll wait for five more minutes." She points at Scott. "Time it." It's gratifying to see him check his phone screen. He seems calmer when following instructions. "If they're not back in five minutes, they must be in trouble. The car broke down . . . or there's more flooding further on or something."

"And after five minutes? If we don't see them?"

"We go searching. They could be waiting for us to come help and wondering what's taking us so long."

"To hell with that! Let's go now. Did you see how deep it was? It wasn't bad—I reckon we could walk through it, no problem."

"I don't want to." Hayley shakes her head. "I'll slip and fall into the water, I know I will."

"All you have to do is stay on your own two feet." Scott's voice has an edge to it.

"I can't see what's under the surface. Doesn't it freak you out?"

"No, it's only a road."

"Please, Scott, let's just wait here, like we planned."

"It's only going to get darker. You stay here, okay, don't move. I'll check out the road." Scott starts wading into the floodway. His sneakers disappear, his shins. He holds his arms out for balance, wobbles, then rights himself, swipes his wet fringe from his eyes.

"Oh god!" Hayley cries. "Watch out for holes!"

"What do you think I'm doing?" he snaps.

There's an itchy anxiety in her groin, as she's torn between wanting to join Scott in the brown water and stay in the relative safety of watching him. In the end, the growing gap between them spurs her into movement, and she slides her feet, one in front of the other as if they're clamped onto skis, into the bitterly cold stream. It seeps through shoes and socks, alive and undulating. She's repulsed by the current on her skin, teeming with grass and sticks. Maybe snakes. When she reaches the other side, Scott is glaring at her.

"I thought I told you to wait."

"I couldn't. You're right, we should hurry. What if they've had an accident? They could be injured—they'll need all the help they can get."

"Yeah? What are you gonna do for them?"

There's a rudimentary first-aid kit in the glove box, with Band-Aids and a coil of bandage she has no idea how to use.

"Come on, let's get going, I'll be fine," Hayley urges.

"Are you sure? Why don't you stay here? If you hurt your ankle or something, I can't carry you."

"I'm sure."

Scott releases a loud breath, then falls in beside her.

They start jogging, water squelching underfoot. There are no buildings, no farmhouses or sheds in the distance, and no approaching cars, at least none visible in the gloom. There are no signs or markers, not even a fence line. The roadsides have become mud flats, with quivering grass and short bushes squatting in shallow trenches. Hayley wonders why she wanted to come out here—the middle of uninhabited Australia. They should have opted for a beach holiday like other students in their classes.

They jog for ten minutes, reaching a curved section of road. Her legs are heavy, her breath pounds in her ears, and her belly wobbles. The last time she ran anywhere must have been back in high school. Now they're facing a crisis, and Hayley finally understands why fitness matters. When they make it out of here and get back to Adelaide, she'll sign up for gym membership. First, one of those bootcamps. Livia would be able to run this far without feeling breathless. Hayley's sunglasses slip from their perch on her head, and she catches them before they fall to the ground.

"Wait a minute," she moans. "I can't . . ."

She falls back into a rickety march, telling herself to just keep moving. Rakes her hair behind her ears and watches Scott slog ahead, shoes shuffling and arms pumping. He's soon more than fifty meters away, and whatever they find, Scott will see it first. She picks up her legs to resume running and finds it impossible. Her chest is burning. "Pathetic," she chokes.

Ahead of her, Scott has dropped to a walk too. The farther they move, the slower he becomes until he stops. When Hayley reaches him, she wants to cry in tiredness and exasperation. They must have covered at least a kilometer, and there is no four-wheel drive stuck in the mud waiting for them. Holding back her confused tears, she bends to put her hands on her knees and regain her breath instead.

"Where could they be? This is nuts." There's whining in her voice.

It's the outback, it's February, it's supposed to be bone dry and hot. Not all this unrelenting rain, falling on and on, threatening to send Hayley mad. She wants to be at a table inside the Pindarry, eating hot chips, taking photos of the pub's famed interior. Wearing dry clothes and dry shoes.

"We can't freak out," Scott says. "There's an explanation for all of this. We have to keep calm."

Hayley hears it as a personal warning.

"They've driven away," he says, "and we don't know why. I should never have given Joost the keys to the car."

"It's not your fault. I went along with the idea. Everyone did."

They go quiet, panting beneath the deluge, studying the road ahead.

There's no one, there's nothing. They're on their own.

CHAPTER

15

Andrea

Tuesday, February 7
7 PM

WHEN SHE HEARS a motorbike, her first instinct is to turn off the lantern and crouch in the dark. It's not very grown-up, yet every part of her screams that she has to hide. So she switches off the light and waits, listening intently. Who's on the bike and why are they here now, as a squall is building? It might be Dom or one of his mates; it might be a new rider, Andrea doesn't care—she does not want them here, especially when it's just her and Ethan.

The engine sound grows closer. It's a monstrous intrusion, but it seems like just one bike. It must be circling the car park now, finding the best place to stop. Andrea pauses in the center of Quinn's bedroom, palms held out as if they can expel the visitor. *Please go away*, she thinks, *please, please go away.*

She considers ignoring them. It wouldn't be hard—the whole place is dark and everything is shut up. She could keep quiet, and maybe the rider will eventually drive on.

Her hands trail the walls as she navigates into the living room. With hardly any moonlight piercing the clouds, it's difficult to see where she's going. Her heartbeat feels loud enough to be a beacon.

The engine stops. Nothing can be heard over the drumming on the roof.

Andrea creeps along the corridor to the front bar. Her phone is there. She grabs it, slides down to the floor, and checks its screen. Still no signal. Her hands curl into fists, working to contain a growing fear and outrage at the person who has arrived. Why now? She hates to be in this position. It is an outback pub's unwritten obligation to offer hospitality and safety, so can she reasonably refuse entry? If she does ignore the biker, what will they do? They could let themselves into an accommodation hut, stay the night, and wait for the torrent to stop. Hell, Andrea would be ecstatic to have them stay in a room for free if it meant she didn't have to let them into the pub, connected to her home, to where Ethan is sleeping. However, the huts are locked, and the motorcyclist won't be able to enter without breaking in. If they were to do that, they would've crossed a line. What other lines might they cross? Right now, the Pindarry appears a ridiculous, flimsy old building, with its tacked-on rooms and various entry points. What protection does it really offer? They are miles from anywhere and prey to whoever wants to burst in.

"Calm down," Andrea whispers.

She reminds herself this isn't the same situation as years ago, this isn't the person who attacked her in a car park when she was a young bartender. Yet this would not happen if they were living in the suburbs; she and Ethan would never be this isolated. They would be within shouting distance of neighbors. The phone lines would never drop out and a police car could be with them in minutes. Not here, not at the Pindarry. The police are hours away.

Why did Matt have to leave her and Ethan to go to the aid of a man they barely know? She curses his neighborly spirit, even though she knows he couldn't say no to Greg. If they were in trouble, they would expect the locals to come and help. It's give-and-take in remote Australia, essential to building community credit—although that's usually from battling bushfires together, not floods.

And why did Quinn go to the Durand farm today, on the eve of a storm? Andrea should have persuaded her to stay home. Where *is* she? Is it possible she's had an accident?

There's a flutter inside her. Perhaps fear, perhaps the first stirrings of the baby. She wraps her arms around her waist. When Matt gets back, she will definitely tell him about the pregnancy and issue an ultimatum. They need to move to a larger town before the birth. She doesn't have the courage or resilience for this isolation anymore. The stress can't be good for her pregnancy either.

Tap, tap. The visitor knocks at the glass half of the front door. Andrea has to clench to stop from urinating with nerves. *Get a hold of yourself.*

The tapping comes again, harder this time, on the wooden frame.

She can't stay huddled down here; this is ridiculous. If Matt or Quinn could see her now . . .

Whoever it is, they won't give up just because the pub is dark. This is the only haven for miles.

The front door is cold when Andrea places a hand to it. The vinyl blind is pulled down over the glass window, and combined with the lack of light, it shields her face from whoever is on the other side.

"We're closed!" she calls out, trying to modulate her voice to sound firm and upbeat.

"Hello, love." A male voice. "Sorry to disturb ya—I thought you'd still be open, being a pub 'n' all. I was here at lunch with the boys. Remember?"

She freezes. So it is one of the bikers from earlier.

"We all split up," he continues. "This weather has played bloody havoc! Some of the crew are going north, some heading back south. I decided to come here. The roads are dangerous, it's getting wild and woolly. We shoulda known!" There's a self-deprecating laugh.

Andrea stays silent. The rushing downpour is the only sound.

"You still there?" the voice asks.

"Yes," she says.

"Can I come in? I'm soakin'."

"We're closed. Sorry."

"I just need somewhere to kip for the night. Please."

"Like I said, we're closed."

"I won't bother ya, I promise."

Andrea covers her eyes with one hand. What can she possibly say, how can she refuse? There's nowhere else to go and the man is right—it is dangerous to travel. And even if she doesn't open the door, he won't necessarily leave. He might stay around, knocking and pleading, waking Ethan and adding to her anxiety. Like Matt with the bikers earlier today, Andrea needs to be hospitable, to assume the best in people, not the worst. Professionalism is the only armor there is.

"All right," she says. "You can stay in one of the huts . . ." She's posing a question and waits for an agreeable response.

"Bloody brilliant," the biker says. "Thank you. I appreciate this."

Andrea stretches to unlatch the bolt over the door.

16

Livia

Tuesday, February 7
4 PM

LIVIA GRIPS THE handle above her window as if it will keep her grounded. Her eyes dart, checking the speedometer, the road ahead, the growing gap they are leaving between them and Hayley and Scott.

"Okay, very funny," she says. "Can we stop now?"

"I am glad you agree this is funny," Joost says. "This makes me very happy."

His left leg bobs up and down. He's humming with energy.

"This is a massive prank, I'll give you that." Livia works to lighten her tone. "I think we've scared them enough now, Joost. Let's turn around and go back. Scott will be pissed off, but he'll laugh eventually. You got him, you got him good!"

Joost doesn't respond. He stares through the windscreen, the ridiculous beanie pulled down low. Looking at his blank expression makes Livia boil once more.

"*Joost!*" she shouts. "I said this is enough. *Turn around!*"

He brakes sharply, and the rear of the four-wheel drive slides. They fishtail over the road, and a scream rips from Livia's throat. They are about to lose control, and she braces herself with her arms; she forgot to put her seat belt back on. Her body could catapult through the windscreen, shattering onto the hard road. In the next moment, though, the car rights itself and speeds through the hammering rain.

Even as her pulse throbs out of control, Livia draws the seat belt across her body and clips it into place, breathing hard. From head to toe, she's shaking.

"Good girl," Joost says. He sounds out of breath too. "Safety first."

Tears fill her eyes. "I hate you."

He cackles. "Get a grip." He adjusts his position on the seat, and she's afraid he'll lose control and they'll begin sliding again. She crosses her arms over her chest, her bare arms and legs cold and vulnerable.

What must Hayley and Scott be thinking? Do they realize something is going on? Have they crossed the flooded road themselves, or are they still waiting where Joost left them and their belongings? Maybe their phones are working and they've called for help. If not, Hayley could panic soon. Livia pictures her, clothes stuck to her stocky frame, plastic sunglasses perched on her head. She imagines Hayley's distress, and it adds to her own. The Australian girl hasn't been anywhere before and put so much time and love into planning this trip. Now this insanity has arrived. Livia's nails dig into her palms. Scott better not blame Hayley; he better not be lashing out at her right now. This is all Joost's fault, nobody else's.

How long have they been driving? While it can't have been more than a few minutes, they're covering ground rapidly. Livia presses herself against her door and watches Joost from the corner of her eye. Maybe if she stays silent and shows no emotion, he'll grow bored and turn around. If she seems tense or scared, it could fuel his weird adrenaline. He's taking the joke too far, that's all—it's his odd Dutch sense of humor. Joost thinks everyone will admire his mischievous audacity when they're all reunited. He wants this to be a legendary anecdote of their trip. Well, Livia won't laugh about this later. She's not going to forgive Joost for this, and certainly won't be spending any time alone with him. It was reckless to get into the car with him, too trusting. How could she have ignored how creepy he had been earlier in the day? She is a victim of her bravado.

Her family would be distraught to know what's happening right now. If they hear about it later, her parents might not fund any of her future overseas travel. Her father was especially worried about the boat from Darwin, and it took Livia days of wheedling, supported by Camila and her mother, to gain his blessing and money for this tour. Little did they know the Darwin boat might not be the most perilous part of the Australian leg. Perhaps it would be best never to share this. In fact, she decides to forget all about this episode herself. Once she parts ways with Joost, she'll never think about him again—except to post a warning on travel forums. This boy can't be allowed to treat anyone else like this.

"Having fun?" he says.

Livia regards it as a minor triumph that Joost broke the silence.

"No, I'm not having fun," she says tersely. "How can you even ask me that?"

"I am having the best time." He smiles.

"Well, what now? You're gonna keep driving? How far? This is just wasting fuel, Joost."

He is silent.

"You better hope nothing bad happens to Hayley and Scott," she says.

"Shut up, would you?"

Her pulse races. "You know you've stolen a car?"

"It does not even belong to them. Scott borrowed it."

"It doesn't belong to *you*."

He bounces one leg. "You are starting to be a real downer."

"Do you even have a plan?"

"Oh, I have a plan, Miss Livia."

His words send a ripple of terror through her. Livia leans to look at the fuel gauge. The tank is three-quarters full, thanks to their stop in Minnarie. It makes her want to cry in fury.

"It is so good to be alone. Shall we kiss now?" Joost puckers his lips.

Livia moves away in disgust.

"I need the toilet," she declares. "Pull over."

"You are lying."

"I'm not, I swear. I'll wet myself. Please!"

"That is okay with me. I would like to see you piss your pants. I dare you."

"You're revolting."

Livia remains pressed against her door, creating as much room as possible between them. Joost is twisted, that much is clear. She was bluffing about needing to pee, but now she's raised the subject, there's a twinge in her bladder. It's maddening to think he has control over her. He hums and taps his thumbs on the steering wheel, and she wishes he would be still. Whatever aimless tune he's enjoying, it's penetrating her skull.

"Hey, at least the Aussies have plenty of water." Joost watches her as if she will join in with his laughter.

"What about when it gets dark? They'll be wet and freezing," Livia says. "Not to mention scared and confused."

"Didn't you notice—they took their tent out of the car. How funny is that?"

"What's wrong with you? Hayley and Scott are good people; they don't deserve this! They could get hypothermia, and you'll be in huge trouble. Huge."

"*They're good people . . .*" Joost whines like he's imitating her.

"You'll be arrested," she continues. "Kicked out of the country and never allowed to come back."

"Promise?"

"You could be in trouble at home too. Maybe spend time in jail. This is serious."

Joost takes one hand from the steering wheel, resting back on the seat like he's at the cinema. "I am not going to jail."

"Ha. Good luck with that."

"Livia, this is just a joyride."

"Actually, it's kidnapping."

"You got in the car with me; you made that choice. I did not make you, I did not grab you."

"And I've asked you a dozen times since then—let me out!"

"Hayley and Scott saw you get into the car," he says. "You were happy and mucking around. They know the true version of events."

Anger surges through her. "They know you're a weirdo and I wouldn't leave them behind!"

Joost hardly reacts. "A weirdo, huh? That's okay, I don't care what anyone thinks of me. Never have, never will."

Livia wedges her hands between her thighs to halt her trembling, tries to control her breathing. This isn't working. She needs to keep her head and think about the situation. He's not listening to her, and it's time to take a different tack.

"What about your parents? They're paying for this trip, aren't they? They must love you and care about you—your parents don't want you driving around the outback like a maniac. They don't want to see you in prison. What would they say about what you're doing to me?"

Joost's face is drooping. Whether he's feeling glum or bored, Livia can't tell.

"Do you have any brothers or sisters?"

"I do not have anyone I care about," he says. "Except you. You're my number one." He lets his tongue hang from his mouth like a panting dog.

Livia turns her head, determined not to let him see the distress on her face.

The rain slows, and the weak, drained sunlight casts a discomfiting glow. Livia waits for a car or a building to materialize. There are no lights anywhere. It's as if they're on an uninhabited planet. What can she do if another vehicle does appear—open her window and wave her arms? Lunge across Joost and hit the car horn? She'd only have a fraction of a second to gain someone's attention, and Joost would try to stop her. At this speed, on this slick surface, they'd inevitably crash. She can't believe how quickly and effortlessly he's trapped her.

Her phone screen shows no service. Joost was right about one thing: technology has not permeated this remote land. How do people live like this? What happens in emergencies?

"You know, we could keep driving . . . go right through the center of Australia without even stopping." His voice is lower, conspiratorial. "You and me. Side by side on our own road trip."

Her lip curls. "Yeah, great idea, my dream holiday."

"It is not so hard to keep driving, all night, all day. Truck drivers go for days."

"That's different. They're used to it and they *do* make rest stops."

"I am young, I am fit. I am alert. How long do you reckon I could go without stopping?"

"I'm not gonna dare you, if that's what you're waiting for."

"Oh, come on, dare me."

"All right—I dare you to *turn around* and go back for the others!"

His response is loud laughter.

"We're not having a good time together, so why not let me go?"

"Speak for yourself. I am having a brilliant time. The best time I have had in Australia so far. *So far . . .*"

Livia's skin prickles.

They approach a road sign—yellow and black, diamond shaped. It is bent like a tree that's grown on a windy plain. Livia sees the bold words: FLOODWAY.

"See that?" She stabs a finger. "What are you gonna do now?"

She waits for Joost to decelerate. They'll have to stop and check the water level a second time, giving her a chance to escape. What happens after that, she's not sure—it's one step at a time.

He doesn't ease his foot from the accelerator, and the water-covered road looms.

"Hey! You're going too fast! Didn't you see the sign?"

"What am I supposed to do? Stop the car?"

"Yes!" Livia props her feet against the floor as if it'll help her avoid the imminent crash.

There is no time to argue further. Their wheels hit the water, and it gushes around them. The engine labors, and the tires begin slipping. They lose speed.

"You're insane!" she yells. "You're going to wreck the car!"

Livia buzzes the window all the way down, and rain sprays her face. The four-wheel drive growls and chugs as she slips off her seat belt and gets to her knees. She doesn't know how Joost is going to get through this, but she's not staying here with him.

"Right, like you are going to jump," Joost taunts.

It's the final spur Livia needs. She juts her head out the window, preparing to climb out. She feels his fingers rake her shoulder and instinctively jabs an elbow backward. It doesn't

hit a target, but it gains her some space. She thrusts one leg
through the open window and bends so her head and torso
can follow, straddling the door like she's astride a horse. The
car struggles through the floodway, moving slowly, and Joost
curses.

Livia stretches her left leg farther, her toes reaching
water, then hauls the rest of herself out, hopping. At the
last moment, her right foot nearly catches on the window
frame and she pulls it free, falling out sideways. Her arms
flail. All she can think is *Don't let me get caught under the
car*. A hip and elbow slam painfully into the new swamp,
and when she opens her mouth to yelp, it fills with floodwater. She splutters, finds her feet, and scrambles away,
nursing an elbow that's shrieking in pain. She's in a nightmare where her body won't move as fast as it needs to. The
car is meters ahead, liable to lose traction and slide toward
her at any moment.

Livia reaches the scrubby roadside.

What a fucking mess, she thinks, furious again.

She should've known it was risky to team up with Joost.
He brought joints on this trip; maybe he's taken pills too.
His eyes don't look right. That must be it—Joost is high. It's
the only explanation for this madness. The best thing to do
is reserve her energy and be ready for whatever comes next.

She sinks to the ground, face to the sky, seeing a patch-
work of slate-and-auburn clouds furled and angry, glimmer-
ing at the edges.

Joost nudges the car forward, water spilling from the
inner fenders. He's a lofty figure behind the steering wheel,
head almost touching the ceiling. If he can't drive the car
the whole way, if it gets stuck, he will have to leave it too.
What then, with them both stranded here without transport?
Maybe other travelers are taking this same route; perhaps
they'll collect Hayley and Scott on their way. They could
arrive soon, and they'll be angry at being left behind. Hayley

will be distraught, perhaps teary, and that's okay. Livia will soothe her, she'll explain everything. And then they can report Joost to the police.

Maybe.

Livia isn't sure how her story will sound. Will anyone believe it? It's like Joost said—she willingly got into the car with him. It gave her a buzz, she felt daring, and for some stupid reason she didn't want Joost to think her as timid as the Aussies. It seems so juvenile now.

The four-wheel drive regains traction and crawls onto drier ground. While it's a relief the car is all right, Livia is afraid of what may happen next. Joost is unpredictable, but at the very least he'll try to sweet-talk her back into the car. She won't get in unless he lets her drive, will insist he hand over the keys. Maybe he'll admit he's not sober and she can urge him to let her take the wheel.

A tremor overtakes her body as the car comes to a halt. She rises and walks a few meters away before the driver's door opens and Joost stumbles out. He seems injured until he begins laughing, slapping the bonnet of the vehicle like it's his buddy in an adventure movie.

"Woo! We made it!" he screeches. He points and starts to approach her. "Check you out, Wonder Woman. You jumped out of a moving car."

Livia scowls, breathing hard. "Stay away from me."

"What do you think I am going to do?" Joost's eyebrows form a pitiful triangle. "Livia, please. I am not going to touch you."

"You already have touched me! Remember this morning?"

"Come on . . . don't be like that," he croons, but stops before he gets too close.

"Let me drive," she says. "Give me the keys."

"I don't think so."

Livia waits for sudden moves in her direction. Instead, Joost saunters to the mud at the opposite side of the road, widens his legs, puts one hand down his pants, and takes out his penis.

"You're a pig!" Livia averts her eyes before she sees him urinate.

Joost cackles. "You know you want to watch!"

Livia thinks about her next move. She shouldn't stray from the car. The engine is still running. If it comes to a physical tussle for the vehicle, Joost will win. She can't fight him off; he's much taller than her and could beat her up if he wanted to, although Livia is convinced it won't come to that. She just has to end this craziness. If she can get to the car first, she can drive back to collect Hayley and Scott and they can figure things out from there. That could give Joost time to come down from whatever drugs he's taken.

She monitors him from the corner of her eye. How long is he going to take?

His head twists and he catches her. "Like what you see?"

Livia snorts, steps over the wet ground, her expression sulky as she pretends to reluctantly head for the passenger door.

"Good girl, I knew you were smart," Joost says. "See? We are unstoppable. The real road trip is about to start, and it is going to be incredible."

Nearing the car, Livia struggles to maintain a calm mask, to control the adrenaline coursing through her. This must work; the timing has to be perfect. She's within reach of the hood when her energy explodes, powering her to lunge for the driver's door, still hanging ajar.

"Hey!" Joost yells.

Livia swings around and onto the driver's seat. The key is in the ignition, a dangling metallic savior, and she's yanking the door closed when Joost appears, his face looming like a monster from a children's story. He grabs the door with two hands and peels it back, inserts his thin body into the gap. His eyes are wide and wild.

"Don't be stupid," he wheezes. "Get out of the car!"

Livia loops an arm through the steering wheel, head down, determined not to be removed. He's a writhing beast, grunting hard against her, and she kicks out with one boot. It makes a connection.

"Fuck!" Joost doubles over. One of his hands comes loose, and Livia fights to win the door. If she can only get it shut, then she can slam down the lock and the car will be hers. Pain flares in her elbow, which is still sore from her leap to the ground, yet she clings to the steering wheel tightly, straining for the handle with her other arm. The metal wobbles back and forth between the two of them.

"Come on, girl, give it up," Joost grunts. He seems to be enjoying himself again, and his grin terrifies her. "You know strength always wins!"

A spark of hatred flares inside Livia. And then she recalls a childhood game.

She releases her fingers. The door flings back and strikes Joost in the face. He shrieks and clutches his nose, and Livia stares in horror. She wanted to gain control, and now she is stalled at the sight of Joost's blood. Did he break something? Has she gone too far, does he need help?

Livia has one foot dangling out the door, one arm still threaded through the steering wheel. Joost has staggered back. He might lash out in a second, try to hurt her for hurting him. This is no time for indecision—this is her chance, this is the moment to close the door and drive away, to go back to Hayley and Scott.

Her fingers reach for the handle at the same moment as Joost's howling morphs from pain to fury. It's an animalistic cry, and Livia feels its reverberation inside her. She stretches, straining to close the gap. Her fingers find only air, and then Joost is on her again.

17

Hayley

Tuesday, February 7
4:30 PM

THE GROUND IS hard and damp, but Hayley is grateful
for some sort of shelter.

It was her idea to erect their tent and wait inside, and
Scott wearily agreed. Drenched and defeated, they tramped
back to their pile of belongings, the return feeling so much
farther than their initial jog. They dithered for a while on
where to make camp. Close to the road, where they might be
spotted and more easily hail any vehicles? Or farther away,
at a safer remove, to avoid being struck by a driver battling
to see through the weather? In the end, they settled for a few
meters off the shoulder.

After Minnarie, Hayley and Scott had a better idea of
how to pitch the tent. It wasn't a pleasant exercise, working
while saturated—and minus Livia's helping hands—but they
got it up with grim determination. They lugged the backpacks and other belongings inside, everything soaked and
hefty.

Now Hayley is huddled with Scott under the canvas, hopeful its distinctive color will be a beacon to any passing traffic. Her sodden clothes stick to her, immensely uncomfortable and constricting. She'd prefer to sit closer, but Scott leans away, one elbow on his pack, treating her like she's contagious. If this is how he behaves in a crisis, she doesn't appreciate it. He's as cross with her as he is with the others.

Hayley attempts to brighten things. "It's lucky we grabbed the tent out of the car."

"Yeah," Scott says. "We are *so* lucky, I feel hashtag-blessed right now."

She exhales. She wanted to be out of the weather and is glad for this minor achievement. If the rain's off her head, she can take a moment and think about what to do next. Scott, though, seems more intent on brooding than brainstorming.

"What if we're here for hours? It's gonna get properly dark," Hayley says. "Do we have a torch?"

"Pfft. What do we need light for? Nothing to see out here."

"It would be less scary."

Hayley plays with her shoelaces, thinking, picturing Livia climbing into the four-wheel drive with Joost. What happened inside that car? Where did they go?

"So, what do you want to do now?" Scott growls.

"I dunno. Do you think they'll come back?"

"They haven't come back yet, have they?"

"This is nuts."

"Tell me about it."

"I don't understand how Livia could leave us. She seems so nice."

"Anyone can appear nice when they want to."

Hayley throws her hands up. "Livia is *amazing*. She's a climate activist! I read her blog, I follow her Instagram. She loves animals, loves nature—there's no way she would leave us here."

"And yet she has."

"This is Joost; it must be his idea. Underneath everything, he's a bully, don't you think?"

"He's a dickhead, that's what he is."

"Hey, what if they're hooking up? Do you think it's possible? Maybe they wanted privacy, though there are less drastic ways to—"

"Will you shut up?"

Hayley shrinks, wounded. It's understandable that Scott is tetchy; he's afraid too. But does he have to take it out on her?

She reaches for her bag, unzips it, and removes a block of chocolate, waiting for Scott to tell her off. Lately, he's been remarking on her weight. Instead, he offers his palm. She breaks off a row each. The familiar sweetness makes her feel better, and her tongue explores her mouth to make sure she has all of it.

"When we get home, I am going to eat the hugest bar of chocolate—Cadbury Caramello," she says. "And I'm gonna take the *longest* hot shower. Maybe at the same time."

"Good idea." Scott sniggers.

"This holiday sucks . . . we'll laugh about this later. Hey?"

Scott looks at her, and it feels like the most thoughtful consideration he's given in a long time. "I guess it will make a good story."

"When it's exam time, we'll look back and *wish* we were here!"

"If you say so."

"Last year of uni." She nudges her boyfriend. "It's gonna be great. After we graduate, we'll get amazing jobs, we might even work in the same accounting firm or government department. And we'll go on brilliant holidays, nothing like this one, no cheap road trips."

"Holiday where?"

"Overseas. We'll go to the most crowded cities in the world—places packed with people so there's no way we can get stranded. Paris. London. Tokyo. And we'll go by plane, first class."

"How would you afford all that?"

"I told you—we'll get good jobs. That's why we're going to uni, right?"

"You told Livia you wanted to volunteer. Go visit some villages and stuff."

"I know. There's no reason I can't do both."

Without warning, Scott flicks the tent flap aside and clambers out. She crawls after him. Fat raindrops are falling and the air has become cooler, a welcome freshness that revives her.

"Scott, what are you doing?"

"I can't just sit and wait here all night." He swings his arms in agitation.

"What choice do we have?"

"I'm gonna walk until I find them. Or find somebody."

"You're what?" Hayley squawks. "That could take hours."

"Yeah, maybe. It's better than hanging around here, shivering our arses off."

Hayley surveys the road, a gray strip that is beginning to blend with the dimming light. It's hard to imagine walking it, with such immense and unknown space on either side, the great wet sky overhead. Somehow, the feeble tent anchored in the scrub represents safety, a fragment of civilization.

"When you get lost in the outback, you're not supposed to go wandering," she reminds him.

"That's if you *still have your car*!" Scott barks.

Hayley flinches. "Why are you getting mad with me? This isn't my fault."

"Oh, yes, it bloody is."

She is stunned by his words. "You're being a real jerk . . ."

Scott hops forward with an arm half raised, and for a second, Hayley thinks he's going to hit her. He has never done it before, she's never imagined this, and she reels back. Their eyes lock, Scott's shining with fury, then he drops his arm and spins to the road. What is happening to them?

"Wait!" she shouts. "I'm sorry. I don't want to fight."

He walks fast, doesn't look back.

"Please, Scott. Stay here, we need to stick together!"

She could follow him, yet she's tethered to the tent, unable to make herself leave it.

She watches until Scott is a distant shape, until he is enveloped by the mist.

18

Andrea

Tuesday, February 7
7:30 PM

"THANKS, LOVE. I'M sorry to rock up in the middle of the night like this," the man says.

He looms in the dark doorway, black helmet dangling from one hand like a bowling ball, a new contentment already in his voice. He's in jeans and long sleeves, skinny, taller than her. The sinking sun is smothered by cloud, and Andrea cannot make out his face. The rain is a shower symphony around them, striking the verandah roof, the car park, the desperate gums ringing the buildings.

Andrea hurries behind the counter, finds a second emergency lantern and switches it on. She's under a spotlight now, but it's the only way to find what she's looking for. Footsteps echo in the near-empty front bar. The man has followed her inside.

"I'm trying to be quiet," Andrea says evenly, trying to appear unruffled. "My family is asleep." She crouches behind the counter, where a compact cupboard is secured with a keypad. Presses in the four-digit code, opens the door, and selects a room key from a hook.

"Matt has conked out, hey?" The man chuckles.

Andrea looks up, sees the blue eyes, the slack holes in the ears. "Oh, it's you."

"It's me." The biker holds up wriggling fingers, a macabre children's entertainer. "Rosey."

The biker who took Ethan for a motorbike ride, the man she was raging at earlier. Of all of Dom's friends, why did it have to be him returning? Andrea huffs angrily, holds back her spluttering. She wants to shove him outside, push him back all the way to the mucky car park and slam the door closed. She should have listened to her instincts and not opened the door.

Andrea drops the key onto the counter. "There. It's the first hut, just head around behind this building, you can't miss them."

"Thanks, love. What about my bike? Is there somewhere dry I can stash it?"

She thinks for a second. "The big shed. It's not locked; you can slide the door open and park it in there."

"Perfect."

A flicker of lightning sends glints of brightness around the building.

"What's your name?" Rosey asks, sounding cheery.

"Andrea."

"Andrea, nice to meet ya—properly this time." He places his helmet on the bar, leans his elbows alongside it. "How about a coffee? I need something to warm me up."

She gestures to the black ceiling above. "Sorry. The power is out."

Rosey slaps his forehead. "Of course. Why else are we standing in the dark? Kinda spooky, innit? No streetlights around here, no traffic neither."

"Look, I really have to close up."

"Jeez, I'm freezing, Andrea. If I can't have coffee, how about a Scotch?"

"I don't think so."

"I could even go a nice drop of port. I can't remember the last time I drank port, probably not since I was a kid and stole some from my granddad. Heh-heh."

"Like I said, the bar is closed."

"Pretty please?"

Reluctantly, Andrea turns to examine the shelves. The sooner he's served, the sooner he'll move on. His eyes are probably on her backside, but she refuses to allow nerves to take hold. This isn't the same man who attacked her years ago, nothing bad is going to happen, Rosey just wants a drink, this is her job, and it's completely ordinary. She lifts a sealed bottle of port. It has been there so long it's dust covered. She wrenches the lid off and pours a measure into a short glass.

"There you are—your warming drink." A peal of thunder vibrates in the distance, a giant rock rolling across a floor.

"You're a good woman." Rosey raises the glass to her. He tastes the liquid, coughs, and wrinkles his nose. "Old man's shit. Like I said, my granddad used to enjoy a drop. He's not with us anymore."

"You don't have to drink it." Andrea screws the lid back onto the bottle tightly, as if to say *That will be all for tonight.*

Rosey remains leaning on the bar. The worn lines of his face are like yawning scars. "Nice gig you got here, Andrea, running this place. Away from the hustle and bustle of the city."

"It's all right."

"I guess you and your hubby meet people from all over the world? Tourists exploring the great outback, hanging out to see a kangaroo or wombat, heh-heh. How many visitors would you get each week, do you reckon?"

"I'm not sure."

"Weather like this makes a difference, I s'pose. Not many people on the road right now—it's deserted."

"And that's partly why we shut up for the night."

"Got anyone else staying tonight?"

Andrea ignores the question. She wants this to be over. Rosey's manner has shifted from grateful to relaxed, almost entitled, as though he has all the time in the world to enjoy his drink. She wishes Matt would come home now; she'd give anything to see his headlights approaching through the storm.

Rosey hunches around his glass protectively. The port looks like blood in a vial.

"Can't believe the fellas wanted to keep riding," he says. "It'd be different if we were in cars, ya know, but my jacket was getting so heavy I was struggling to keep hold of the handles, heh-heh. Dunno where the boys are now. That's their problem, innit? I wouldn't be surprised if one or more of them come a cropper. This is my safe haven, right?"

"Mmm. As I said, you can stay in the first hut." She pushes the key across the bar and closer to Rosey.

He doesn't look down. It's as if she hasn't said a word.

"So how's your boy going? Cute kid, very quiet, friendly enough. He was excited about gettin' on the bike, I can tell you that much. How's he goin'? All tucked up asleep . . . like Matt?"

Andrea's heart pounds, enormous in her chest. "He's fine." She pictures Ethan asleep, breathing softly, his cute nose, eyelids shut fast, oblivious to the growing storm. This unwelcome visitor.

"I didn't mean to scare ya before. Boys his age, they dig bikes. Boys my age too, heh-heh! We were just havin' a bit of fun, Andrea, no harm done."

"Well. You should have asked for permission first."

"Okay. Can I take him for a ride tomorrow morning?"

"Absolutely not."

"Why? Because of the weather?"

"No. Because I don't want him on a motorbike. He's too young."

"No such thing as too young." Rosey downs the port and raps the glass on the counter. "One more. Please."

Andrea clutches the bottle neck. "Tell you what. How about I give you the bottle and you can take this back to your room and enjoy it there?"

"For free?"

"Yes."

"Don't you like my company?"

"It's late, I'm tired."

"Are you kidding? It's still early. We may as well hang out and keep chattin'. I'm enjoying myself, and I don't think I'd enjoy myself being alone in one of them teeny rooms."

"We didn't plan to be open tonight, and I've been working all day."

Rosey regards her with hooded eyes. "It's funny how your hubby isn't here. He always let you work alone? I wouldn't let my wife take the night shift by herself. I'd take better care of her."

"He fell asleep, he's exhausted. We've been sandbagging all day."

"Or maybe he's afraid of the thunder? What do you reckon?"

Andrea pretends to tidy things around the bar.

Rosey eases his wet jacket from his shoulders, lays it next to the helmet. He pats the stool beside him. "Pull up a seat, Andrea. Have a drink with me. C'mon, stop fussing around."

Andrea keeps her chin up, thinking, *He doesn't believe that Matt is here.* Still, there's no way the biker could know for sure. There is a large shed outside, and any number of cars could be parked in it. Indeed, their spare car is there. She moves the bottle closer to Rosey, trying to seal the deal. Like the room key, he refuses to pick it up. He keeps one elbow glued to the bar, blue eyes fixed on her.

"You tryin' to get rid of me, Andrea? C'mon, you can be more friendly than that."

19

Quinn

Tuesday, February 7
6:30 PM

QUINN PULLS AWAY, thrusting a boot at the man's chest, not caring about his injuries. The stranger cries out and the hand clutching her wrist loosens, but he doesn't entirely let go. Quinn hears Bronte barking from the car and wishes she had let her dog out.

"Let me go," she gasps.

"Please." It's a weak voice. "Help me."

Quinn freezes, confused. It's not what she expected to hear. The hand releases her, she scrambles back, and the man doesn't pursue her. His arm falls to the wet road, and he moans loudly. His eyes and one side of his mouth are swollen. His face looks so battered and bloodied it makes her feel ill to look at it. She stands a few meters away and watches, waiting for him to make another move, scanning the low saltbush at the roadside for anyone lurking there. It doesn't appear to be a trick. The man can't truly hurt her, he can barely see, yet she remains rattled by his touch.

She edges closer. "I'm trying to help you. Just don't grab me, okay? You scared me. I'll call for help . . ."

She sprints back to the car. As soon as she opens the door, Bronte springs outside—there's no stopping her. Quinn scoops up her phone and checks the screen. No coverage.

"Shit." She stamps one foot on the ground. There's a two-way radio fixed beneath the dashboard, but they're too far out of range to reach the Pindarry.

Bronte sniffs the stranger warily.

"Bront—get away." Quinn slaps her leg and whistles, drawing the dog back to her side.

She wonders what to do. She isn't strong enough to haul the man into her car, and if he's dragged anywhere, it could injure him even more. Yet it's dangerous for him to be lying out in the rain. His body temperature will already be dropping, and that could lead to hypothermia. First, he needs to be sheltered from the downpour. If they're lucky, someone else will arrive soon.

She opens the driver's door, coaxes Bronte back in, and starts the engine. Carefully, she reverses the vehicle closer, terrified of running over the man. Perhaps that's what happened to him in the first place, a hit-and-run, yet surely those accidents only happen in the city? There are no pedestrians out here. It's more likely that somebody beat him up and left him to die. Why? Who is he?

When the car is as near as she dares drive, she leaps out, opens the back hatch, and retrieves an old picnic rug, the type with a plastic base. She returns to the man and raises the rug over them, having them take refuge beneath the improvised tarp together. She studies him; he's unconscious once more. Their faces are only centimeters apart and it's intrusive to be so close, as if she's crept into his bedroom to watch him sleep. Crouching next to him, she prays for a car to come by.

*   *   *

Quinn thinks of the last time she waited by a roadside, years ago, in very different circumstances.

It was the Christmas season and a scorching-hot afternoon. Quinn and her mother, Trish, were returning from a weekend of clothes shopping in Port Augusta. Ryan was at a cricket carnival with friends in Adelaide. They were only sixty kilometers from home when Quinn was startled by a thudding noise beneath them and the car broke down.

"It's okay, the engine just needs a rest," Trish reassured her, easing to the side of the road.

They climbed out of the vehicle and were assaulted by the heat of the day. Quinn felt the yellow sun burning her neck as she watched her mother prop up the hood and probe the car's innards. She was afraid they wouldn't discover what was wrong, then heard a triumphant "I've worked it out!"

Her mother beckoned Quinn closer. "See this? It's a piece of fan belt. It was fraying—that happens sometimes—and now it's come lose. That's what made the banging noise."

"That seems bad," Quinn said.

"It is—luckily, your mother is always prepared." Trish made the googly-eyed smile Quinn adored. "This will be a good chance for you to learn more about cars, love."

They moved to the boot, and Trish pushed shopping bags out of the way to pull out a plastic crate of spare parts. She rifled through until she found another fan belt. Quinn remembered feeling smug because her parents had grown up in remote Australia and were always ready for tricky situations like this. Soon they would be back inside the air-conditioned car and on the way home.

"All right, let's do this," Trish said, bending under the hood, concentration stitched across her face. "I don't get it," she muttered after a few moments, angling her head to examine the faulty fan belt.

Quinn moved closer. "What's wrong, Mum?"

"I can't see where I undo the casing."

"Can I take a look?"

"Sure, go ahead," Trish said, sounding distracted.

Quinn stared at the torn fan belt, looking for a miraculous answer to what Trish couldn't find.

"Shit!" Trish cried. "I'd be able to fix this if the engine wasn't all upside down!"

"Upside down?"

"Well, it's not right . . . the fan belt doesn't usually sit like that."

Her mother stood with her hands on angular hips. She was wearing her city outfit of tailored shorts with a crisp white blouse, a jade necklace gleaming at her neck. Trish didn't wear jewelry around the farm. She studied the empty road for a moment. "We need to call for help. We can't stay out here much longer—we'll roast."

"Who can we call? Dad's busy." He was a volunteer member of the Country Fire Service, like most locals, and was helping fight a scrub fire three hundred kilometers away.

"Dad couldn't fix this anyway," Trish growled.

"Sorry."

"No . . . I'm sorry, sweetheart." Trish frowned at the fan belt again, as if it might have changed position. Her shoulders sagged. "We have to try the auto service." She tapped at her phone. "Let's just hope they don't take long."

After the call was placed, Trish put their water bottles into a bag and plucked a blanket from the back seat. They pulled on hats and moved to a clutch of mallee trees, the only shade for miles around. First they examined the orange dirt for snakes or aggressive ants, then Trish folded the blanket into the bulkiest seat possible for the two of them, and they sat to wait in the thick heat. Quinn's mother rested with her knees up, held together by her thin arms, softly swearing at the cloudless sky.

"It's okay, Mum." Quinn patted her ankle. "Maybe they'll be here soon."

"I just know I could have fixed it," her mother said, "but these modern engines and the bloody idiots who build them . . ." A sob caught in her throat.

"It's not your fault, Mum. Nobody could fix it."

"I wanted to be home. I was planning to put the cooling on, put the shopping away, have dinner ready for your dad. He's out there battling a fire, and I wanted to make sure everything was ready when he got home. And I don't like you being out here in the heat."

They waited for more than an hour, Trish regularly asking her daughter if she was okay. Their clothes stuck to their skin, and Quinn wished she could douse her face with some of her drinking water. When the auto service arrived, the first thing the mechanic did was hand each of them a chilly bottle of water from an esky in his passenger footwell. Quinn pressed it to her neck. Then the mechanic spent less than a minute under the car hood.

"Nah, I can't fix that here," he told them. "I'll need to tow it to the shop and pull it apart."

Quinn watched her mother's body relax. She was relieved it wasn't an easy fix, because she could maintain her pride. Yet she soon looked vexed, upset about getting home later than planned, and was huffing as they transferred their shopping bags into the mechanic's truck. The adults talked about the broken-down car and then cricket while Quinn perched between them on the bench seat, trying not to sway into the mechanic as the journey lulled her.

When they finally reached the farm, Trish insisted the man stay for a sandwich and cup of coffee. She asked about the scrub fire, and the mechanic said it had been contained hours earlier.

"I wonder where Dad is, then," Quinn said.

She never forgot those words. The tension and disquiet in the room. The way her mother stared vacantly out the window.

"He'll be right," the mechanic said. "Probably helping to mop up."

"Yeah." Trish nodded. "He'd stay to help."

*   *   *

Now instead of facing dangerous heat, Quinn is trapped by the side of the road in unremitting rain. The sky is growing darker and the droplets feel harder. What would her father make of this weather if he were still alive? Would his farm be better prepared for it? Would he see this freak storm as an opportunity, or would it be another weather curse, beating him down?

Bronte snuffles against them, and Quinn raises the picnic blanket to let her in. The dog's breath is clammy on her neck, her coat carrying her familiar dusky scent. Quinn puts tentative fingers on the man's forehead, and it is icy in contrast.

"We can't wait here, can we, Bront? Nobody is driving around now, and this bloke is freezing. We have to go."

Quinn leaves the picnic blanket, returns to her car and opens a passenger door, then races back and prods the man.

"Hey, can you hear me?"

He turns his head and mumbles.

"Can you walk?"

There's no response, and she releases a frustrated sob. She can't lift him; she is too short and slight. "Hey." She shakes him more vigorously. This is their best option. "You have to wake up."

His bulging eyes shift behind closed lids.

"You just need to take a few steps. Come on!" Quinn grabs an arm and tugs. The body begins rolling, and she thinks it is her doing, then it keeps moving and the man sits up. "Yes! That's good, keep going."

She ducks under his arm and heaves, and together they rise from the ground, swaying slightly. Quinn summons all her strength to get him moving, shuffling for the open door.

He lets out a piercing cry, and she almost drops him. Bronte barks, dancing on her paws. Somehow, the man flops onto the back seat. Quinn rushes to the opposite door and tows him across the vinyl. He yells in pain and she blocks out the sound, closes both doors carefully. He's in and they can be on their way.

Behind the steering wheel, Quinn pauses. Where should they go? The Durand farm is closest; they could turn around and be there in fifteen minutes. But there's nobody to help them at the vacant property, and little food or medical supplies. She would be alone with the stranger and this storm could continue for hours, maybe even days. Her other option is the pub, an hour's drive away, and Andrea and Matt have great first-aid training.

Quinn starts the engine as the rain lashes the windscreen and clenches the steering wheel in frustration. The journey will take longer in this deluge—it's a challenge to see a few meters in front of her.

"We're going to the Pindarry," she tells Bronte.

The tubby dog whines, sounding as anxious as Quinn feels.

20

Hayley

Tuesday, February 7
5:30 PM

THE WIND HAS gained power. It batters at the canvas along with the rain, and Hayley flinches at every strange sound. What made her think she could stay here without Scott? This tent is no protection from anything.

She clamps hands over ears, trying to block out the flapping and cracking. If she weren't so set on conserving her phone battery, she'd listen to music. She begins to sob, wishing her parents were here. They would make everything better. With phone reception, she would call them and they would come up with a solution, even from miles away in Adelaide. She'd love to hear their familiar voices. If somebody was coming for her, if other people were aware of her situation, it would make the waiting more bearable.

But nobody knows, and right now, with Scott walking away, it's as if nobody cares.

First, Livia and Joost left her. Now Scott. He didn't ask her to come with him, didn't plead, he didn't even look back.

Is he trying to be courageous? Maybe he wants to be her hero, to fetch help and return as soon as he can. Or maybe he's putting himself first. Another example of Scott pulling away from their relationship.

Back in June they had a miserable patch, with weeks of leaden skies and wet leaves on the ground. Without the buffer of classes, they were cooped up together in the house. Hayley tried to coax Scott into taking walks with her, to sit on the sofa and watch Netflix, to visit the pub for half-price beer and a free band.

"I don't feel like it," was his constant refrain.

Finally, she asked him, "Are you getting sick of me? You spend all your time gaming; you barely look at me. You're going to dump me, aren't you?"

"No. What makes you say that?"

"You never want to spend any time with me."

"We live together!"

"That doesn't count if we don't talk. We don't do anything together."

Scott pushed his laptop away, rubbed his eyes behind his glasses. "I don't know what you want from me, Hales. I'm going through so much shit. Uni. Work. All that."

"Well, the same stuff is happening to me and I don't sulk all day."

He looked at her, slumped in his seat, weariness and softness in his eyes. "Look, I'm sorry, okay? I'll try to do better."

Hayley felt bad. She put her arms around him and they kissed, then eventually moved into the bedroom and made love while bleak sunlight spilled over the mattress. That night, they walked to the pub for dinner and she felt lit up inside, full of things to tell him. At the table, he didn't look at his phone once.

Over the following weeks, their connection was strong, and she was reassured. Then, leading into Christmas, Scott became miserable again, barely able to speak to Hayley, let alone show affection. The road trip was supposed to unite them again, but perhaps he's truly had enough of her.

Hayley wipes her eyes. One of her new nails has broken—an ugly angle that has ruined the whole look. New to professional manicures, she forgot to pack an emery board. Sighing, she draws out her phone. No signal and no social media doesn't mean she can't record her turmoil. She feels compelled to write. In the Notes function, she begins an entry as if it's an Instagram caption. It's calming, and before long, she has tapped out several paragraphs:

> *Alone in the bush.*
>
> *Some holiday this turned out to be! Weeks of planning and everything goes to shit because of the weather. Like it's not even supposed to rain out here. I thought there was a drought and it turns out that was a massive exaggeration and it's actually raining too much!!*
>
> *That's not the only problem. Livia and Joost took our car and drove away!! I still cannot work out why they left. Are they insane? Maybe they're in love and they've eloped and that's nice for them but what about us? hahahahaha*
>
> *Scott blames me and now he's taken off. Fucking incredible. GRRRRR. What kind of boyfriend leaves his girlfriend like this? Maybe it's for the best. He's such a grumpy bastard. You wouldn't know he's on holiday because he keeps lashing out at me. I should've known this was coming because he was acting all weird before we even left the city.*
>
> *So now I'm alone in the dark and any old creep could turn up . . .*

*   *   *

The diary begins to frighten her, so she stops typing, sits still, and listens for any new noises. She hasn't been paying attention—anything could be happening out there. But no, it's the same frantic weather assaulting the canvas.

The phone battery should be conserved, but she can't resist scrolling through her camera roll. There's a picture of Livia, Joost, and Scott standing by the four-wheel drive on the sunny morning they left Adelaide. All three are squinting in the brightness. Joost looks lofty and angular, so much taller than any of the others. Livia has her duffel bag by her feet, and the corners of her mouth are upturned, more determined than happy. Ready for her next travel leg, ready to save the planet.

Another image captures Livia and Joost talking on the shaded porch of the Minnarie food store. Joost towers over Livia, who's cradling a pack of bottled water. In another, they're relaxing around the Minnarie campfire after dinner; Joost has made a peace sign, and Scott's mouth is open as if he's midsentence. It dawns on Hayley that she doesn't appear in many photos. She's included in the next one, only because it's a selfie at the campsite with everyone in the background. Close to the camera, Hayley's face is garish. Her cheeks are pink from the flames and the wine. It's not fair. The others got to pose farther from the lens, appearing calm and cute.

Did anyone take photos of Hayley? Was anyone interested? Livia is fixated on taking pictures of plants and animals, and Scott has barely used his phone. Actually, he's taken only a handful of photos of her since they met.

She digs through her backpack, finds a bag of soft sweets and rips it open. The lollies spill into her lap. She was going to share these with everybody, but now she thinks, *Fuck you!* She eats furiously, shoving one piece of confected fruit into her mouth before another piece is even swallowed.

She studies the last picture on the camera roll.

The sky is overcast and the image slightly out of focus. There was probably rain on the lens. Livia is at the back of the four-wheel drive, its red brake lights glowing. She is half crouched, having fun with the camera. There's a bluish shape inside the car—the back of Joost in the driver's seat. The picture surprises Hayley; she had forgotten it. Given her situation now, it seems foolish that she was taking photos, although she understands why she wanted the distraction. Seconds later, Livia would hop into the car and drive away. Hayley puts her fingertips to the phone and stretches the image so Livia's face fills the screen. What do they know about her? Is Scott right—could Livia be a mean girl? The older Brazilian with rich parents. She could be laughing in a motel with Joost right now, and it'll be hours before Hayley and Scott can report the missing car to police. Does this mean their whole trip is abandoned, that they'll return to Adelaide as failures?

This is Livia's fault, Hayley tells herself. She feels a rush of resentment. This has nothing to do with poor holiday planning and everything to do with Livia, who has Joost wrapped around her finger. Traipsing around in her tight shorts. Shaving off all her hair, as though she's so pretty she doesn't need it, not like other girls. Globe-trotting on her parents' dime, pontificating about the climate. Asking for the name of a dumb brown bird Hayley has never seen in her life before. Why should Hayley know its name? Hayley has nearly finished her university degree, has a career in accounting ahead of her, a long-term boyfriend. She's independent of her parents. And she's years younger than Livia. So who is the real overachiever? There's no reason Hayley should feel inferior.

"I did everything right," she murmurs. "We were having a great time."

Her belly queasy, she pushes the packet of sweets away. Scott must be exhausted. He's been walking on his own for twenty minutes. How far has he gone? At least he's trying, and he might be nearing a farmhouse or a roadhouse or something, while she hides away in this stupid tent. What is wrong with her?

Hayley gets to her knees and probes deeper into her backpack. She can't stay alone here overnight; she needs to hurry, find help before sundown. Scott was right to keep moving.

Her hoodie is still wet, so she puts on an extra T-shirt, then a long-sleeved cotton shirt. Reties her shoelaces in readiness before crawling out of the tent.

Out in the wind and icy rain, Hayley almost changes her mind.

It is dark—strangely dark for six PM in summer. Thick clouds have obliterated the sun. There are no streetlights, no house lights. Hayley activates the torch function on her phone and picks her way through the ankle-high bushes. There's only forty-one percent battery left, so once she reaches the road, she turns the light off.

One foot in front of the other. Hurry up, she tells herself. Just keep moving, and soon she'll be reunited with Scott. It's not fun, walking in the wet, forging ahead in the gloom, but it's progress.

Hayley tries to remember exactly where they were on their route. The map function on her phone won't work without a signal. They'd reached this secondary road to the springs with no further turnoffs, and the Pindarry is in the vicinity, maybe less than fifty kilometers. She's unsure. Imagine if it's within walking distance and Scott's there and he's told people about her. Rallied a rescue party. She might not have to walk as far as he has.

Should she forgive him? He was so mean and blamed her for this fiasco, yet *he* handed the car keys to Joost. He practically waved his grandfather's car goodbye. If Scott hadn't been so cranky around Joost all the time—if he'd tried to be a real mate instead of a competitor—maybe they'd still be in the car together. While she stews over how Scott has let her down, she's also anxious about how cold and tired he is now, perhaps even more afraid than Hayley. He's never really been the one to take the lead.

Chin up, she marches at a determined clip, counting her footsteps under her breath: *one-two, one-two.*

Ten minutes on, her pace slows and she rubs her arms to ward off the chill. "Come on, come on, come on," she urges herself.

Twenty minutes later and her feet feel rubbed raw by wet socks, her clothes as saturated as a wetsuit. She pushes herself onward, thoughts wandering. What if there's someone crouching in the bushes, monitoring her, following her? She's in the middle of a straight road, they wouldn't have any trouble spotting her, and if they attack, there's nobody around to help. What would Scott say now? *You listen to too many true crime podcasts.* She shivers and recalls the cocoon of the tent left behind, wonders if she's doing the right thing.

She hunches into herself to shrink from the rain. Her skin feels glacial, and she wishes she had brought more clothes with her. She could have piled on layers of T-shirts to maintain some heat, wrapped a few around her head and neck like balaclavas. Her sneakers clump over puddles. When is the rain going to stop? It can't be normal—it's more than they get in Adelaide. What if she's still out here at nightfall when the temperature drops but the rain persists? This was a bad idea.

Somehow she picks up speed, shuffling, trying to outpace a new dread. Where is Scott? Is it even possible to catch up?

This road goes on forever. There's no place to rest, nowhere to take shelter from the rain and the cold; she's completely exposed. Feeling very sorry for herself, Hayley begins weeping. The moan works its way out of her, from her stomach to her chest and past her lips. She walks and sobs, hardly watching her path. Her nose clogs and her breathing is ragged. It was reckless to leave the tent. Now she's made everything ten times worse.

A glow appears ahead. It's a light moving steadily nearer.

Hayley stops in her tracks. Is she seeing things? She stares hard. It might be Scott, it's his phone light, he's coming back for her. Scott! It means he didn't find help, but at least she's no longer alone.

Somehow the darkness seems more threatening now, as if it will suck Hayley down before she can reach her boyfriend's side. She begins jogging. The light grows stronger, then it splits into two, bright and white. Headlights. It's a car! Hayley whimpers in relief. She hears the engine. The car's lights are on full beam, and her arms wave high in the air.

"Help! Stop! I'm here!"

It's a large car, a four-wheel drive, she's sure of it. Scott's grandfather's car! He found Joost and Livia. They're all back together, they've come to collect her, and at last she'll find out what happened.

Hayley sobs, midway between laughter and anguish, and moves to the side of the road, bouncing and waving. The car slows and it's recognizable now, the color, the shape—it is definitely their car.

There is only one figure inside.

21

Andrea

Tuesday, February 7
7:30 PM

ROSEY PATS HIS thigh. "Come over here. Have a drink with me."

Andrea tries to sound gruff. "Don't be ridiculous."

"I thought you were a friendly chick."

"I am friendly. I let you in, didn't I? I gave you a free bottle of port, you have a room key—now please go so I can lock up."

They pause, in a standoff.

Andrea wants to walk away, though there's nothing to stop Rosey from following her. Once more, she prays for the sound of Matt's car returning. For the sound of anyone approaching, as long as she isn't here alone with this creep.

"Why don't you ask Matt to kick me out?" Rosey winks.

"Excuse me?" Andrea's throat tightens.

"Your husband. You said he was at the back. Why hasn't he come looking for ya?"

"He's asleep, I told you that."

"And your little boy too? Is he asleep back there?" Rosey rises from his seat and cranes his neck, as if he can see all the way down the corridor to Ethan's bed.

Andrea stands taller. "Get out. I mean it, it's time to leave."

"Aw, c'mon, darling, don't be silly—"

"I said get out!" She marches around the bar and opens the front door. Cold air and a spray of rain rush in. "You're trespassing now."

Rosey settles onto the stool. He doesn't look contrite, only amused.

Andrea doesn't know what to do next, so she shivers in place, unwilling to close the door and admit defeat. She needs to get tougher with Rosey. How? Perhaps by reclaiming his room key, revoking his shelter for the night. That might get him moving at last.

There's a light at the corner of her eye, and she spins around.

Her heart leaps. A vehicle is approaching.

"Matt's back. You're in trouble now!" Andrea announces, something like gloating in her voice.

"I thought you said he was—"

Not waiting for Rosey to finish, she rushes outside and shelters impatiently under the verandah, willing the car to arrive faster. Her teeth begin to chatter, from the chill or the tension. Is it Matt? Sheets of rain obscure her vision. It's a four-wheel drive, but it seems smaller than Matt's Toyota. It could be Quinn home at last. What a relief it would be, to know Quinn is safe and to have her and Bronte to help boot Rosey from the premises.

As the car nears, she sees dark paint, a compact bull bar, windscreen wipers swabbing fast. It's not Matt or Quinn, it's another visitor, someone else seeking safety from the storm. Andrea pushes aside her disappointment. Whoever it is, she is grateful for company. Rosey will stop harassing her when there's another customer at the bar.

The car lurches to a stop, and Andrea strives to see inside. A door opens, two legs emerge, and then the driver sprints beneath the torrent and onto the verandah.

"Hello!" Andrea says, trying to be heard above the hammering on the tin. "How are you?"

"Woo!" The driver sounds cheerful. A tall young man, he whips a gray beanie from his head and ruffles the flatness from his hair. "What a day! Is this the Pindarry Hotel?"

"Yes." Andrea nods eagerly. There's never been a guest as welcome as this one.

"That is great news. I thought I might be lost." He surveys the verandah. "You have a lot of sandbags. Do you think it will rain so much?"

"I'm not sure. If it does, we're prepared." Andrea peers past his shoulder at the car. "Is anyone else with you?"

"No, it is just me."

"Okay, then. Come inside!"

The stranger leaps ahead of her, and Andrea pulls the door closed behind them, shutting out the storm.

"Thank you!" He wipes his shoes on the doormat and takes in the muted surroundings. Empty tables and chairs, two battery-powered lanterns, and a bleary-eyed biker sulking on a barstool amid the long shadows.

"Sorry—the power's out," Andrea explains. Her eyes flick to Rosey, who has one hand still clutching his port glass. He already looks diminished compared to the towering, youthful arrival. The biker scans him from head to toe, his expression sour.

"I am so glad you are open," the newcomer says.

"No worries, you're most welcome." Andrea is chirpy. "Wait here a minute, I'll grab you a towel."

Rosey grunts. "Didn't offer me one . . ."

"Don't pay him any attention," Andrea calls over her shoulder. She rushes to a storage closet in the kitchen and back, offering a towel meant for overnight visitors. She notices a nasty cut along the top of the young man's nose, dried blood at the nostrils like he's walked into something. "Oh no, what happened to you?"

He touches his skin, looks sheepish. There's a large, modern watch on his wrist. "I went hiking in the bush and fell over."

"Oops." Andrea grimaces. "That's easy to do. Do you want it cleaned? I've got first-aid training."

"No, it is only a few scratches. They are a souvenir!"

"Fair enough. Is that an accent I hear?"

"Yes. I am Dutch. My name is Joost."

"Joost," she repeats tentatively. "I'm Andrea." They shake hands.

"And I'm Rosey," the biker grunts.

Andrea sighs loudly. It'd be great to eject Rosey now, but how? She offered him a room for the night, but he's been so lecherous he doesn't deserve a bed. How can she withdraw that offer?

Joost watches the two of them quizzically, rubbing his head and arms with the towel.

"Can I get you a drink?" she asks.

"Yes, thank you. A coffee would be very good," Joost replies.

"I'm sorry, the coffee machine isn't working. I could make you an instant on the stove?"

"Sure."

"Warm milk?"

"That would be nice."

"Milk?" Rosey scoffs. "Sure you don't want somethin' stronger?" He puts a hand on the bottle of port.

"No. I am alcohol-free today."

"Alcohol-free? I never heard of it."

"I can see that," Joost says, and the smirk falls from Rosey's face.

Grinning, Andrea goes to the kitchen, puts a pot of water on the stovetop, then dashes out to check on Ethan. He's curled on his side beneath the dinosaur sheet, eyes sealed shut. She kisses his head, then trots back to make Joost's coffee. Checks her phone and is dismayed once more. How is Matt? Will he be home soon? And what about Quinn, so much later than usual? Something isn't right.

Back at the bar, Joost has turned away from Rosey and is holding a lantern, studying a large map pinned to the wall. Andrea is glad the two men haven't become friendly in her absence. Rosey's face has taken on a metallic tinge. He doesn't have Andrea to himself anymore and he slumps on his stool, wearing his disappointment badly. Although he's no longer a looming threat, she knows not to let her guard down.

She nods at Joost. "Your coffee."

He chooses a stool at the other end of the bar from the biker, and Andrea puts his mug down. She pours herself a large glass of water and sits beside him. Tiredness begins to pull at her. She'll wait for Joost to finish his drink, then work out what to do with the pair. She looks forward to falling into her own bed beside Ethan.

"Are you traveling alone?" she asks.

"Yes."

"That's unusual, if you don't mind me saying."

"Is it?"

"Overseas tourists usually travel in groups to share the cost of fuel, plus it's safer. It's good to have friends with you in case you get into any trouble."

"Mmm, I will remember next time." He sips his coffee.

"So, how long have you been in Australia?"

"A few weeks. I flew into Sydney, and then I spent time in Adelaide."

"Adelaide—that's where I'm from."

"It is a nice town. Very . . . organized. Wide streets."

"That's a fair description. And where are you driving? Are you doing the Stuart Highway?"

"Yes, exactly. I am driving right up to Darwin, in the Northern Territory."

Andrea tries not to laugh because Joost has told her where Darwin is. "Have you got a place to stay there?"

"Actually, I am joining a boat. It is an environmental ship. We are going to film illegal fishing; perhaps you have heard of that? Like Greenpeace?"

"Wow, I'm impressed. Good for you. Won't it be dangerous?"

Joost grins. "Everyone needs to fight for our planet."

"Ah, you're one of those hippies, are ya?" Rosey interrupts.

"No, not a hippie."

"Pfft, sound like one."

"Actually, climate demonstrations are a very good way to meet pretty girls . . ."

Rosey laughs loudly, slapping the bar, and Andrea is taken aback, until she decides the Dutchman is joking, baiting the older biker. One of the emergency lanterns flickers, then resurges. It won't be long before it needs replacement batteries.

"Where is everybody else?" Joost asks.

"Ah, most travelers have been frightened away by the storm," Andrea says.

"Do you have staff? Chef, waiters, that sort of thing?"

"I run this place with my husband—"

"And he's sleeping back there, so don't get any funny ideas." Rosey sniggers.

Andrea frowns at him. "Why are you still here?"

"I'm a customer, just like him."

Andrea and Rosey lock eyes. She considers telling him what a piece of shit he is but doesn't want to make Joost uncomfortable. He just got here, and she wants him onside if things start going haywire.

She turns back to Joost. "We have one employee, Quinn, who lives here and who's just wonderful. And we have casual staff during the busier times."

"And you like it out here?"

"Of course."

"It is a very isolated place. It can be scary for a woman."

Andrea laughs. "Steady on."

"How far is the nearest town?"

"Near enough. We can drive there and back in a day if we need to. We stock up on plenty of supplies, so we don't often go to town. We get hotel deliveries trucked to us too." Andrea is surprised to find herself defending their remote location after weeks of fretting about it.

Rosey stands and stretches. "Don't get up to anything exciting while I'm gone," he chuckles, shambling toward the men's toilet.

As soon as he's left the room, Andrea leans closer to Joost. He smells sour, like old clothes.

"That bloke has got to go." She keeps her voice level.

The young man blinks at her. Up close, he has pleasant light-blue eyes on either side of an unfortunately snub nose.

"What did he do?"

"He's been . . . you know, hitting on me. It's making me very uncomfortable."

"What?" His eyebrows shoot up.

"I've been asking him to leave, and he won't. I'm so thankful you arrived when you did."

"So your husband is *not* here, then?"

"No, I've been lying to make Rosey leave me alone. Can you help me, please?"

Joost stares straight ahead at the shelves of liquor.

"I don't want you to grab him—nothing like that, nothing physical," Andrea says. "I just need you to back me up. I don't think he'll argue with me when you're here too."

Joost straightens up on the stool, raps the bar with his knuckles. "Absolutely. I can help you. Whatever you need."

"You're a lifesaver." Andrea gives his arm a quick squeeze.

She takes Rosey's hut key, which is still resting on the bar, and returns it to the key safe. Swipes the port bottle away too and back onto its shelf. When Rosey returns, she has resumed her position behind the bar, her back stiff.

"Don't bother sitting down," she tells him.

"I'm still drinkin'," he says.

"Not anymore."

"Aw, not this again. You said I could stay the night!"

"Not with the way you've been behaving."

"I didn't do anything."

"You've been a sleaze, and you know it. You're not welcome, and I'm not going to argue about it."

Rosey jerks his head. "What, you got a young lover boy now?"

"Don't be revolting! This pub has rules, and you've broken them." Andrea looks at Joost. "I'm sorry about this."

"Why are you so nice to him?" Rosey rearranges his expression to look pathetic.

"Get out."

"Are you sure?"

"Yes, I'm sure!"

"It's too bloody wet to ride."

Joost shrugs. "The weather is not so bad now."

The rain on the roof has softened to a patter.

"He's right, this is the perfect time to leave," Andrea says. "Goodbye!"

Rosey's eyes dart from her to Joost and back again. The young man turns on his stool to watch them both. Andrea holds her breath, wondering if Rosey will continue to protest. Will they have to get physical? Then the biker snatches up his helmet and jacket.

"Wait till I tell everyone about this place and what a bitch you are." As he stomps to the exit, he kicks a chair, sending it scraping across the floor.

Andrea rushes in his wake, closes and bolts the door behind him. She peels the window blind aside, watches as Rosey dons his gear and starts the engine. He sits in the saddle for a moment, her bogeyman in the shadows, then flicks his stand, and the bike rolls away. She tracks the journey of his headlight until it disappears, feeling tension drain from her body. She hopes to never see the man again. "Good riddance," she says dourly.

There's the sound of slow clapping behind her. Joost is grinning from his seat at the bar.

"Well done. He is gone."

"Thank you." Andrea bows.

"You are a very brave lady."

"Well. I couldn't have done it without you."

22

Quinn

Tuesday, February 7
8 PM

THE DRIVE IS slow going. Quinn hunches over the steering wheel, navigating the slick roads with care, trying to see beyond the sweep of the windscreen wipers. The storm has created a foreign landscape, and wind buffets the compact four-wheel drive. Bronte is restless alongside her, unsure about the marauding weather and the stranger lying behind them.

"Are you okay?" Quinn sings over her shoulder. It's not the first time she's asked, and again there's no response from the unconscious man. It feels wrong not to try.

She considers stopping to check that he's all right, then decides getting to the Pindarry, and fast, is the best idea. The storm might worsen, making driving impossible. And she hasn't forgotten the shock of the man grabbing her wrist earlier. What if he's a bad person? Maybe he attacked somebody and got hurt in the struggle. Quinn has no idea who she is transporting.

The road makes a wide curve, and Quinn takes it slowly. She despises this rain, lets herself admit it. Memories of the flood at the farm flicker in her mind. Is this storm as bad? Worse? She will never erase the images of calves imprisoned in the mud, the fatigue in her father's face. Wet weather is not always a good thing—she knows it, her family knows it, everyone around here knows it. Rain isn't always a relief, bringing life and succor. It can be overpowering and smothering, bringing down livestock, washing everything in its path—more killer than lifesaver. It ruined everything for her father, arriving unexpectedly as it did, adding to the long list of battles the farm already faced. It may as well have poured into his lungs and drowned him.

There are happier memories. Her family gathered for Sunday lunch, arguing good-naturedly over how much gravy was left in the jug. Movie nights, with blankets and pillows strewn over the living room. Birthday parties, with presents her parents had kept hidden for months. Will she ever build her own family? Where will they live? Quinn never dreamed her life would become this, with her brother Ryan on the other side of the country, her mother down south, and her father in the ground. It's understandable why Trish couldn't stay, why she couldn't wait for the farm to sell. They tried, for a time, but their life had changed too dramatically. All three of them felt lost, and while she expected the grief, she was shocked by the rage and resentment. How dare her father leave them. How did he expect his family to go on? They each ruminated over what they might have done to stop him. Her father was selfish. A coward. They could have all left the farm together, built a new life elsewhere.

She despises him. And she loves him and misses him, and would give anything to have him back.

Trish moved to her sister's, closer to the city, with more noise, vineyards, and tourists. She needed different walls, different trees, different vistas. Yet that has only added to

Quinn's sense of abandonment. How can a family shatter like this? How is it they are no longer close and protecting each other? Quinn dreams of starting her own family one day. The fantasy of raising children on a successful farm sustains her, but she has to meet somebody first. And she wants to know what it's like to truly be in love, to feel connected.

While Thommo was fun, they weren't in love. He was another local kid, a School of the Air student like Quinn and Ryan. They'd never taken much interest in each other growing up until one Christmas holiday, when Thommo and Ryan got their driver's licenses and had more freedom to roam. Thommo became less prone to teasing her, less prone to burping competitions with Ryan. He began wearing a men's fragrance and took more care with the shirts he wore, tucking them into his jeans. Later, Quinn realized her rush to lose her virginity had kick-started the relationship. She was almost eighteen, curious and keen, and after their first time together, Thommo turned up at the farm every day until the family accepted they were an item. He was allowed to stay over, although only if he slept on the floor of Ryan's room. Still, with little fanfare or conversation, Trish drove Quinn to the nearest medical center for a contraceptive implant. Quinn marveled at her mother's practicality, appreciating her support, even if she was unable to look her in the eye for several days.

At Christmas, Thommo gave Quinn a thin gold bracelet. She adored it. It was a fragile chain—a sharp tug would have broken it—and while it wasn't expensive, it made her feel sophisticated. It glinted on her wrist as she walked around the place, signaling to everyone that she was growing up and somebody's girlfriend now.

January came with a summer inferno that made everyone weary and move with a sheen of sweat over their skin. They kept quietly alert for news of bushfires. By mid-February Thommo's visits were less frequent, and March brought his first year of university. They kissed goodbye fiercely on the

Durand verandah. They texted each other, hourly at first and then daily, then weekly, until they stopped communicating altogether. There was no official breakup, just a growing disconnection over hundreds of kilometers.

And now that she's twenty, Thommo remains her only relationship. Sure, there have been a couple of one-night stands while working at the Pindarry, waking with regret and a hangover, slinking from one of the huts and praying Andrea and Matt didn't notice. Quinn hasn't chased anything long term because she hasn't met anyone who seems worth the effort. It's tricky being single in such a remote area.

She has no idea where that flimsy gold bracelet got to, and she doesn't care.

The car reaches the turnoff to the pub, and Bronte wriggles her backside in anticipation.

In the hours that Quinn has been gone, things have become almost unrecognizable.

The light is all wrong.

The ground is all wrong.

It's as if a crane has lifted the Pindarry and placed it in the middle of a brooding swamp. Dimly lit by her headlights, most of the car park is underwater, and the pub is hemmed in by walls of sandbags like ancient stones fortifying a castle. There is just one visitor car, a faint outline near the huts, and Quinn's skin prickles with apprehension. Her body is sore from the tension of the drive, yet there's real relief at having made it. Andrea and Matt can help now, and with any luck, their phones are working, they can call for a doctor or even an ambulance, and then the police can sort this out.

Bronte quivers, ready to be freed.

Quinn checks the back seat. The man is lying on his side, knees pulled up, one arm hanging to the floor.

They park close to the verandah, an area usually kept for visitors. "We're here," she announces. "I'm going inside for a minute. I'll be quick, I promise."

No response.

As soon as she opens the car door, Bronte leaps over her lap and out onto the mud. Quinn isn't far behind, hopping onto the verandah. "Andrea!" she shouts. "Matt! I need help!"

She bursts into the front bar, which is lit by two lanterns. They must have lost power, but what about the generator? There's nobody at the tables or on the stools and no one behind the bar. And who does the strange car belong to?

"Andrea?"

She rushes through the kitchen. Rainwater drips from the range hood onto the stove, but there's no time for that now. She continues down the corridor, calling out. It's dark back here, airless, and she takes care not to stumble into furniture. The couch is empty, the TV screen blank.

At her bosses' bedroom, she taps at the closed door. "I found a man—he's hurt."

No response. Maybe they can't hear over the rain on the roof. Why are they in bed so early? Quinn pushes the door ajar. Ethan's still form lays on the mattress alone. Where are Andrea and Matt? They wouldn't leave their son. This doesn't make any sense.

Trepidation rising, she retreats and heads to the small yard off the kitchen. Immediately, she sees the generator sitting in water. That explains the blackout. Matt will be cursing his lack of foresight.

Back in the bar, she spots Andrea's phone on the counter and picks it up slowly, as if it's a foreign object. She presses the screen, and a photo of Ethan in an oversized Akubra looks back at her. No signal, just like her own phone. "Andrea?" she hollers. She checks the men's and women's toilets. Both are empty. Nobody answers her calls, but Bronte appears, wet and panting.

"Where is everyone?"

Apprehensive, uneasy, she runs back to her car. The rain is still falling. Andrea and Matt aren't here to help her carry the man inside—what is she going to do now? She bends into the back seat, and the dull interior light illuminates the crumpled body, the pummeled face. She prods the stranger's arm to rouse him.

"I'm sorry, you have to get up."

His groans, his eyes stuck shut.

"I'm the only one here," she says. "You have to wake up and move. Please!"

"What's going on?"

Quinn shrieks and spins around.

Andrea is there, her black curls wilting in the downpour. "It's only me! Where have you been?"

Quinn throws herself into Andrea's arms, and they hug tightly. It's the first time she has ever embraced her boss, and Quinn feels a long hug in return. She buries her face in Andrea's shoulder and wishes it were possible to stay there.

"Hey, are you all right?" Andrea says.

Quinn moves back. "I found a guy."

"What do you mean?"

"He was lying on the road."

"Shit. Who is it? Is he hurt?" Andrea moves past Quinn and peers into the back seat. "What happened?"

"I think he's been in a crash."

"Oh my god. Are you hurt, Quinn?"

"No, I'm fine, I wasn't in the crash. I found him just lying there."

"And you moved him?"

"I had no choice! It was raining, he was getting colder. I couldn't leave him out there."

Andrea leans over the man. "Hello, can you hear me?"

Quinn paces over the mud. "What are we going to do?"

"We have to call for help."

"Do you have a phone signal?"

"No." Andrea shakes her head. "We can use the sat phone."

Quinn watches as Andrea's hands roam over the unconscious man, checking him closely for injuries.

"I can't see any bleeding, no broken bones," Andrea says.

"We have to get him inside, warm him up." Quinn leans close, using the car for shelter against the rain. "Where's Matt?"

"He went to help Greg. His place was flooding."

Quinn's stomach sinks. "When's he getting back?"

"I don't know." Andrea sounds terse, tired.

"Are we strong enough to carry him without Matt?"

Andrea slips from the car. "Maybe. We have help." She strides away a few meters and shouts at the accommodation huts.

"Who are you calling?"

"A Dutch guy that's staying here. He only arrived a little while ago—I was just showing him his hut."

Andrea returns to the car, and the two women study the unconscious man for another moment, waiting.

"Where is he?" Andrea murmurs. She moves away once more, shouts "Joost!" more loudly.

A moment later, a lanky figure runs into view, back held straight, feet splatting on the ground. A tall male, perhaps younger than Quinn, copperish hair sticking to his damp scalp. He stops in front of them.

"This is Joost." Andrea points. "Joost, this is Quinn, who works here. We've got an emergency. Quinn found a guy on the road. He's knocked out in the back seat."

The man called Joost moves closer and stares into the car. His eyes are very round.

"Is he . . . ?" he begins.

"He's alive," Quinn says.

"We have to move him carefully," Andrea says. "We could make things worse."

"How do we do that?"

"Stay here, I'll go grab some blankets."

"Blankets?" Quinn says, but Andrea has already disappeared indoors.

Joost's chest rises and falls as he stands in his sodden clothes, still gawking at the back seat. Quinn feels bad about spooking him. This is a big surprise for the tourist.

"Are you okay?" she says.

Joost looks at her, nods, doesn't say a word.

"I think he's going to be all right," Quinn continues. "Please don't freak out. I mean . . . I've nearly freaked out a few times. Do you think it's probably worse than it looks? We just need help to carry him inside, and then we'll take it from there. I'm sorry about all this."

The young man clears his throat and looks at Quinn properly. "Sure. No problem."

Andrea reappears on the verandah, laboring with a folded bundle in her arms. "We'll make a stretcher." She flings blankets onto the floorboards—one, two, three—in long layers, then slings the whole works over one shoulder and returns to the car. Quinn and Joost move aside as Andrea wriggles in.

"Grab the other end, spread it out," she says, and Quinn rushes to obey. They tuck the blankets beneath the unconscious man, nudging him here and there, until he's lying on them. Joost watches, seemingly in a reverie.

"Come on, Joost, you take one end," Andrea tells him, and he finally moves, grasping the blanket corners at the man's head. He begins to slide him out, and Quinn and Andrea get ready to take the legs.

Bronte sniffs around them as they shuffle toward the building. "Get out of the way, girl," Quinn says.

Somehow they make it inside, heaving their patient on the makeshift stretcher. "Keep going," Andrea grunts.

They shuffle through the bar and kitchen and into the living room.

"The couch." Andrea raises her voice to be heard over the rain on the roof. They lower the man down in the darkness. He lies there shivering, his breathing ragged.

"I'll grab a quilt." Quinn runs to her room.

When she returns, Andrea is examining the unconscious man a second time, checking him from his scalp to his shoes, intent on her task. "Can you hear me?" she says. "What's your name?" She receives the same silence Quinn did earlier.

Joost appears with one of the emergency lanterns from the front bar. It casts an eerie blue light over the unconscious man's slack face. Quinn studies him. It's hard to tell how old he is, there's so much puffiness and bruising. It's possible even his own family wouldn't recognize him. Somehow, though, she thinks he's around her age, like Joost.

"His eyes are so swollen, I don't know if he can see anything." Andrea tucks the quilt around the man. "Can you grab the big first-aid kit from the bar, Quinn? And a bowl of water."

Quinn races away, hearing Bronte scrabbling behind her. The poor dog doesn't know what's going on. They reach the bar, and the main door is still ajar, letting the wind and rain rush in like invading ghouls. The posters and maps on the walls are flapping in the gale, and the floor has a slick of water over it. Quinn rams the door closed and locks it, then snatches up the first-aid bag from its spot beneath the bar. In the kitchen, she boils a pot of hot water, pours it into a metal bowl, and drapes a hand towel over one arm.

She ferries everything back to the living room and places the bowl on the floor, near where Andrea is still kneeling by the couch. Joost is by the wall, watching the scene with a hand on his chin.

Andrea opens the first-aid kit, removes the scissors, and pushes the quilt aside.

"What are you doing?" Quinn says.

Andrea is too busy to reply. She takes the bottom of the man's T-shirt and begins cutting along the center to the neckline, exposing a torso of purple-and-black bruises, then does the same with his jeans, revealing legs that are unmarked. She dips the towel into the water and dabs at his face, painstakingly removing blood and mud, making him appear slightly less damaged.

Quinn stands by, uncertain of her role.

"Can you call for help now?" Andrea doesn't look away from her task.

"Is the telephone working?" Joost asks.

"No, we have a satellite phone. Hurry!"

Quinn hasn't used the satellite phone before, but Andrea once gave her a demonstration. She sprints to the bar and hunts through the lower shelves until finally she sees the red metal box. She removes the phone, switches it on, and presses the emergency number.

"Help, I need help," she says, as soon as she hears the operator's voice. Her story comes tumbling out. "I'm at the Pindarry Hotel. I found a man on the road, he's injured, he's got injuries all over . . ." She listens, then answers the operator's calm questions. "Yes, he's indoors now. My boss is looking after him. No, I don't think he's bleeding . . . at least not that we can see." There's more questions and answers. "Yes, he was awake, but now he's unconscious again."

She listens further, reaches for a notepad and begins scrawling down instructions. Bronte reappears and sits beside her.

"When are you coming?" Quinn asks the operator. "Are you sending the flying doctor? The power is out, so I can't put the lights on for the plane to land. Or do you send a helicopter? Sorry, I haven't done this before . . . Are you sure? What time should I call? Okay, then, thank you."

Quinn cradles the phone to her chest, eyes squeezed shut. Bronte nudges her with a moist nose. She packs the phone away. Her limbs feel heavy walking back to the others.

"What did they say?" Andrea is using a cotton swab and bottle of antiseptic liquid, gently continuing her efforts on the patient's head.

"It's too dangerous to fly. It's the lightning. They never fly in conditions like this."

"This is an emergency! Look at the state of him."

"They reckon everyone is overstretched; they're getting lots of calls for help. The roads are no good either, they're closed because of flooding, so we're cut off."

"Fuck."

"They said to call in the morning. They'll reassess the weather then."

"What's that?" Andrea nods at the paper in Quinn's hand.

"Instructions on how to look after him, but I think you're already doing all this."

Andrea reads the note and sighs. "Yeah . . . I've got it covered."

Joost shuffles, and Bronte growls.

"Bronte!" Quinn looks at her dog, startled and embarrassed. "Sorry," she tells Joost.

Andrea rifles through the medical supplies and rips open a packet of plasters.

"How did he get into this state?" she mutters. "He looks like he's been in the boxing ring."

"Dunno, he was just there, all by himself," Quinn says. "No car, no bike, nothing. He was just lying there . . ." Her hands link tightly together. She's so grateful Andrea has taken over but still anxious about the man.

"You did good, hon," Andrea tells her.

"Thanks."

"Who could he be? Did you check his pockets?"

"Yes—there was no wallet, no phone. No ID at all."

"I wonder if he was robbed, then?"

"Maybe. This is horrible." Quinn shivers. "Who would do something so fucked up?"

"Probably had a fight with his mates and they dumped him. Maybe they didn't realize how dangerous it was."

"Whoever did it, you don't think they're still around, do you?"

"I think they would have fled—they'll be miles away. It's amazing that you spotted him."

"He wasn't far past the farm turnoff."

"How did you get him into your car?"

"He was awake for a bit—I helped him walk."

"He was awake?" Joost asks. "Did he speak to you?"

Quinn shakes her head sadly. "Only a few words."

"Did he say what happened?"

"He couldn't tell me much. He wasn't making any sense."

"Did you call the police?"

"When I found him? No, I had no signal."

"What about with the satellite telephone just now?"

"I called the emergency number and spoke to some ambulance people. At least, I think they were ambulance . . ."

"Will they tell the police?"

"I'm not sure."

"Police can come later. We have to concentrate on his medical issues first," Andrea says.

The man moans, and Andrea puts her face close to his. "Hello, can you hear me? You're at the Pindarry Hotel. My name is Andrea. We're going to take care of you, okay?"

There's another moan, then a cough. He touches a hand to his temple.

"Is he waking up properly?" Quinn leans closer. She'd like nothing more than for him to speak. To be okay.

"Maybe he's thirsty. I'll go get water." Andrea leaves the room.

Quinn watches Joost, his face pale, serious, his lips stitched together. It's no wonder he's unnerved; he must have heard a few outback horror stories—most travelers have. And now he's walked into one.

"I wish this rain would let up," she says, attempting conversation. The constant shower is making her feel boxed in. What happens if emergency services can't reach them in the morning? Surely this man needs better care than they can give.

Andrea returns with a jug and plastic tumbler and kneels by the couch. "Here you go, have a drink."

The man struggles to raise his head, and she puts one hand beneath it and slowly drips water between his lips. He splutters, and Quinn thinks he has swallowed some. He lifts his arm slowly, like a weight, and lays it over his forehead.

"That has to be a good sign, right?" Quinn says.

"I'm not sure." Andrea readjusts the bedding.

"What do we do now?"

"We wait until morning when help gets here." Andrea gets to her feet. "I'm hungry. Let me check on Ethan, then I'll make us some food—"

"Who's Ethan?" Joost says, frowning.

"My son."

"You did not mention a son. How old is he?"

"Three."

"Ah. He must be very cute."

"He is, especially when he's sleeping. Now, let me get on with it. This is going to be a long night."

23

Andrea

Tuesday, February 7
9:30 PM

A NDREA SLIPS INTO her bedroom, crawls over the mattress, and wraps herself around Ethan. His warmth, his slight form, make her want to cry. She'd like to stay here, but there's too much to do, and when she closes her eyes, Rosey's leering face appears. She snaps them open again. Where is he now? The nearest shelter is a roadhouse more than 100 kilometers south; perhaps he'll head there. He'll be sodden, probably exhausted, and she doesn't care. He has no empathy for others, and she feels sorry for anybody in his life. Did he say he had children? The thought makes her ill.

Thank goodness for Joost. The young man has been a prize since he arrived. It's such a relief to have Quinn back safely too. What about their patient? He's brought more havoc. Hopefully the weather will improve tomorrow and medics will be able to retrieve him early. Andrea doesn't like the look of him, but she tried to mask her concern because Quinn is already jittery. He could have internal injuries, bleeding, and clearly he has head injuries. What if he gets worse through the night? What if he dies before help gets here? Her first-aid knowledge didn't prepare her for something as daunting as this, and she feels the pressure of being in charge.

Andrea considers where the plane can land. When she and Matt took over the pub, the owners showed them the so-called landing strip—just another long, treeless surface nearby, marked with white tires at eighty-meter intervals and a wind sock hanging from a pole. Andrea surveyed it, hoping they would never have a reason to need the runway. Now she wonders if it will be impacted by the day's rain, so water-logged the plane can't land at all.

She goes into the en suite. Once she's flushed, she washes her hands and face, studies herself in the mirror. Her eyes are anxious, her hair a matted mess. She grips the smooth edges of the sink.

"Please come home, Matt," she whispers.

How different it would be if her husband were here. Matt and his affable, calming presence. Just being able to grasp his hand, feel his callused skin, bask in his reassuring smile. Not every couple could live and work in each other's pockets the way they can. They enjoy it, they feed off each other's energy and support, and that's one of the things Andrea loves about living here—their closeness. She should remember and appreciate that more.

The building has become colder beneath the streaming rain. Usually it would be at least thirty degrees at this time of year; now it seems below twenty. Andrea pulls on a jumper.

When she exits her room, Quinn and Joost are sitting, watching the patient. She gives them a comforting smile.

"I won't be long."

In the kitchen, she lights two long candles, which cast a golden glow over the benches and hanging pots and pans. She uses a handful of tea towels to mop up water from the stovetop, hoping it's the only leak.

Bronte trots in.

"You must be hungry too."

Andrea bends to pour biscuits into the dog's bowl, watching as she chomps them down. At the front bar, she checks to make sure the doors are securely locked. She hasn't heard any engines yet can't be sure Rosey isn't lurking, waiting to try again for a bed. With her face close to the nearest window, she feels the chill of the glass. The sandbags are in podgy rows around the verandah, soaked and standing firm. She scans outside, though it's so dark it's difficult to see anything at all. There's the outline of Quinn's car to her left, the edge of Joost's car closer to the huts on her right, no other vehicles. No sign of Matt. She watches the road for a moment, willing him to appear. The rain falls in sheets, and Andrea chuckles as she thinks of how wet Rosey must be. When she showed Joost to his room, there was a growing puddle around the accommodation area. It was shallow enough to walk through, yet she was jolted by the impact the storm was swiftly making.

Andrea collects her mobile phone from the bar and checks the signal. Nothing and no messages. Back in the kitchen, she puts a pan of water on the gas stove for coffee and begins preparing two sandwich plates, munching slices of food as she works. She's ravenous, eating cheese and cucumber and bread.

Joost appears in the doorway, the top of his head almost touching the lintel. His arms hang wearily, and his face is flushed. Andrea feels bad. She had scolded him about the dangers of driving in the outback alone, and now he has been through nothing but drama since he arrived. He probably wishes he had kept driving.

"Do you want anything for that cut?"

Joost puts tentative fingers to his nose.

"No thank you, it will be okay." He glances around. "Your husband is not back?"

"No, unfortunately. With the weather the way it is, I wouldn't be surprised if he stays at our neighbor's place tonight."

"He hasn't called you?"

"He wouldn't have a phone signal either."

"Well, I will go to my room for a while. I have some things to get organized."

"No worries. You must be tired. Here, take this with you." She offers him a sandwich.

"Thank you."

"Joost, I don't want to cause you any more bother. Stay in your hut and get some sleep. Quinn and I have everything covered here."

"I would like to help. I will be the man of the house!" He smiles humbly.

Andrea chuckles.

"After a short rest, I will come straight back," he says.

24

Hayley

Tuesday, February 7
9:30 PM

HAYLEY FLEXES, TRYING to keep her arms and legs from cramping and fight off the cold. Earlier, feeling suffocated, she wriggled out from beneath the blanket that had been dropped over her. Now she wishes she could claw it back. Rain thrums on the car roof, and the temperature inside feels glacial. Every now and then, the vehicle rocks with a blast of wind. Her wrists and ankles are bound with cable ties, and she can scarcely move without slicing herself.

Her lips are stretched and painful beneath the packaging tape. She's tried moving the lower half of her face to loosen it, but Joost has smoothed it down tightly. She wanted to screech for help earlier—especially when she heard other voices—but her efforts were smothered.

When Scott's grandfather's car arrived, Hayley had thought she was saved. Even on discovering only Joost in it, she expected a good explanation, that Scott and Livia must be waiting elsewhere and he had been tasked with collecting her.

Joost had lowered a window and smiled widely. "Get in!" he urged, and Hayley had rushed to the passenger door and hauled herself inside. All she felt was relief. She wanted nothing more than to get out of the rain and climb aboard, and she was ready to forgive everyone for everything. She would hear the whole story soon, but in the meantime her nightmare was over. No more walking alone in an outback storm in the dark.

She pulled her seat belt on. "What's been going on? Where's Livia? Did you see Scott?"

"Just wait. I will tell you everything."

Joost swung the car around to do a U-turn, and Hayley fell back onto the seat, gripping the handle over the window, relishing the comfort and stability of the ride. She had only been outdoors for half a day; it felt like a week. She wanted to laugh. It was going to be wonderful to be reunited with everyone. She reached to turn the heater on, savoring the rush of warm air. Her feet ached, and she bent to remove her sopping shoes and socks.

"It is lucky I found you," Joost said. His face and clothes were mud spattered.

"I know! I'm so relieved. It's awful out there! I'm soaked, I was freaked out, I couldn't see a thing. This whole day . . . it's been so crazy! I knew you guys couldn't have left us."

"Yep."

"I was waiting in the tent, then that seemed silly. Scott left before me. You saw him, right?"

"Yes, I found Scott already."

"Oh, thank god. Is he waiting for us? With Livia?"

"Yes. The whole gang will be together again." Joost kept his eyes trained forward, headlights showing their path through a murky landscape.

"Why did you leave us, Joost?" Hayley rubbed her cold hands in her lap, eyes darting to and away from him, not wanting to begin an argument but so keen to know.

He chuckled. "Were you scared?"

"Yes, of course! Scared and confused. Why did you do it?"

"You could have stayed in the car with us."

"Ha! We *would* have stayed if we had known you were going to take off like that—"

"But you were happy for us to take the risk. To drive through the water."

She wriggled on her seat. "Oh, Joost, it wasn't like that. I warned everyone, you remember. I was worried—"

"About the car?"

"Not just the car. I was worried about someone getting hurt. And then everyone agreed it was the best plan, and I went along with it."

"Do you still think it was a good plan?"

"No, I guess we should've stayed together." There was an uncomfortable hitch in Hayley's chest. This was an awkward reunion, and Joost seemed on edge. "So, where did you go? Why did Livia go along with the joke? I thought she didn't like stuff like that . . ."

Joost had lapsed into silence, seemingly hypnotized by the windscreen wipers. She wondered about the empty back seat. "Have you found us a place to stay? Is that where Scott and Livia are?"

"Livia and I broke up," he said.

"Excuse me?" Hayley thought the phrase was odd. "What do you mean, broke up?"

"We split. Went our separate ways."

"Okay, I am *so* confused right now. Did you two have an argument? Where did you drop her off?"

"I can show you. Soon."

Hayley's fingers tapped over her thighs. Joost liked games, Livia had said that, and it was clear he was playing—speaking in riddles, parceling out pieces of information. She wriggled her bare toes to help warm them, told herself to be patient.

After a few minutes, Joost broke the silence.

"Scott walked away and left you."

"That's right," she grumbled. "I wanted to stay with the tent, and he disagreed. He's probably gonna tease me about it. I guess he's somewhere dry, eating a hot meal?"

"What sort of boyfriend leaves you alone out here?"

"I know, right?"

"Hayley, he does not really love you."

She stiffened. "That's a mean thing to say."

"You should accept the facts."

"You don't know anything about us!"

She glared out her window, even though there was little to see in the dark. The hum of the engine and *whump* of the windscreen wipers were the only sounds.

Joost smirked. "What's the matter? Do you not want to talk anymore?"

"Not about my relationship, no." Hayley turned back. "I can't believe you said that."

"I am just telling the truth. That is what friends do."

"We're friends, are we?"

"Of course."

Hayley didn't want to continue this conversation. There'd be plenty of time to rake this over with Scott later. She fiddled with her phone. "Hey, do you have a signal?"

"No."

"Me neither. It's annoying."

"So you have not called anyone?"

"Nope, I haven't had a single bar on my phone for hours." Hayley pointed her phone at Joost. "Here, let me take a photo of you," she said, eager to change the subject.

He knocked the device out of her hand.

"Joost! What the hell? Why did you do that?"

"Do *not* take my picture."

"All right, all right. You could have said that; you didn't have to hit me."

"I did not hit you."

"You know what I mean."

"You have no idea what a hit is."

Hayley frowned. "Excuse me?"

Her phone had fallen into the footwell, and she bent down, her fingers striving to reach it. As she twisted, she gained a different view of Joost's muddy face. A blood nose. Scratches. She pulled herself up.

"Oh my god, did you have an accident?"

Suddenly Hayley was thrown forward, then back, her head whipping with her, the seat belt burning her chest. She screamed and flung her arms out. The car came to a stop and Joost leaned close, his breath hot in her face.

"Shut the fuck up! Just stop with the questions!"

Hayley shrank away and stared at him—the grazed face, the wild eyes. She nodded, lips pressed, not daring to make a sound.

"Yap! Yap! Yap!" Joost pounded the steering wheel three times, and Hayley recoiled with each blow. "Why do women talk so much? Can you control your own mouth?"

She froze as he drew in long, harsh breaths. Then she heard thudding. Not from Joost's fists. From the rear of the car.

"What's that?" she said, dread forming in her gut.

He glared. "I told you to shut up."

"But . . . what's that banging?"

"Nothing."

Thud! Thud!

"It's not nothing," Hayley said. "Please . . . just tell me what's going on."

Joost opened his door and sprang from the driver's seat, slamming it behind him. Hayley watched him tear around to her door and wrench it open. He unclipped her seat belt, and she screamed as his fingers grabbed the back of her neck and he yanked her from the car and into the freezing rain.

"Let go!"

Her eyes bulged in panic and she squirmed, trying to double over and break free, clawing at his hands. His grip only tightened, pinching her painfully as he shoved her ahead of him toward the cabin of the car.

"What are you doing?" she croaked. "Let me go!"

"You want to know what that noise is?" Joost said. "Come on. Come on, then!"

He threw her to the ground face first. Stony dirt raked the palms of her hands, and she felt a crack in her wrist when she tried to soften her fall. She cried out, but Joost had already turned away. He hauled the hatch open, spitting out words in his own language. The interior bulb shone, illuminating the bottoms of his legs. Hayley righted herself, drawing her bare feet closer, crouching and preparing to flee. Would her body obey her? How far would she get before Joost caught up?

Joost bent his knees and grunted loudly, lugging something. It was a large shape, bigger than their backpacks, and when it was halfway out, Joost let it drop to the ground.

It was a person.

Hayley howled in horror.

Joost jumped to her side and grasped the back of her neck again, forcing her to look down. "There he is!" he yelled. "There is your perfect boyfriend!"

Hayley sobbed. She didn't want to look, didn't want to understand what was in front of her. The same shape, the same hair, the same clothes, yet not the Scott she knew. A grotesque mask obscured her boyfriend's face—purple, black, and red, puffy and misshapen. He was unconscious and seemed so far away from her.

"Scott!" She hunched over him, soft hands cradling his face.

Joost watched her cry for a moment, then grabbed her shoulders. She flailed at him, and he yowled as her nails raked his face. His grip loosened, but before she could step away, he raised a hand high and struck her across the cheek. It felt like she had run into a wall as her head snapped back. He smacked her again, this time finding her nose. It rang with pain, and water spilled from her eyes. She tasted blood. The world lurched sideways and she crumpled onto the hard road.

"You wanted to see him!" Joost was spitting. "Are you happy now?"

Hayley closed her eyes, tried to breathe through the sparks of agony. A sledgehammer struck her side. Joost had kicked her. She curled herself into a protective ball, not feeling the rain anymore. There was ringing in her ears.

Joost pulled her into a sitting position, pushed her against a rear tire, and she held her arms over her head, petrified of being attacked again. He rolled Scott over into the mud like a discarded rug.

"There," Joost said. "Say goodbye to Scotty. He is no longer part of the road trip."

"No! Don't leave him there!"

Joost knelt beside her, puffing. "Now, do you want to know what I did with Livia?"

She wrapped her arms around herself, weeping, refused to look him in the eye.

"Well, she is not going to make it to Darwin," Joost said. "I did those fishermen a favor!"

Hayley didn't want to hear, didn't think she could bear it. Her body tensed, waiting for Joost to strike out, as she thought of Scott nearby. She couldn't reach him, there was nothing she could do, but perhaps in a moment Joost would calm down. Maybe he would even drive away and leave them both and she could check on Scott.

Instead, he dragged her up, turned her around, and forced her arms behind her back. Thin plastic strips bound her wrists, sharp, and she yelped in pain. She heard something ripping behind her, and when he spun her around, he was holding a strip of gray tape. She tried to duck away, but he pressed it over her lips. She focused on breathing through her nose to keep the panic and nausea at bay. Finally, she was blinded by what felt like a sleep mask. Everything tilted as Joost maneuvered her into the space where Scott had been minutes earlier. She fell among the travel bags, just another dumb object.

"You know what—you really are fat," Joost grunted.

Two hands pressed around her skull. She peed herself. Then everything disappeared.

* * *

She doesn't know how long the car has been parked here. Where is she? Is this a public place, or has Joost taken her to someone's home? She heard voices. Why isn't anyone coming, why hasn't anyone found her yet? And what is Joost doing? She's sure she'll wet her pants again if she thinks about him and what he could be planning. Perhaps something spooked him and he's run away.

Her thoughts leap to Scott, his lifeless form lying on the roadside in the storm. She tries not to cry, knowing it will clog her nostrils and make it more difficult to breathe. Why did she decide on a driving holiday with strangers? She'd felt pressure to go traveling, to see Australia, and now she doesn't know if her boyfriend is alive or dead. He didn't deserve to be treated like that. There's so little traffic—will anybody find him? And where is Livia? What did Joost do to her?

A door opens, and sleet sweeps in. Hayley screeches behind the tape, kicking out, trying to resist whatever's coming.

Two broad hands press down on her shoulders from above. Joost's repugnant scent arrives, and she bucks harder.

"Stop it," Joost hisses.

25

Quinn

Tuesday, February 7
9:30 PM

THE MAN ON the couch twitches under the covers. Quinn hears "Hey," then moaning. He's rousing or having a dreadful dream, she's not sure.

"It's okay, you're safe." She strokes his arm, and it seems to calm him. "I'm Quinn. I brought you here—do you remember? You woke up, you walked to my car. You did well."

She falls quiet, feeling foolish. This guy doesn't want praise, he doesn't want babble, he wants a doctor. He seems to be breathing more peacefully—he might be stable, as they say in the movies. His dark hair is nearly dry, his skin less pale. At least there's no bleeding she can see, and he doesn't seem to have broken bones. His swollen face is distressing, but it's improved since they applied ice. Someone must have struck him several times. She stares, thinking, listening to the insistent rain.

Andrea returns with two plates and two mugs on a tray. She lowers the tray to the coffee table, then drapes a throw rug around Quinn's shoulders.

"Here, have something to eat."

"Thank you," Quinn says. This motherly treatment from Andrea is something new, but it's tender and welcome. They each settle into an armchair, chewing their sandwiches. Quinn is boosted. She didn't realize how empty her stomach was.

"How was the farm today?" Andrea asks. "Will it be all right in this weather?"

Quinn nods. "Yeah, it'll be all right. At least the dams will get some water. Might make it easier to sell. The real estate photos will definitely improve . . ."

"Are you getting many offers?"

"Nothing serious."

"Still, that gives you plenty of time to pack up, I suppose."

"That's the bright side. I like doing it, I like spending time at the farm."

"Plenty of happy memories, right?"

Tears spring to her eyes, and she hopes Andrea can't see them in the gloom. "Very happy," she says. "Most people think it would be sad to be in the empty house. They don't understand."

"I know I've said this before, and I mean it—I was so sorry to hear about your dad. It must've been so difficult. A traumatic time for everyone."

"The worst."

"It's not your fault, you know that?"

"That's what people say."

"It's hardest for the people left behind."

"I know."

Quinn dusts crumbs from her hands, then tweaks her soiled T-shirt. "I'm going to get into clean clothes."

Bronte follows her to the bedroom and arranges herself on her bed in the corner. She watches her owner with attentive eyes framed in long lashes.

"Good girl," Quinn murmurs.

She changes into fresh jeans and a flannel shirt, leaving her wet garments hanging over a bedpost. Checks her reflection in the bedroom mirror. Her medium-blond hair is tied in its customary lazy ponytail at the nape of her neck. She pulls the elastic band off, tousles her hair to get rid of some wetness, and ties it higher, on top of her head, where it will be out of the way. Her skin has the caramel glow of summer, and there are freckles over her nose—a stubbly nose that she regards as ugly, even though her father always told her it was cute. Fathers are supposed to say things like that. "Quinny-quinn-quinn," he used to coo. She whispers it to herself now, testing to see if it will bolster her. It doesn't work. It creates a hollow feeling instead.

She checks her phone, certain her mother would have tried to call her by now, but coverage hasn't returned. Trish knows all about wild weather, and if she can't reach her daughter, she might try Ryan. The thought makes Quinn snort. So immersed in Canberra life, her brother likely has no idea about the deluge in South Australia. He'll want to get Trish off the phone as quickly as he can to return to drinking with his new mates at that swanky city bar.

Quinn understands why Ryan has spurned his old life, but that doesn't mean she doesn't resent it. He chose not to live like their parents did—the stress, torment, and toil was enough to endure during childhood, and Ryan has no interest in maintaining the family tradition. How, though, can he thrive in such a different lifestyle? He pushes more paper than wheelbarrows these days. How can he tolerate his city-born colleagues, the endless emails and meetings, being confined to a desk indoors every day? Quinn would much rather have her part-time, live-in job here, especially when the hotel is busy. It stops her from thinking too much. Yet it can't last forever. One day Matt and Andrea might give up the pub lease. What if they move on and the new managers don't want Quinn around? She needs to have a backup plan for a more independent future, for getting her own home one day, and it won't be done on a pub salary.

Whenever Quinn ponders her future, her mind grows foggy. She would rather go back than forward, back when there was plenty of feed on their property, when the livestock team arrived, when she helped her mother make towers of sandwiches, when her father's boots sounded over the verandah and he twirled her through the air. *Quinny-quinn-quinn.*

Back before the shopping weekend six years ago with her mother, when Trish couldn't fix the torn fan belt. Back before they learned her father wasn't out helping fight scrub fires. Back before Trish found him hanging in the old shed.

*   *   *

Bronte patters to the doorway and looks at her owner. It's the signal to be let outside to pee. "Okay, come on." Quinn pulls on her ankle boots and fetches a wet-weather jacket from the back of her door.

Andrea is napping in a living room armchair, her legs curled underneath, head tucked in the crook of one arm. Quinn considers telling her to go to bed, but if she's sleeping already, what's the point? The man looks as comfortable as a battered person can look, his chest rising and falling gently.

Bronte trots ahead, claws clacking on the floor, and Quinn follows. Midway down the corridor, the air is different, cooler, with an alien, earthy smell. They reach the bar, see the front door blown wide open, dark pools lapping like an oil slick. Bronte jumps over the threshold.

"Shit!"

Quinn ducks outside, sees water sluicing around the verandah, bypassing sandbags and reaching past her into the building. She races back to the living area and shakes Andrea's shoulder.

"Quick! There's rain coming in the front."

Andrea springs to her feet, and they hurry to the pub entrance. A wave of dirty water rushes beneath their shoes.

"We gotta get more sandbags!" Andrea gasps. She whips an elastic band from her wrist and binds her curly hair into a rough ponytail.

Outside, the squall strikes Quinn's face. She hunkers down into her jacket.

"There!" Andrea points to the far end of the verandah, where spare sandbags sit in a neat, rectangular pile. A wheelbarrow leans at one side of the stack. Andrea sets it upright, and the pair begin heaving bags into the tray. Quinn's breath rasps with the effort. While she's a hard worker and fit, this is an exhausting exercise—each bag weighing about fifteen kilograms. Her fresh clothes are soon soaked, and her lungs and limbs burn. She recoils as thunder cracks overhead. The storm is flying directly at the building, a volley of water.

Joost appears, making Quinn jump back. She had forgotten about him.

"Help us!" Andrea pants.

Joost bends and grabs a sandbag. He struggles to stand, then transports it directly to the pub doorway.

"It's quicker this way." Andrea points at the wheelbarrow.

They form a production line, filling the barrow with the cement-like bags before Joost pushes it, wobbling, to the doorway. Then they all muck in, transferring sacks to the wall of sandbags already there. After a minute, Andrea heads back inside and uses a large broom to sweep the water, directing it between the sandbags and over the step.

"C'mon, we've got to move!" Her face is strained.

Out of the corner of her eye, Quinn sees Joost laboring with the effort. He might be tall, but he's underdeveloped and perhaps not used to grunt work. Another flare of lightning illuminates the yard, and Quinn braces for an explosive bang.

Ethan appears behind Andrea, an ethereal little figure, barefoot in pajamas, his eyes round.

"Ethan!" Andrea says. "It's okay, buddy, we've got it under control. Sit here, please don't move." She hoists him onto a bench.

Quinn applies robotic dedication to the task. Her arms and legs are caked in mud, her jeans and boots weighing her down. Joost stumbles past, almost losing his footing on the slippery boards. Thunder growls another warning.

"I will get more bags!" Hands on the barrow, he hustles away.

Ethan puts his ghostly face to the window. Quinn gives a reassuring wave, and he only stares back.

After a few exhausting laps, Andrea shouts above the storm, "I think we're all right now."

Quinn agrees. The reinforced walls are holding the water back. She stands, hands on her head, recovering her breathing. Joost slumps to the verandah floor.

"I'm going to check round the back," Andrea says.

"I'll come," Quinn says.

Joost looks up. "I will help too."

"No, that's okay, you rest, we're just giving everything a quick once-over," Andrea says. "Can you make sure my son doesn't come outside, please?"

The Dutchman seems about to argue, then he nods as Andrea rests the broom against the wall. She grabs an emergency lantern sitting nearby and goes to the side of the building, passing Joost's car. Quinn feels like her body can't possibly keep moving, but she follows her boss. Around the corner, there's the outline of the accommodation huts, a rippling pool before them about twelve meters long and two wide. They march closer and discover the water is shallow. Thankfully, the huts, the nearby bathroom block, and the sheds are on concrete blocks, raised slightly up off the ground. And earlier that morning, Quinn helped Andrea and Matt line the accommodation walls with sandbags, which have not been breached.

Andrea spins around. "Let's check the sheds."

Quinn nods. They move behind the main building, mud splatting on their legs, the lantern beam dancing around them. They check the shed perimeters, and Andrea holds the light high while Quinn opens the doors. They inspect each shed, scouring the shadows of vehicles, benches, and tool and supply cupboards. There's a puddle at the entry to the largest shed, but it hasn't made its way inside.

"This all looks okay," Andrea says.

"Great, I need a break," Quinn puffs.

They trudge back to the stone pub building. As the oldest structure on the property, it's suffered the worst, but the newly placed sandbags are doing their job.

Bronte waits for them on the verandah, ears attentive. Andrea ushers them all inside, and Quinn closes the door firmly, relieved to see bare floorboards beneath her boots. The watery crisis has been averted.

Joost stands behind the front bar, still breathing hard. He's not very fit at all, perhaps used to a more comfortable life back home. He holds up a whiskey glass.

"I thought I would have a drink." His shoulders are bony beneath his wet T-shirt.

"Absolutely. You've earned it." Andrea collapses beside Ethan on a bench seat, kisses the top of his head. Quinn sits opposite, Bronte by her leg, and she scratches the dog's neck absent-mindedly.

"Would anyone else like a drink?" Joost says.

"Water, please!" Quinn eases off her drenched shirt. Joost brings full glasses to the table, and it feels novel to be waited on, as if he's staff now, an addition to the family.

Andrea must be thinking the same, because she says, "Joost, do you want to kip inside with us tonight?"

Joost raises his eyebrows. "Excuse me?"

"Would you like to sleep in here?" Andrea explains. "I think we should stick close together. We could pull out the spare mattress. You don't have to, of course. It's up to you."

Joost nods, considering the idea. "Yes, I can do that. Thank you for the hospitality."

"Thank *you* for all your help."

"When do you think the rain will stop?" Joost asks. "Will I be able to drive tomorrow?"

"The roads might be okay, who knows."

"I'm gonna check on . . . the guy," Quinn announces, still unsure what to call him. She strips the boots and socks from her feet and pads past Joost with Bronte in tow.

In the living quarters, the lantern has dimmed. It must be running out of battery. Quinn gazes at the stranger on the couch, her quilt pulled up to his chin as they left him. It's good he didn't wake while they were fighting back the flooding. It would have been disorienting to him to find himself in this room alone. Quinn pauses and leans closer. He's still. Too still.

Dropping to her knees, she puts her ear close to his mouth. She can't hear or feel a thing. A peal of panic rings inside her as she places fingers to his throat. She doesn't want to break his slumber but presses more firmly, searching for a pulse while her own begins to race.

"Hey." She grabs his T-shirt, shakes him. "Hey, wake up. Are you all right?"

His eyes are sealed shut, his body as unresponsive as the sandbags outside.

"Andrea!" Quinn screams.

Andrea comes flying down the corridor, Joost thumping after her. "What's wrong?"

Quinn jumps up, points to the man on the couch. "He's not . . . I don't think he's breathing . . ."

Andrea falls to his side to check for vital signs. "Get Ethan back to bed," she says.

Quinn lifts Ethan away from the doorway and into Andrea's bedroom. Bronte dashes in after them, and Quinn closes the door.

"The man—" Ethan says.

"Yeah, a man." Quinn's voice trembles. "Your mummy is helping him. Everything is going to be all right."

She hoists Ethan onto the bed, sits with her back against the headboard while the boy flops onto her. Bronte springs onto the mattress, and Quinn doesn't push her away. Warm bodies, that's what she needs, warm bodies all connected together. She pulls a blanket over their legs, grateful for the pelting on the roof because it means Ethan can't hear what's happening on the other side of the door. Yet Quinn is burning to know and her body is taut, every cell on high alert. Is the man okay? When did he stop breathing? Will he die because they were busy fighting the flooding?

At last Ethan's breathing grows louder as he falls asleep. Quinn eases him onto a pillow, and Bronte watches with one eye open.

Then the door opens, and Andrea beckons Quinn with one hand.

* * *

"I can't believe it," Quinn keeps saying. "He almost died." She can't stop pacing the room.

Andrea is perched by the man's side, one protective hand on his leg, drained, her body slumped like a question mark. "He's okay now," she murmurs.

"It is a rotten thing." Joost looks down at the couch.

"I don't get it. He was okay. What happened? Why did he stop breathing?"

"He's in a terrible state, you know that," Andrea says. "He might have internal injuries we know nothing about."

"We should never have left him alone."

"It's not your fault. It's not anybody's fault. We got distracted by the floodwater."

"Maybe I shouldn't have moved him from the road at all! That's what they say: don't move the injured person. I could have made his injuries even worse. But I couldn't leave him out in the rain; he could have got hypothermia—"

"That's right," Andrea says. "You did the right thing, Quinn, the only thing you could. Please, sit down, you're making my head spin."

"Sorry." Quinn reluctantly lowers herself onto the coffee table, and Bronte immediately settles beside her legs. "Should I call emergency services again?"

"What would you say to them?" Joost asks.

"That he stopped breathing! Surely it makes him more of a priority."

"It is still raining. The weather has not changed since the last phone call—it is worse."

Andrea sighs. "Joost is right."

Quinn's palms press together. There's a current of worry traveling her body, and she can't make it stop. "Well, I'm not going to leave him alone, that's for sure."

"You can't watch him all night," Andrea says. "Let's take shifts."

"You look so tired already."

"I can keep watch too," Joost says.

"Are you sure? You don't have to."

The young man nods emphatically. "I am sure. I want to help. The guy has suffered, and we all need to take care of him."

"That's very thoughtful of you," Andrea says.

"How long should the shifts be?" Quinn asks.

"Two hours? Three?"

"Three sounds okay."

"Good." Andrea looks at Quinn. "Is it okay if I have the first sleep?" There's no color in her cheeks, and her arms and legs are painted with mud.

"Yeah, of course."

Andrea disappears into her bedroom, and Quinn scans her patient. She checks the quilt, puts a hand to the man's chest to feel it rising and falling.

"Look at you. A real nurse," Joost says.

Quinn smiles only out of politeness, puzzled by the mocking she hears in Joost's voice. Perhaps it's his harsh accent. "Where did you say you come from?"

"The Netherlands."

"And you're out here on your own? Jeez, we don't see many solo travelers here. It's a bit risky."

"Andrea said the same thing. The highway is one long road in the center of the country. I do not think it is a complicated travel plan."

"Did you hear about the storm warning?"

"Yes. I did not expect this much rain."

Quinn shrugs. "I don't think any of us did. Hey, the spare mattress is in my room. We should set you up for the night."

She leads Joost to her bedroom. Bronte follows at Joost's heels, growling once more, and it irritates an already nervous Quinn. "Stop it."

Joost looks at Bronte as if she's a problem to be solved. "Is it yours?"

"Yes, she is."

"Australian cattle dog, correct?"

"Yes. Usually called a red heeler, because of her color." Quinn strokes Bronte's broad head, taking comfort. Her dog is soft and strong at the same time, a repository of resilience she draws on.

"Will it go outside to the kennel now?"

"She doesn't have a kennel; she lives inside with me."

"Is that not against the law in Australia? A dog in a hotel?"

"No," Quinn scoffs.

"At my home, dogs are never allowed inside. They are dirty, not hygienic. You should put the dog out."

"She won't bite you. She's just on edge because of the storm."

"Please, do not mistake me, I am not scared of a dog. Animals should never be in the house, that is all."

"Well, I disagree. Now are we going to grab this mattress or not?"

The mattress is under the base of Quinn's single bed.

"I can move it alone," Joost says.

"Don't be silly. I'll help."

They bend, grab a corner each, and drag it out across the floor.

"So you live here?" Joost asks as they set the mattress on its side to get it through the doorway.

"Yes. A job and board. It's a good deal," Quinn says.

"You, Andrea, and her husband? What about a boyfriend?"

"That's none of your business."

Joost gives a short laugh.

They lay the mattress behind the couch, where it won't block access to the bathroom or other doorways. Quinn tosses a pillow and spare bedding on top.

Joost grins. "Are you going to make my bed for me?"

"Get stuffed." Quinn is beginning to wonder if Andrea was right to invite Joost to stay inside the pub. This is the staff sanctuary—a guest has never been allowed to stay in here before. Why not let Joost go to his accommodation hut? They can holler for him if they need him. Then she thinks again. Maybe Andrea is spooked by the freak storm and Matt's absence; she's exhausted, having just saved a man's life. Fair enough.

"I do not mean to argue." Joost's tone is friendlier.

Quinn gives a grudging smile. "Me neither."

"You should go to bed now. I can take the first shift."

"I'll stay here a while longer. You need rest, and Andrea said—"

"I know what Andrea said. I can take care of myself!"

She's taken aback by his abruptness. He's on the edge of an armchair, knobby knees splayed wide, arms forming sharp triangles, like a gargoyle perched on a castle wall. Quinn's scalp prickles under his harsh gaze, and for a second it seems he's going to yell at her to go to her room, like a strange, overzealous big brother.

Then, just like that, he smiles.

"Sure thing," he says. "We can stay up together. Like a pajama party."

26

Andrea

Wednesday, February 8
5 AM

WHEN ANDREA WAKES, the first thing she thinks of is Matt. She stretches an arm out, fumbles for the phone on the bedside table. There is no signal, but somehow gleaming text messages have arrived overnight—the best present she has ever received.

Andrea gulps back tears, wriggling upright with care not to wake Ethan, and hurriedly reads.

3:10 AM: *Sorry, love, had no reception. xxx*

She laugh-cries.

Stayed at Greg's. We're watered in, looks like an island out here, we should have a second honeymoon.

Then, a final text, minutes later.

Hope everything is ok there. Is Quinn back? Will call you in the morning, going to get some kip now. xxx

Andrea rereads the texts several times, smiling widely, a glow in her belly. Matt is all right, of course he is, and he will be home later today. When all this drama is over, she will tell him she's pregnant and they can celebrate. What happens in their lives after that, she doesn't know, but it is a moment to look forward to.

With a start, Andrea thinks about the time. It's after five AM. Quinn and Joost have let her sleep for hours. Why didn't they rouse her? Perhaps they felt they could take on the shifts without her. She climbs out of bed and goes to the en suite, a fresh checklist running through her mind. Rain drums overhead, though softer than yesterday, the type of morning wet that's usually welcome, that usually makes her want to snuggle under the covers. But she needs to check on the stranger, check the Pindarry for flooding, and when the sun rises in about ninety minutes, she can make the short drive to the airstrip to see how it looks. She prays a doctor will be able to fly in this morning. Then there's the task of feeding herself and everyone else, and looking after Ethan.

There's no time for the luxury of a shower right now, so Andrea just pulls on clean clothes and boots in the gloom, casting regular glances at Ethan. She removes a T-shirt and track pants from Matt's side of the wardrobe, ties her thick curls back with a hairband, grabs a light jacket, and tiptoes from the room, gently closing the door behind her.

The emergency lantern has gone out, and yet Andrea can make out the pile of bodies in the living room. There's the unconscious man on the couch, turned on his side now, one arm crooked across his chest. Quinn has pulled two armchairs together for an awkward bed, and her head is slumped on one shoulder. Andrea tuts; she should've known Quinn wouldn't leave the guy's side. Two long legs appear from behind the couch—Joost, on his mattress. And last of all, Bronte on the rug in the center of the room. She raises her head to stare at Andrea.

"Good girl," Andrea whispers.

Squatting by the unconscious man, she places Matt's folded clothes on the floor. They can help him get dressed later. She checks his breathing, the bandages, uses her phone light to assess his color. *He almost died*, she thinks. *We were supposed to be looking after him, and he almost died.* She runs it through in her mind: the resuscitation, her breathing into his slack lips, pressing his chest, striving to revive him while Joost watched. She had practiced CPR so many times in first-aid classes. Last night was the first time she'd actually had to apply her learning, and she felt messy and inept and useless while doing it, but it worked.

Andrea creeps down the dim corridor to the kitchen, where water still drips through the range hood. She will have to deal with that before she can cook any breakfast. She opens a fridge door, grabs a yogurt tub and spoons it down while walking to the front bar. It's a relief to see the additional sandbags worked— the floor is dry. Seeing the room so empty in the eerie calm after so much rain makes her yearn for their usual sunny days, even those that bring searing heat, dust, and sweat. It would be wonderful to see happy travelers relaxing at tables, sharing driving tips, taking selfies. To watch Matt stop at a table to have a chat, turning up his Aussie twang for the international tourists, making her laugh. She has taken it for granted.

Andrea presses a light switch; still no power. Shame; she would have liked a frothy machine coffee. She'll take another look at the generator soon, maybe ask Quinn if she knows more about it. There's a familiar tapping on the floor as Bronte ambles into the room.

"Want to go outside?" Andrea slips into her jacket, opens the door, and lets Bronte trot past. The early morning is a shock of cold on her neck, and she pulls her collar high as she steps onto the verandah amid a maze of sandbags. Wait until Ethan sees this; he will want to clamber over it like a mini fort. The lantern glowing behind her is the only light around, the moon and morning stars still muffled by cloud. Bronte disappears around the side, and Andrea ventures out a little farther. The car park is wet, but rain isn't threatening the pub as it did earlier. She brings the hood of her jacket over her head, tucking her hair inside, and wanders near to where Joost has parked his car. It's a mud-spattered four-wheel drive, an old model, and she wonders where he got it. It can't be a rental. Perhaps he bought it cheaply from another backpacker. They often buy vehicles for driving holidays and onsell them before they head home. She circles the car, peering into windows, feeling nosy. She can't see much. It's messy inside, with hats and water bottles and items discarded over seats and floor. He's not a tidy traveler.

Eventually the chill is too much, her nose like ice. "C'mon, Bronte," she calls. "Time to come back in." The dog doesn't reappear, and Andrea grows impatient. "Bronte!" she calls, a little more loudly.

There's a knocking noise. Andrea turns, trying to locate it. Bronte reappears, wiggling her backside, mouth hanging open happily.

"There you are." Andrea turns to go back inside, and the knocking starts up again, insistent.

There's no ignoring it; she has to check it out. She approaches the row of accommodation huts, wondering if one of the doors has been left open. But what would make it swing? The wind has calmed. It's difficult to see this far away from the front bar lantern, so Andrea retrieves her phone from a pocket and uses the light function to guide her. It illuminates the dirty pool around the huts, and she sees that all doors are firmly closed.

The sound resumes. *Knock, knock, knock.* Andrea stops in her tracks. An unsettling current runs from her fingers to her scalp, and she's glad of Bronte's solid presence beside her. "What is it?" she mutters.

Knock, knock, knock. Her feet move toward the sound.

The banging is coming from Joost's hut.

She glances back at the Pindarry, half expecting Joost to appear. Should she open the door? He's rented it for the night; he has purchased his privacy. But what's making that noise? Perhaps he brought a pet with him and it's trying to get out, poor thing. He wouldn't be the first traveler with a dog.

Feeling uneasy, Andrea reaches for the doorknob, grips it, begins to turn. The handle won't budge. It's locked, of course.

She leans close to the door.

"Hello?" She's almost too quiet to be heard.

The knocking pauses, then it resumes at a faster pace. Frantic. Andrea feels a cold sweat. A dog would bark or whine at least. Something is very wrong—there's someone inside.

"Hold on," Andrea says. "I'll be back in a sec!"

She rushes away, her jacket hood flying from her head, staggers into a pothole, righting herself quickly. She runs with Bronte in tow, onto the verandah and inside. Her mind is racing. Should she fetch Joost first or grab the spare key and take a look now?

Although she isn't sure what's going on, something tells her to investigate on her own.

She throws herself around the corner of the bar and kneels by the secure key cupboard. She punches in the passcode, finds Joost's hut number, and clutches the key in her palm so tightly it stabs her. Without thinking much longer, she dashes outside again.

Back at the hut, the knocking continues.

"Hang on, hang on," Andrea says.

The rain has begun to fall harder, beating against the hut wall and washing over her shaking hands. Andrea slips the key into the lock and turns the handle. In the open doorway a wave of rank air hits her—it's like entering the toilet block of a music festival. Bronte yaps and Andrea pushes her away, then steps inside and closes the door. Holding one sleeve over her mouth and nose, trying not to gag, she waves her phone light.

The beam lands on a squirming figure spread-eagled on the bed. Andrea sees cable-tied wrists and ankles, a muss of hair, terrified wide eyes. Bare, fleshy legs. A teenage girl with packing tape covering her mouth, screeching from behind the plastic.

"Oh my god." Andrea falls to the bedside and carefully peels the tape away.

A rasping, sobbing sound fills the room.

"It's okay, it's okay," Andrea soothes. "I've got to get something to cut you free. I'll be quick!"

She sprints to the large shed that contains their tool collection, keeping her phone light trained low, fearful of alerting Joost. Fuck! He's got a girl trussed to the bed! Andrea can't reconcile that image with the clean-cut young man who, for the past twelve hours, has been helping her. She flings open a toolbox, her fumbling hands locate the cutting nippers, and she runs back. The girl makes mewling noises as Andrea drops her phone on the mattress and snips the bindings away in the artificial light.

As soon as the girl is free, she releases a fist that catches Andrea in the chest. Andrea falls back, raising her hands to protect herself.

"Don't be scared," she gasps. "I'm helping you!"

The girl squirms away to huddle against the wall, tugs down her short skirt and stained T-shirt, trying to cover herself. One side of her face is bruised and swelling, there's blood around her lips, her knees are covered in angry scrapes, her legs in dried mud.

"What happened?" Andrea tries to sound as gentle and unthreatening as possible. "Who are you?"

She hears sobbing. Then a hoarse voice says, "Hayley."

Hayley

Wednesday, February 8
5:30 AM

HAYLEY'S LIMBS SCREAM with pain after being tied for so long. The corners of her mouth are dry and sore. A woman with curly black hair kneels by the bed, gawking at her. Hayley blinks rapidly at her and the strange room. Her prison cell.

"Where is Joost?" It's difficult to speak. Her throat rasps and her hands go to her neck, her right wrist jarring in agony.

"He's inside," the woman says. "Did he do this to you?"

Hayley stares. "You know him?"

"I met him yesterday. I don't know anything about him. I didn't know you were in here, I swear!"

"I have to get out. I can't be here when Joost comes back. You've got to help me! Call the police!"

The woman nods. "Okay, okay. We'll do that—"

"We can't let Joost see us." Hayley slowly pushes to her feet, wincing. Her underpants are caked to her. She is dizzy.

"Here, let me help." The woman scoops her phone from the bed and takes her elbow.

Tears slide down Hayley's misshapen cheeks. It's like they belong to somebody else. The hearing has gone from her left ear. She's a giant walking bruise.

The woman pushes the door open, and a rectangle of soft light appears. A red-and-brown dog waits on a step outside, whining its concern. The woman shushes it away, and they move into the fresh, damp air. Hayley gingerly steps down to the mucky ground, her eyes darting over the landscape. The sunrise is muted by brooding clouds. She wonders what time it is.

She sees the outline of Scott's grandfather's car and wants to scream. The woman notices her flinch and rests a cautious hand on her arm.

"It's okay. Like I said, Joost is inside. He's asleep."

Hayley sees a toilet block about twenty meters behind them, seemingly made of concrete squares. Ahead of them and to their left is a long building, old stones at its corners, the beginning of a verandah. The sky pelts her, reminding her she's vulnerable here, exposed. The dog turns and runs for shelter.

"We have to hide. Now!" Hayley grasps the woman's arm, holding tight.

"Come with me," the woman says.

Hunching alongside her rescuer, Hayley works hard to be quiet, to tamp down the shriek that wants to leave her body. If Joost sees her, he will kill her. Her body is both racked with pain and powered by adrenaline, and the ground sucks at her sneakers as the woman leads her behind the old building. There's a shed door ahead of them. The woman pulls it aside and they scurry in. The rain is louder in here, it echoes and bounces from corner to corner, and Hayley's nerves jangle.

Hayley keeps moving, leading the way now, retreating from the doorway and deeper into the shed's dankness.

There's an old fridge, a quad bike, shapes she can't distinguish. She sinks into a corner between a workbench and a beaten old wardrobe, stone-cold concrete beneath her. It's only a matter of time before Joost senses her here, she's sure of it. Her trembling is like an alert signal, and he will track her down. Hayley makes herself as invisible as possible, cradling her injured wrist.

Last night when Joost cut her ankle bindings and dragged her blindfolded from the boot, she had no idea where they were. Released from the car, she tried to pull away, but he grabbed her hair. She was defenseless, useless, mind and body flooded with hot panic. He jostled her up some steps, bumped her through a narrow entrance, and she heard a door close. He'd shut them out of the storm, sealing them indoors together, and she was certain he'd kill her and terrified he would rape her too. She screamed from behind the tape.

"Shut up!" Joost hissed into her ear.

He tore away the eye mask and shoved her onto a bed. She fell onto a thin mattress. Where was this room? Was this some kind of motel? Why weren't there any people to help her? Hadn't anyone seen what Joost was doing? She wriggled to the wall, as far away as possible, yet Joost only needed one step to reach her.

He laughed, creeping close. "Where are you going?" He stared at her, unblinking. She squeezed her eyes shut, turned her head away.

"Hayley, what's wrong?"

She squawked from behind her gag. He slapped her.

"Stop it," he said. "There is no need to be so hysterical. Livia was not like this."

She sobbed at the mention of that name. Livia. Someone from a lifetime ago.

"Behave yourself," he said. "Or I will really hurt you."

He sat astride her backwards, his weight on her torso making it difficult to breathe. She squirmed while he grappled each leg down and cable-tied her ankles to the lower bed rail. Then he turned around, tilted her to cut the wrist tie, and reapplied a new one to secure each arm to the bed. He held cable ties between his teeth while he worked, blank faced, as if it were an everyday task.

Hayley had never felt as exposed as when completely bound to the bed. Her short skirt had ridden up, her T-shirt revealed her belly. Her underwear was soiled. She couldn't pull her clothes down, couldn't cover herself.

Joost took the cable ties from his mouth and climbed from the bed, checking his work.

"I know what you are thinking," he said, "I make this look easy, right? It is surprising how many videos online show you how to tie up a person. I might make my own video after this, ha-ha. What do you think, Hayley? Will you star in a film for me?"

She struggled to draw her knees protectively together as Joost gazed down at her with something like disgust. Then he jerked away suddenly, head cocked toward the door. Hayley froze and listened too.

"Joost!"

Someone was calling his name. Wherever she was, these people knew him.

He put his face close to hers. "Do not make a sound," he warned, pressing the tape harder over her mouth. "I will be right outside. If you make any noise at all, I will be back to hurt you. Instantly. Believe it."

Then Joost left. Hayley heard the click of the door being locked and lay still, ears straining, trying to get a sense of what was happening outside. The storm got in her way, thrashing the roof and walls around her. She thought about twisting on the bed, making it rattle, making some sound to raise the alarm. Maybe people would come running to rescue her.

Unless they were Joost's friends.

Unless they already knew she was in here and didn't care. Maybe they were bad people too. Maybe they had expected her arrival.

She turned her head, taking in the room. There was one square window up high, bordered by a muted grayness that spoke of the light outside.

She began crying, thinking of her parents, thinking of Scott. She fell into a tortured inertia.

* * *

Later—Hayley couldn't tell how many hours later—when she realized Joost wasn't outside, he wasn't returning as swiftly as he promised, she felt brave enough to make noise. She discovered she could draw her arms and legs together slightly, arch her back, and make the cheap bed frame strike the wall. It might draw Joost back, it might not. She had to face the truth that Joost was going to keep hurting her. He'd done something to Livia, and she couldn't wait around for it to happen to her.

And then at last, the woman with black curls appeared.

"My name is Andrea," the woman whispers now, crouching beside Hayley in the shed. She's staring at Hayley as if she's a bomb about to explode. "Tell me what happened. Did Joost do this to you?"

"Yes," Hayley croaks. "I think . . . I think he killed my boyfriend."

"I don't understand . . ."

"He bashed him up and threw him out onto the road, right in front of me! He wasn't moving when we left him—he was just lying there."

Andrea looks like she might be sick.

"And Livia is gone too," Hayley continues.

"Who's Livia?"

"She's another backpacker. She was with us on the road trip. She got into the car with Joost; they drove away from us. I haven't seen her since yesterday. She wasn't in the car when Joost picked me up last night."

"Joost . . . attacked your boyfriend and your friend, Livia," Andrea says slowly. "And he tied you up. Do you have any more friends out here?"

"No!"

"Why is he doing this? How do you know each other? Have you all been taking drugs?"

"No drugs! Listen to me," Hayley hisses. "I don't know why this is happening . . . Joost is an animal. Call the police."

Andrea holds her face with two hands. Hayley knows she's grappling with her story—it does sound crazy; it does sound too much. Will Andrea believe her? When is she going to get help?

"I have to tell you, Hayley—we're a long way from any-where, and the storm has made roads impassable. The police might not be able to get here for a while."

"How long?"

"Hours."

Hayley moans softly, wants to disappear inside herself. "No, no, no . . ."

"It's not just washed-out roads; it's the distance they have to cover," Andrea says.

"Where's Joost, what is he doing? He'll come looking for me."

"He's inside the pub."

"The pub?"

"Yes, this is the Pindarry."

Hayley stares. The Pindarry. The hotel, the safe haven on their itinerary. She's going to be all right, she's back in civi-lization. There will be bar staff and tourists and men inside, and this can all be over.

She grabs Andrea's arm. "The people in the pub will help us. We're gonna be okay!"

Andrea looks sad. "That's me. I own the pub."

"What?"

"I'm here with Quinn and my little boy. There's nobody else."

28

Andrea

Wednesday, February 8
5:30 AM

THE GIRL LOOKS like a frightened kitten, and her fear is contagious.

Joost had her tied and gagged in the hut, and now he's inside Andrea's own home, meters from Ethan, from a sleeping Quinn. She invited him in, insisted he spend the night. She's put everyone in danger. Normally so attuned to threats, how could she trust a stranger so soon?

The unconscious man must be Hayley's boyfriend. Quinn found him by the side of the road. Andrea decides not to mention him, because the girl is already on the edge of hysteria and Andrea could be wrong. And what about the person called Livia? There's a lot to piece together. Were these kids on some sort of sick road trip? How did Joost do all this, and why? Perhaps he's a criminal who's fled to Australia. All Andrea knows is Hayley was captive, bound to the bed, while Joost has been acting like nothing is amiss. She thinks she might throw up.

Hayley's shivering, and Andrea wants to pull her into a hug and tell her everything will be all right, that she will keep her safe. But she can't promise that.

"What do you mean, it's just you here?" Hayley asks.

"My husband had to leave to help one of our neighbors," Andrea says.

"What about Quinn? Is that a guy?"

"No, it's a young woman who works and lives here."

"And that's all the people you have? Where are all the staff?"

"We don't have anyone else. We don't need them until the busy season."

Hayley hides her face in her knees, rocks back and forth.

Andrea can't comfort her any longer; she has to move before Joost wakes and discovers what's happening. Quinn called emergency services earlier, but that was for a doctor. The police need to know what's going on—there's an apparent maniac among them. Storm or no storm, the police have to come.

She takes her phone from her pocket and wants to cry in frustration. "The phones are still out," she whispers. "I have to go inside and use the satellite phone behind the bar."

"You're leaving me?"

"I don't have a choice."

Hayley takes a sharp breath. "I'm scared."

"Me too. I'll call the police as quickly as possible, okay?"

"And they could take hours?"

"The sooner I call them, the sooner they're here. Just stay here, stay hidden, that's all we can do right now."

"Does Joost know you're out here?"

"He was still asleep the last I saw him."

Hayley hugs her knees to her chest. "Please be quick. I can't handle this."

"It's important you stay here, stay out of sight." Andrea looks into Hayley's eyes. "Understand? I won't let him come in here, I won't let him hurt you."

Hayley nods.

Andrea reaches for a plastic tarpaulin on the top of a cupboard and unfolds it around Hayley. She wishes it could be a soft blanket, that she could bring Hayley inside and care for her properly.

"Take this, hide under it. I'll be as fast as I can but don't know when I'll be back."

Hayley whimpers as she withdraws beneath the tarp.

Andrea gives her one more look, then runs from the shed, thinking of Ethan and Quinn, wondering if Joost has woken. What will she say to him? How will she act? She needs a plan. Most importantly, she needs to keep him away from Ethan.

Andrea careens around the verandah and, at the last second, decides to lift up a sandbag and carry it with her.

It was the right decision.

Joost is between the front bar and kitchen, unmoving, like a predator in stasis. He grips a bottle of water in one hand. It takes all of Andrea's willpower not to cry out and drop the sandbag. She has to pretend she doesn't know what's going on, pretend she doesn't know about Hayley. She can't afford a confrontation; that would bring everything to a head, and who knows what Joost might do. She will behave normally to protect everyone and phone for help as soon as she can.

"Oh . . . good morning." Andrea expels a breath and hopes he thinks she's puffing from exertion rather than terror.

"What are you doing?" Joost asks.

"We had a little leak." She drops the sandbag by the doorway, wrestles it into place. "It's all good now, though."

"Just one bag?"

"Yeah . . . it's done the trick."

"You should have called me. I would have helped." He takes a long slug of water. She watches his neck working.

"I didn't want to wake anyone. I got it sorted on my own." There's a tremor in Andrea's voice, and she prays Joost doesn't hear it. Her eyes meet his. The scarlet scratches on his face appear in a new light.

"It is still raining," he observes, rotating the bottle between his palms so it cracks loudly.

"Yes, it's not as heavy. It might stop soon."

"So the roads will be better?"

"Yes, I think so."

"What about the doctor? When do you think he will arrive?"

Andrea doesn't know how to answer. If Joost thinks help is imminent, will he want to take Hayley and run? What will he do once he realizes she's escaped? He might lash out. Andrea knits her fingers together, thinking of the satellite phone beneath the bar. It could take hours for police to get here. She needs to make that call.

"I should phone the emergency line again."

"Why?"

"To check the doctor is coming," she says.

"Okay."

To her dismay, Joost climbs onto a stool. He jiggles his knees, controlling his energy. He's less than a meter from where the satellite phone is stowed. Is he deliberately waiting here? Perhaps he was monitoring her from a window, he knows exactly what's going on, and he's working out his next steps. All this time he has been putting on a facade. How could anyone pretend to be kind and helpful, as he has, while they have a girl captive in their room? Andrea feels a stir of fury. Joost tied Hayley spread-eagled to the bed. He's disgusting, he's inhumane.

She wishes he would jump into his car and leave, but that would mean going to his hut first, where he'd discover Hayley has gone.

"Are you going to make the phone call?" he asks.

"In a minute. Why don't we head into the kitchen? I really need coffee . . ."

Joost places his bottle on the bar and follows her.

She holds the pot beneath the tap, fighting to keep her hands from shaking, convinced she's going to drop it any second.

Joost takes an apple from a bowl without asking, watches her as he chews.

"Keep an eye on the water, would you?" she says as she puts the pot on the stove. "I need to check on Ethan."

Andrea feels his eyes on her as she leaves. She moves past the stove and benches, into the short corridor and the living room. She breathes in through her nose, out through her mouth. Her legs want to fold beneath her. How long can she keep this up? When will she have a chance to use the satellite phone? Hayley is outside alone, waiting for Andrea to do something.

The living room is still dim, and Andrea spies the outline of the stranger on the couch. Is he Hayley's boyfriend? Would she recognize the bruised man lying there? If he couldn't defend himself against Joost, what hope does Andrea have?

Quinn is not in the armchair where Andrea last saw her. Her heart beats even faster. She rushes to Quinn's bedroom and pushes the wooden door open.

"Oi!" Quinn spins around, pulling a blue tank top over herself.

"Shh!" Andrea closes the door and steps across the room.

"What's going on?" Quinn lurches back. "Is the guy okay?"

"Listen to me." Andrea grabs Quinn's arm, speaks in a harsh whisper. "Joost is dangerous."

Quinn's eyes widen, but she keeps her mouth closed.

"I've just been outside. He had a girl tied up in the hut," Andrea says.

A sound escapes Quinn's throat.

"I left her hiding in the big shed."

"In the shed? We have to help her!"

"Quinn, we've got to be careful. Ethan is here; I don't want anybody to get hurt."

"We should call the police."

"Yes, I know, but even when we do . . ."

They exchange looks. Quinn understands how isolated they are. They're on their own for now.

"Who is she?" Quinn asks.

"She said her name's Hayley."

"Is she Joost's girlfriend?"

"No—I don't think so."

"Is she hurt?"

Andrea nods. "She's not bleeding, but, yeah, I think he hit her around."

"Fuck! Why is he doing this? What's wrong with him?"

"Who knows?"

"What about Matt? He could be home soon?"

"Yes, he might." Andrea starts pacing. "But it could be hours."

"We've gotta tell Joost to leave."

"Is that an option?"

"If we tell him we know what he's done, then he'll want to get out of here."

"What if he says no?"

"There's two of us, one of him."

"What, we're going to force him out? I'm not going to wrestle him, are you? He beat Hayley up. And I've got Ethan to think about." Andrea tries not to raise her voice.

"Okay, you're right. We could lock him outside."

"Hayley's outside. And it wouldn't be hard for him to break back in—he only has to smash a window."

"Well, we've got to do something!" Quinn grabs her anorak from the bed.

Andrea moves to block the doorway. "We have to act normal and call the police without him knowing. We wait until help arrives, and until then we can't let Joost think anything is going on."

"I can't act normally. Can you?"

"Not sure . . ."

Quinn perks up. "The guy on the couch—he was trying to talk a few minutes ago."

"What did he say?"

"He was mumbling; I couldn't make it out. I gave him more water, and he was almost sitting up. He looked around the room. Reckon he's going to be okay."

"That's good, but he's in no state to help."

"I know, I just wanted to tell you—"

"We don't have much time. I left Joost in the kitchen. He might already be suspicious."

"Shit. Should I go watch him?" Quinn hugs her arms to her chest. "I'm scared. I don't know if I can do this."

"I have to check Ethan, then I'll come with you. We can do this if we do it together. We've got no choice."

29

Hayley

Wednesday, February 8
6 AM

I T IS IMPOSSIBLE to keep track of time.

Rain rattles the roof, and a draft of cold air swirls beneath the stiff tarpaulin, lapping at Hayley's bare legs. When did the woman, Andrea, leave? Was it ten minutes ago? Was it more? Why is she taking so long? Has she managed to call the police? Andrea said even without flooding, the police could be hours away. They're in the middle of nowhere.

Hayley hugs her knees. She's racked with pain and the terror of more pain to come. She's sure Joost will find her. She angles her head, trying to hear past the tarpaulin, to hear over the shower. Is he coming? He's going to hit her again, he's going to be angry that she escaped the cabin, and he'll drag her out of here. She wants to be back in Adelaide, back at uni, back in class. With Scott. Hearing him complain and fret about assignment deadlines, seeing him at his PC with his headphones on, gaming controller in both hands. She wouldn't even resent all the hours he spends online. He doesn't have to be a big macho man, exploring the outdoors, getting a suntan, working on a buff body; he doesn't have to take her out, join her on the dance floor; he can do whatever he wants to do. Except now, he is probably . . . Hayley pushes the thought away.

This is her fault. They shouldn't be out here so far from the safety of the city. The Pindarry isn't a quaint pub full of chatting tourists; it isn't a refuge from this nightmare. The outback is just as scary as it is in horror movies.

No. It's worse.

Andrea is taking a very long time. Something is wrong.

Joost is inside the pub, and Hayley knows what he's capable of. He must have attacked Andrea, and now he's tying everyone up. Who did Andrea say lived here? Something about a little boy. Hayley trembles. They'll all be captives, and Joost will have plenty of time to do whatever he pleases before the police arrive.

She cannot wait here. She has to do something.

Hayley lifts the tarpaulin aside, nervous, unsure if it will make any rustling noises. She gets to her knees and scrabbles over the dusty ground, grit on her palms, trying to keep as low as possible. She crawls stiffly, then pauses, listening for any movement outside. At the shed door, she clings to the doorframe, the earth spinning.

She doesn't know how long she waits. The rain slashes at her, falling in diagonal sheets, and she gasps, drinks in the frosty air.

Just get to the car, she tells herself. *Find your phone, quick!* There might be a signal. She could call for help.

Hayley stares at the back of the Pindarry, the pub celebrated in so many Instagram photos and travel blogs. It seemed charming back then, the quintessential outback destination with its soaring tin roof and tipsy customers propped on the verandah sipping beer while sheltering from the Australian sunshine. She's bitter now, incensed at its uselessness. There should be more people here, there should be crowds, staff, tourists. She never thought this spot would be so deserted.

She keeps surveying the area. There's another shed to her left. To her right is their car. The thought of climbing back into it is petrifying, but she needs her phone above all else. It's at least twenty meters away. How fast can she move? She's in so much pain simply standing here.

The pub is closer than the vehicle. She must run there first.

Before she can talk herself out of it, Hayley lumbers into the storm, moving as swiftly as she can, supporting her sore wrist. She reaches the stone-and-brick wall and rests against it, breathing in great shudders and trying not to collapse. There's a window alongside her and she steers away, in case Joost is on the other side. Imagines his pale eyes drilling into hers, his hungry sneer.

It would be easy to stay stuck here in her terror. She needs to move, has to get her hands on her phone. She crouches, slithers beneath the window. One hand tracing the wall, she creeps on until she reaches a second window, this one smaller, higher, perhaps for a bathroom. She ducks before passing beneath it.

Now the four-wheel drive is closer. Hayley draws a big breath, rushes across the empty space, and huddles by the car at last. She slides down against a tire and cries silently. Each movement terrifies her, yet she's so relieved to have made it this far. Water strikes the puddles around her, the shower meditative, almost hypnotic.

Move, Hayley, she thinks. *Get your phone. Stop wasting time.*

She wonders how to open a car door without setting off the interior light. Impossible. She can only hope Joost isn't watching. Then another thought occurs to her. What if the keys are still in the car? She could drive away, leave this place.

Would that be a terrible thing to do, to abandon Andrea and the others? Would she be capable of starting the engine and driving away before Joost raced out to investigate? To chase her down? Her wrist, which may be broken, means she can use only one arm, and she's not a very experienced driver in the first place.

She goes to the driver's door, rises slowly, and tries the handle. It lifts in her hand. She jerks the door open, leans into the stale air, and inspects the ignition. It's empty. No key. As she expected, the light globe has automatically come on. Hayley wriggles into the car, closes the door, and a second later the cabin is dark. She scrunches down, foraging for her phone. It was with her when she climbed in; she tried to take a photo of Joost and he knocked it from her hand.

The chip packet is still stuffed in the pocket of the door. There's a sports cap on the back seat, empty water bottles over the floor. Mementos from a happier, naïve time, only twenty-four hours earlier.

The light blinks on, and the car is filled with the sound of the storm.

"There you are," Joost says.

CHAPTER

30

Andrea

Wednesday, February 8
6 AM

ANDREA MARCHES TO her own room without breaking stride, without looking at the sleeping stranger. She feels bad; it's like the man is invisible, though it's the others who need protection now.

Her bedroom is dark, and the familiar furniture shapes are there. It's a world apart from what's happening outside. Ethan is breathing deeply, eyes closed. The pub is often rowdy, he's accustomed to sleeping through it, and she prays he will sleep for another hour yet. Her son, who celebrated his third birthday just a few months ago. They made the trip to Adelaide to see her parents, to throw him a family party around a gigantic store-bought cake. She took him to the city things he was missing out on: a play café, swimming pool, even a ride on a metro train. Ethan was overcome with much of it, subdued, clingy, except for the beach. He loved the beach. He ambled over the white sand in brand-new bathers and sun hat, sun block smeared across his nose, letting Matt hoist him and dangle his feet into the frothy tide. Andrea can still hear his excited squeals.

Joost mustn't go anywhere near Ethan. A rush of terror floods her body like hot pinpricks. She has to do this, has to carry on as if this is simply another morning while surreptitiously phoning the police, waiting until help arrives. Waiting until she can retrieve Hayley from her hiding spot. The girl is already on edge; Andrea can't leave her alone much longer. Maybe she could move her to another hut, lock the door, apply some quick first aid.

How long can it be before Joost discovers the girl isn't trussed to his bed?

She soundlessly withdraws from the room. Quinn is waiting in the corridor, eyes bright, a determined tilt to her chin.

"Come on," Andrea whispers.

They head to the kitchen, expressions stony.

Joost is not there. The two look at each other and continue on.

They are nearing the front bar when they hear screaming.

"That came from outside," Quinn gasps.

"Hayley," Andrea says.

She's frozen to the spot. Too much time has passed, and somehow Joost has found the girl. Part of her wants to run to her, part of her wants to rush back to Ethan. Her indecision is disrupted when Quinn charges ahead.

"Quinn, be careful!" Andrea hisses, following.

They reach the empty front bar. The sky should be growing lighter by now; instead, it remains dim as more stifling clouds arrive. The gloom is held back by an emergency lantern, its light fading too. Quinn gets low, scrambles across the floor to a window seat.

"Get down, he might see you!" Andrea says.

She joins Quinn against the wall, the floor below them patterned with dried mud from the night before. Andrea raises her head as much as she dares to gauge what's happening. Outside, the ghost gums are bending beneath sleet. Quinn's car is on their left, Joost's car slightly farther away, to their right. The internal car light is on, but no people are visible.

There's hollering. It's Joost. Andrea can't understand what he's saying, though it's clear he's angry. Then there's barking.

"Bronte!" Quinn says. "Oh my god, he better not hurt her."

"I can get to the sat phone."

"So what? There's no time to wait for anyone to—"

Hayley screams again.

"We have to go out there *now*." Quinn's face is pale.

"I know, I know," Andrea whispers.

She scans the room, heads back to the bar, scuttling along the floor like a spider, examines the shelves, looking for any sort of weapon. There's a large, hefty torch she could hit Joost with. That seems pathetic. What does she hope to do—run outside and strike him down? She tries to contain her shock and think clearly. There are knives in the kitchen, large blades for the meat, but it wouldn't take much for Joost to knock a knife from her hands, and then he would have it. Maybe the threat of the knife would be enough.

Quinn arrives at her shoulder. "What are you doing?"

"Searching for a weapon. We need something!"

"How about a gun?"

31

Quinn

Wednesday, February 8

"A GUN?"

Quinn nods. "Dad's old gun. It's in the back of my car."

"Shit, Quinn, I didn't know—"

"It's been locked up at the farm. I packed it yesterday."

"Do you know how to use it?"

"Yes, but . . ."

"But what?"

"I haven't fired it in years. Dad showed me how—we used to practice in the back paddock."

"I dunno . . ." There are smudges of mud on Andrea's face, and she looks like she hasn't slept in weeks.

"You're looking for a weapon, right?" Quinn says urgently. "What could be better?"

"Are you prepared to . . . you know . . . shoot him?"

"I'll shoot it in the air, and Joost will run. I bet you he will—anyone would."

"Is it loaded?"

"Not yet. The cartridges are in the car too."

"Oh, far out. How are you going to do this, Quinn? He'll see you."

There's more screaming and shouting from outside. More barking from Bronte.

"Andrea, we have to help!" Quinn stands up. She has to move, has to do something.

Without waiting for a response, she runs to the door and cracks it open. The car park is a swamp shining with the beginnings of sunrise. Bending low, as if it will make her invisible, immune to harm, Quinn sprints outside, the cool air quickly shrouding her.

She pauses by her front wheel, listening, trying to ascertain if Joost saw her. The smell of mud fills her nostrils. When she looks back, there is no sign of Andrea. The screaming and shouting has stopped, the rain has softened into a mist. Then Bronte barks—a deep, aggressive woof Quinn has never heard before—doing her best to be big and intimidating. Quinn wishes she could tell Bronte everything is going to be okay, she's coming, she hears her.

Then, "Hey, Quinn!"

Quinn freezes, heart thudding.

"Come and get your little dog. Before I bash its head in."

"Don't touch her!" Quinn roars.

"Oh, Quinnnnn!" Joost sings. "I know where you are, Quinn."

She clenches her entire body, steeling herself. She needs to get to the back of the car, needs to fetch the rifle.

"Why are you hiding, Quinn?" Joost calls. "Is this a game? Would you like to play hide-and-seek with me?"

She wishes he would stop using her name.

"I love Australia!" Joost continues. "I am having so much fun here. But I am sick and tired of this rain. I mean—I thought this country was supposed to be in drought. I came for a summer holiday. How funny is this?"

It sounds like he's moving position. Bronte yaps again. She must be okay. Where is Joost now? Is he creeping Quinn's way? She looks left and right, left and right again. Then there's another voice.

"Hey, Joost, what's going on?"

It's Andrea.

Quinn peers around the side of the car and sees her employer step off the verandah, her face a mask of concentration. She is so slight in stature, so exposed, yet resolute. Quinn cranes her neck farther to watch Andrea nearing two blurry figures. Joost stands over a teenage girl, one hand spread on her head to tame her as she sits on her backside in the mud. Her T-shirt and skirt are sodden and filthy, as if she's been plucked from an underground hole. Dark blood cakes her nose, and she's cradling one arm like she's holding an infant. It's a vision from a horror movie poster.

"Joost. Let her go, please," Andrea says loudly, squinting in the emerging sunlight.

Quinn retreats behind her car. While Andrea is distracting Joost, she inches around the vehicle, eases the boot ajar, and climbs in, pushing bags and packages aside until she finds the long rifle lying in its special gun bag, an innocuous blue and gray. Quinn pulls the zip down, notch by notch, and removes the rifle. It smells metallic and dusty, an object both foreign and evocative. For a moment she thinks of her father, how he showed her how to load it, how to hold the gun, how to lean in and look through the gunsights. There's a smaller red nylon bag beside it full of cartridge boxes, which she also opens. Any second now, she expects Joost to burst in and pull her onto the ground. She removes two cartridges from their neat stack, battling to steady her shaking fingers and insert the cartridges into the chamber.

Andrea continues to distract Joost. "Joost, she looks hurt. Let us help her." She's incredibly brave.

Quinn only hopes she can be brave too.

When the rifle's loaded, safety off and cocked, Quinn climbs from the car and creeps around to the side. She carries the gun in two hands, barrel pointing down. Sees Andrea, meters away. There is Joost. And there is the girl, Hayley, still on the ground, crying. Bronte springs around them, snapping and snarling. None of them have noticed Quinn, who's hidden behind one corner of her four-wheel drive.

She stares at Joost. He's a different person; he's not a friendly, obliging traveler, a naïve young backpacker crossing Australia alone and at risk. He is the risk. He's revealed himself, and Quinn sees someone ugly, malevolent. A threat to everyone here.

"You should go!" Andrea urges. "The police are coming."

"Oh, really?" Joost laughs. "Where are they? Just down the street?"

"We called them ages ago."

"You are lying, Andrea."

"It's the truth."

Joost presses his palms together as if in prayer. "Andrea, why are you treating me like this? I have been helping you since I got here. I scared that ugly biker away. I carried sandbags to save this shithole from the rain. You could not do any of that without me."

"What did you do to Hayley?"

"Oh. *Hayley?* So you two know each other?"

Andrea brushes slick curls from her eyes. "This is my place, and I don't want you here anymore. Get out of here!"

Joost's tone changes. "Do not tell me what to do. I am the one who is in charge. Now I am tired of this. We are all going to go back inside."

He steps toward Andrea. It is time for Quinn to reveal herself. She shuffles forward and plants her legs wide, hoists the rifle up and fights to keep it stable.

"Joost!" she shouts.

32

Andrea

Wednesday, February 8

A LL HEADS SWING toward Quinn. The young woman stands steady in the mud, eyes sparking, pointing a rifle at Joost. Relief and terror wash through Andrea. Quinn has her father's gun, but it raises the stakes. What happens now? What is Joost's next move?

Andrea slowly begins to slide out of range of the weapon, edging closer to Quinn. She wants to support the young woman and is unsure what to do. The feeble sunrise is behind Quinn's shoulder, clouds are massing together again, and the scene is cast in slate.

Joost shifts from foot to foot. It's not nerves, it's excitement. Glee.

"Ah, there you are, Quinn! A gun? What are you doing, Quinn?"

"Get out of here!" she says.

"Where did you get a gun? I thought they were banned in Australia. I am so glad you have found one—you can shoot that noisy little dog of yours."

He's goading Quinn. The more she has to think about, the greater the chance for confusion. Andrea prays Quinn will remain focused, prays the shouting will not wake Ethan and draw him outside.

"Joost, this is serious," Andrea says. "Quinn knows how to use the gun, and she will if she has to. You should get in your car and leave as fast as you can."

He shakes his head, chuckles. "That is not going to happen."

"Get in your car, or I will shoot your fucking head off," Quinn warns.

"You are not going to shoot me. I have not done anything wrong. I am a tourist, I am not harmful. You women have all of this confused; you are hysterical about nothing. Put the gun down."

Hayley snaps to life, her face a snarl. "What about Scott? You beat him up! You left him lying on the road!"

"Scotty boy? Actually, he is fine. He is nearby."

Hayley stares up at him. "You dumped him. I saw you."

"Scott is alive and well."

"You're lying."

"Who's Scott?" Quinn says.

Joost gives a slow laugh. "That pathetic person you have been playing nursey with. The boring, sleeping guy. He is Hayley's boyfriend."

Andrea's heart races. It's as she guessed. And all this time, Joost has been pretending to care about Scott's condition. He helped Andrea and Quinn to babysit the man, yet he's the one who beat him and discarded him. Did he mean for the man to die? Andrea suppresses the tremor taking over her arms and legs. The threatening sky, her cold skin, the thought that Joost could be a killer.

"You like fussing around him, don't you, Quinn?" Joost says. "You thought you were a real hero, finding him on the road. Well, I was the one who put him there, you silly bitches."

"Why?" Hayley screams. "Why are you doing this? What's wrong with you?"

"You would not understand," Joost says. "You and your tiny brain."

Andrea holds up her phone like it's a grenade she's about to throw.

"The police are on their way." Her voice wavers so much that she wonders if anyone will believe her.

Joost leers. "I will tell you what happens next. Quinn will put the gun down. Then we can all go inside and talk."

"No way." Quinn is resolute.

"Do you want Hayley to freeze? Look at her—she needs to be inside." Joost prods Hayley's head, and she yelps.

Bronte darts in close, a red blur, latching on to Joost's calf. He bellows, and they turn into a writhing, furious tangle. Joost hammers blows onto the dog, bending from his great height, straining to beat her off, while Bronte slews left and right, her determined jaw clamped shut. Quinn racks the bolt of the gun, points skyward, and pulls the trigger. There's an explosion in Andrea's ears. Bronte tears away, tail down, disappearing around the side of the pub. Quinn staggers, then corrects herself. Joost clutches his bitten leg, breathing hard, his face twisted in agony and anger. Good, Andrea thinks, he's suffering now.

"Is that supposed to scare me?" he screams at Quinn.

"Hey!"

It's another voice. A man's voice, coming from the Pindarry.

They wheel around.

The stranger, the unconscious man Quinn found, is meters away on the verandah, propped against one of the pillars.

"Scott!" Hayley cries.

33

Quinn

Wednesday, February 8

QUINN STARES. "You're awake."

The man she found on the road. Scott. He looks at them through eyes that are slits. He's listing to one side, but at least he's upright. Thunder booms from far away, and Quinn fights an urge to run to him, to support him and stop him from dissolving into a heap. He shouldn't be out here, he should have stayed safely inside.

"Oh, look who has decided to show up," Joost says.

"Be careful!" Quinn tells Scott. There is so much energy coursing through her body that she might drop the gun. Rage and fear are battling for control. Her hands are ice cold, and she doesn't know how much longer she can hold the weapon.

"Oh, Scott," Joost says. "Look at you. You are a mess."

"You bastard," Scott says.

"I have to give you some credit. You are tougher than I thought."

Hayley rises to her feet, and Joost grabs the neck of her T-shirt, yanking her back. Quinn maintains her grip on the gun, looking from person to person, trying to keep ahead of whatever might happen.

"Scott, are you all right?" Andrea asks. She is closest to him and the verandah, five meters separating them, with Quinn farther away.

He doesn't respond.

"I'm sorry," Hayley moans. "I'm *so sorry*. This trip was all my idea, Scott; it's all my fault . . ." She's curled into a shivering ball.

Joost laughs. "All your idea? You still think that? You are so clueless."

Scott lurches off the verandah, holding his stomach and grimacing in pain. Quinn keeps the gun trained on Joost, who's standing and dripping, while her eyes flit back to Scott. He's shorter than Joost, carries more weight too. He's wearing track pants, one of Matt's T-shirts. Nothing on his feet. Despite his wooziness, despite his injuries, he looks angry enough to throw himself at the Dutchman. He might think he's helping them, but he's in no condition to fight.

"Go back inside the pub, please!" Quinn urges him.

"Yes, go back into the pub, have another lie-down," Joost says. "I can take care of this."

Quinn is sickened by Joost. How can he act like he's in charge when there's a wall of people facing him and she's holding a gun?

"You're a traitor," Scott says. "You wanted to get rid of me. You tried to kill me. Twice."

"Oh, come on, I was never going to kill you," Joost says.

"You held a pillow over my face!"

Quinn hears Andrea gasp. Her own mind is working to put the pieces together. Last night, when she found Scott unresponsive, she thought it was because of his injuries. She and Andrea had been checking the outer buildings, and when they returned, Joost was puffed, waiting behind the bar. Close to where Scott was on the couch. They'd left him to look after Ethan. Anything could have happened.

"Look, you are still standing." Joost shrugs. "I have to say, Scott—you play dead really well. Just like Hayley during sex? That is what you told me, right?"

Hayley's mouth falls open. "Scott?"

"Shut up!"

"It is all part of the adventure, right, Scott, my bro?"

"He's not your bro!" Hayley spits. "We hate you!"

"Wrong again, my dumb, dumb, Hayley," Joost says. "Scott is my buddy."

"What are you talking about?" The girl's eyes dart between the two males.

"We're not friends, not anymore!" Scott says. "You tried to get rid of me. You wanted everything all to yourself."

Joost sneers. "Stop screeching like a girl—"

"You drove away! You did it deliberately."

"Hey, I ran out of patience." Joost is unsmiling now. The weather has flattened his hair, emphasized the menacing twist to his face.

"What about Livia? You didn't wait for me. You were supposed to wait."

"Livia is gone. You know that."

Quinn shifts position, blinks the rain from her eyes. She doesn't like the way they speak to Hayley, the confusing story they're weaving. Who is Livia?

Bronte returns, trotting anxious circles nearby.

"Scott? What are you talking about?" Hayley's voice wavers.

Scott glares through puffy eyes. "I told you to shut the fuck up! I don't know how I put up with you for so long!" He doubles over, whether from agony or anger, Quinn can't tell.

"Leave her alone!" Quinn shouts.

Scott looks at her, as if he's just realized she's standing there with a rifle. "Who are you?"

Joost hoots. "Ha—fantastic! He does not even know you, Quinn. You rescued him, and he does not even know you exist."

Quinn stares at Scott. Alive, moving, talking. The man she rescued, the man they've been taking shifts to care for. He's not a good guy; he isn't troubled by Hayley and her injuries. He's not on their side. Somehow Joost and Scott are connected. They had something planned, and Hayley knew nothing about it.

"Ladies, there is no help coming." Joost feigns mournfulness. "Your husband left you here, Andrea. The police are hours away, the doctors have more important things to do . . ."

Andrea steps closer to Quinn's side, says something, and while Quinn can't tell what, she feeds on the reassuring tone.

"Are you going to shoot or what?" Joost says. "You have one bullet left, correct? Do you think you can hit me? You might miss and shoot Hayley. Even if you hit me, I can still come for you. Scott might come for you . . ."

Scott regards Quinn, arms by his side, hands clenched into fists, as drenched as the rest of them now.

Joost pushes his shoulders back, flexing, seeming to grow even taller. "I am not leaving. I have come a long way for this holiday. And I have nowhere else to be."

Andrea's hand presses cautiously on the small of Quinn's back, helping her to stay upright, and Quinn draws strength from the solid warmth.

Joost takes a step in the mud. "Put down the gun. Let us all go inside, get dry. We will explain everything. Maybe you will feel better if you have a drink."

"No." Andrea's voice is a whisp of air behind Quinn.

"I promise, we will not hurt you." Joost takes another step. "We will talk and sort everything out. Let me explain, and you will understand."

Hayley begins wailing, and it's like a spell has broken. Quinn feels a bump against her side, then Andrea is ripping the rifle from her hands. She gapes as Andrea points the gun at Joost and pulls the trigger.

It's ten times as loud as the thunder was.

Joost flies backwards onto the ground.

Nobody moves, trapped inside the echo of the bullet.

EPILOGUE

Quinn

Wednesday, October 4

S PRING IS HERE, the land has dried, and soon they will face the heat again, each day beginning and ending with a flaming sun that seems intent on scorching away their presence. For now though, it's a dusky lightbulb on the horizon, and there are geometric shadows around the two four-wheel drives and the minivan in the Pindarry car park.

Chelsea is behind the bar, keeping an eye on things. Her London accent is chirpy, and from her seat on the veranda, Quinn can hear it floating above the country music playing on the radio. Chelsea's a backpacker with a working visa, intent on soaking up the sun every day. She goes on long walks around the property, and her arms and legs are already more tanned than Quinn's. She knows the Joost story, of course, everyone in the nation does. Except Chelsea doesn't prod for information, and Quinn appreciates that.

They had a dry winter, nothing like the freakish rainfall of February. A February they will never forget. Trade has been busier than usual, with visitors drawn to the site of the tragedy. Their eyes flick over Quinn's face when they meet, nervous about what to say, what to ask, what they're allowed to mention. Later, if they stay into the evening—and especially after a few drinks—their questions emerge.

How is Quinn feeling these days?

How about Andrea? And Hayley? Do they keep in touch?

How much jail time does she think Scott will get?

What was Joost like? Was he charming? Did he really dupe everyone?

What is it like to still live in this isolated part of the world? Is she ever scared?

Quinn has perfected a response.

She offers the slightest of smiles and says, "That's not something I talk about. Now—is there anything else I can get you?"

There's a sign at the entrance: No Media Allowed. Matt put it there, and while it doesn't keep all journalists away, it does set the tone for their pub visitors.

Journalists had flocked to the Pindarry when the news of the "backpacker deaths" got out. They rang so often, Matt took the phone off the hook. Drones flew overhead. The police sent a media manager, who stayed in one of the accommodation huts for a week. They set up a cordon around the car park, and media vans had no choice but to park farther afield, journalists kipping in sleeping bags and slinking to and from the pub's lavatories. Headlines screamed about The Pindarry Killings. The story took up four, six—sometimes eight—newspaper pages. There were photos of the pub, fuzzy far-off pictures of Andrea and Quinn moving around the property, images of Hayley and the others torn from social media sites and used without permission. A portrait of Joost, taken from his university's website, a tidy young man in collar and tie, his pale face-clean shaven, hair slicked back, lips smirking. There was even a photo of Bronte, resting on her haunches with an outback sunset behind her, her mouth hanging open in the grin of every dog that's sure of her place in the world.

Quinn tried to avoid all the stories, until an online piece by the BBC in England helped her make sense of things as the court proceedings against Scott inched slowly on.

It described two unstable young men who met via an online first-person-shooter game. Their misogynistic live chat led to them being banned, and once they were outsiders, they formed a stronger bond. They moved to an app, exchanging dozens of private messages each day. They discovered mutual interests and desires: a common apathy for the world, a frustration with the routine life laid out before them—a boring career, a boring marriage. They were enraged by the young women who posed in bathers and skimpy gym gear on their social media profiles yet refused to chat with them. Joost was the more gregarious, the more aggressive of the pair. Scott was brooding, disaffected, keen to find a comrade who could lead the way. They concocted a plan for Joost to travel to Australia to join Scott, for them both to pretend not to know each other and take Hayley and another young woman to the remote outback. There, they would have the time and isolated setting to play real-world games with the girls.

They hadn't accounted for the storms and flooded roads, and Joost tore up their plan, thriving on the growing mayhem.

Livia first, trapped in the car with Joost. They would never know the full story of what happened to the Brazilian girl, what she thought in her final moments, how hard she fought back. Her remains were spotted by a passing truck driver, thirty meters from the road on a stretch of dirt that had dried up after the rain. Quinn saw Livia's family crying on television and quickly switched it off.

At Scott's trial, they learned Joost had raped and strangled Livia. Then Joost found Scott pursuing them on foot and bragged about what he'd done. They fought and Joost won, throwing Scott into the back of his grandfather's car. Next, he retrieved Hayley as she walked the darkening road.

The BBC story relayed how Quinn discovered Scott. Other news coverage made a lot of that angle—how she had brought Scott to the pub, "nurturing the predator." How she and Andrea had nursed him, all without knowing he was a would-be rapist and killer. TV show panelists talked about the young men's odious plan, shuddering dramatically on camera, speculating as to what else might have happened. As if the events hadn't been terrible enough already. And there were petitions for a government inquiry into the impact of violent online games.

Mostly, the media portrayed Quinn and Andrea as heroines, feisty outback women who could take care of themselves. Quinn, who raced outside and retrieved her father's rifle; Andrea, the young mother holding the fort without power or communications while her husband helped a neighbor fight flooding.

Andrea, who grabbed the gun and shot Joost dead when he threatened them all.

Andrea didn't share news of her pregnancy until weeks later, after the police announced that no charges would be laid against her. She'd been worried about going to court, maybe spending time in jail. Quinn and Matt sat either side of her when she got the call from her lawyer, holding her while she cried tears of relief.

No matter how the media tried—no matter what dramatic music their stories used or how often they stalked the property—they could not capture the terror Quinn had felt. The numbness of seeing Joost fall, blood clouding his torso. How she had removed the gun from Andrea's hands and trained it on Scott. He had been cowed and compliant with his accomplice dead in the mud. Confused, forgetting the gun was no longer loaded. They locked him in a hut.

Quinn doesn't know if she will ever stop reimagining what might have happened. It's not healthy, it's not helping her recover, and still she can't help herself.

Joost had spent the night with them, had slept meters away. Why didn't he attack? Perhaps there was safety in numbers. Perhaps he wanted to dispatch Hayley first. Maybe he was enjoying the power and knowledge he had over them.

There were so many what-ifs.

What if the rain hadn't come?

What if Livia hadn't jumped into the car with Joost?

What if Quinn hadn't packed her father's gun?

*   *   *

At the height of the media frenzy, Quinn slipped into her car one day before dawn, Bronte following. None of the journalists roused from their camper vans, no one pursued her. Bronte licked Quinn's nose, and she laughed.

After more than an hour of driving, the road curved as they neared the edge of the property. They reached the turnoff and took the narrow farm road. They slowed down at the dip, Quinn gazed outside, and Bronte whined and wriggled.

The dam had transformed from a parched basin to a vast pool of bronze water.

"I suppose we better take a quick look."

Quinn sauntered over to the dam's edges. Bronte snuffled along, paws following the perimeter, taking care not to get wet. Quinn knelt and extended her fingers into the water as if checking it was real. It felt incredibly cool, silky. She stayed crouching, entranced.

"Water," she whispered. "All this water and nobody here to use it."

Still, she was determined to get value from it. She took her phone from her pocket and snapped photos of the dam from different angles and texted them to the land agent to add to the listing. Then she texted them to her mother and brother, adding a smiley face. The three of them had been in close contact since the awful event, with Trish joining her daughter in the city when she gave her police statements, holding her hand in the interview rooms, hugging her close in their hotel room at night.

Quinn whistled for Bronte to return to the car and climbed behind the steering wheel, feeling a familiar, expectant tingle as she neared her family home.

When she saw the farmhouse in the distance, she slowed, awestruck.

"It looks so different, Bronte. Take a look at that."

The rain-washed roofs, the budding grass, the moist fields. Milk thistle weeds had sprouted yellow flowers; two crows perched in a river red gum. The storm had turned the place into an inaccurate imitation of the Durand home, a painting using alternative colors. Quinn knew it was the right time to say goodbye.

*   *   *

A week before Scott's second court appearance in Adelaide, Chelsea handed Quinn her tablet.

"I found something," she said. "It's a blog by an investigative journo in the Netherlands. It's translated, but most of it's in English anyway. Looks like Scott kept screenshots for insurance. Either that or it was his sicko diary."

"What does it say?"

"You should read it yourself. It explains a few things. Come and fetch me if you need to talk." She smiled fleetingly and left Quinn alone to read.

The news blog had dozens of online messages exchanged between Joost and Scott more than eight months before

Joost arrived in Australia. The first few were innocuous gossip about their fellow gamers, which soon turned to derision toward female players. Joost began to write about what he wanted to do to two female players in particular, while Scott egged him on. The messages were violent, disturbing in their graphic detail of forced fellatio and more.

At that point the game's moderators expelled them. The screenshots changed format and became their private messages. Then Scott began complaining about Hayley and what she wouldn't do during sex. Joost's replies were taunting and provocative, so much so that Quinn wondered why Scott remained friends with a guy two years younger, on the other side of the world. Joost criticized Scott's manhood and supported him at the same time, somehow keeping him loyal. It was a toxic coaching relationship.

Ultimately, it was Scott who suggested Joost come to Australia. Quinn read the messages at speed, scanning months of correspondence, sickened by their premeditation.

> *You should fly here.*
> *We can get up to some real shit.*

Dude I am not fucking your girlfriend
for you lol she sounds limp

> *It's simple.*
> *We head out bush. No people out there.*

No rules either?

> *Hayley is in.*
> *She legit thinks the road trip is her idea.*

Dang you CAN do something right then?

> *Now we need one more.*

We look online when I am in Oz

> *Holy shit do you think this is gonna work?*

The hardest part will be cleaning up after
Can you lie and keep the lies straight?

> *Dude, I am an expert at lying at this point.*

> *We pretend we ALL got lost.*
> *The girls and us. Happens all the*
> *time here.*

Yeh. Then girls don't get found.
We wander out later

> *Cool.*
> *We need to come out at different places.*
> *That means we split up.*

Are you sure you will not cry about
Hayley?!! Lol

> *Fck off.*

Quinn's hands shook when she turned the tablet facedown on the couch and bolted from the room. She vowed she would do everything she could to ensure Scott spent as much time in jail as possible.

*   *   *

In September, Andrea gave birth to a girl. Quinn made the long drive to Adelaide, observing the parched landscape morph into yellow wheat and barley fields as she traveled south. She stopped at small towns to refuel and stretch her legs, acclimatizing to the growing number of people around her. At the hospital, she wandered the polished floors, trying not to bump into rushing nurses, searching for directions to the correct ward. When she found Andrea's hospital room, Matt wrapped her in a gentle bear hug.

"Congratulations on selling the farm."

"Thanks. I'm so relieved," Quinn said, moving on to embrace Andrea, who was propped up in bed.

"Do you know much about the new owners?" Matt asked.

"No. It's a big pastoral company. They won't even use the house; they just want the land. Good luck to them."

"It's wonderful news—and maybe a little sad too?" Andrea said.

Quinn nodded. "Yeah, it's definitely bittersweet. But it's the best thing for everyone. In a way, we said goodbye to the farm a long time ago. Anyway—congratulations to you two!"

She bent over the crib by Andrea's bed, drinking in the baby's wide face, the tightly shut eyes, the curled fingers—pale pink and gray, like a fresh bruise. Maddie was cocooned in a soft blanket. What life awaited her? Quinn felt a rush of fierce affection; she couldn't imagine how protective Maddie's parents felt.

Matt left to fetch Ethan from Andrea's parents' house, and Quinn and Andrea held each other for a long time.

"So you're definitely coming back?" Quinn asked, breaking the silence. Months earlier, Andrea had shared her misgivings about living at the Pindarry with a new baby.

"Yes. Absolutely." Quinn felt Andrea nodding.

They pulled apart. Andrea's curls were a halo around her face and she looked vulnerable beneath the sheets, wearing a loose nightshirt that exposed her collarbone. "We've had enough of the city—all three of us," she said.

Quinn smiled in agreement, thinking of the countless traffic lights on the way in. Circling the hospital car park below ground, searching for a space. Horn blasts ricocheting between concrete pillars.

"I'm not going to let fear drive me away. Up north is where I want to be," Andrea continued. "It might sound silly, but I've only been in town a couple of weeks, and I'm homesick already."

"It's not silly at all."

"It's like we have our own separate part of the world up there—you know? None of this hustle and bustle."

"I know exactly what you mean."

"Besides, Matt is going to build a . . . cellar where we can be safe in emergencies."

"A cellar? You mean, like a bunker? That could be good for bushfires too. I've heard of farms doing that."

Andrea sighed, relaxed back into her pillows. "I'm so glad you didn't say panic room. I thought you might laugh at the idea. You don't think it's over the top? A bit paranoid?"

"No, it's a brilliant idea. As long as there's room inside for me and Bronte too."

"Of course!"

The pair held hands and grinned.

Hayley arrived ten minutes later, pausing in the doorway with a bouquet of lilies. Her hair had grown longer, soft strands threaded behind her ears. She wore white jeans and a long-sleeved T-shirt even though it was a warm day outside.

"Come in, come in," Andrea urged. "Meet Maddie."

Quinn led Hayley to the cot. Hayley's eyes softened as she contemplated the baby, and the other two let her take her time. Then Quinn pulled two chairs closer to Andrea's bedside.

Hayley smiled as she took her seat. "I feel like I'm at this hospital all the time."

"How do you mean?" Quinn said.

"This is where I come for my counseling. It's on the sixth floor."

"Oh. Is that helping?"

"I think so, though I still have nightmares."

"Me too," Quinn said, "and I'm sure mine are nowhere near as scary as yours."

"Sometimes I'm too scared to close my eyes. I dream about Joost, and that's supposed to be normal. I dream we're at the pub, sometimes other places, but he's always got that . . . creepy smile on his face. So comfortable, so sure of himself. You know?"

Quinn and Andrea nodded.

"In some dreams Livia is there and she's shouting at Joost. She was such an amazing person. She didn't deserve what happened to her."

"I wish I'd met her," Quinn said.

"You would have liked her. I'm sad Brazil is so far away and I didn't have the money to go to her funeral. It felt wrong, you know? That I couldn't be there."

"Sure, but you're in touch with her parents," Andrea said. "You sent them photos of Livia, and we all donated to her climate fund. That means a lot to them."

"I still can't believe what Scott did. I thought I knew him." Hayley studied her fingers. "He was planning to hurt me, he was planning to—"

"Oh, hon, nobody could suspect their boyfriend of anything like that."

"I can't stop going over it, looking for signs. Everything he said, the way he said it. I thought he was going on the road trip to please me. I thought he hated Joost. They tricked me. They tricked Livia."

Quinn and Andrea listened to Hayley while hospital staff bustled past the open door. The sky was bright blue and cloudless on the other side of the windows.

"Scott's mum even phoned our house. She wanted to speak to me."

"What did you do?" Andrea asked.

Hayley stared at the hard floor. "I couldn't do it, I couldn't talk to her. I told my dad to take a message. His sister has texted me a bunch of times too."

"I guess they're trying to understand."

"Maybe I'll talk to them one day, just not yet."

Quinn reached across and held one of Hayley's hands. It seemed to help, because Hayley took a deep breath, mustering a fresh smile.

"You know you can call us anytime," Quinn said. "We'll stay in touch."

"I'd like that."

"I'll give you updates on Maddie," Andrea said.

"And I'll give updates on Bronte," Quinn said.

They giggled.

"Guess what?" Hayley said.

"What?"

"I'm going back to uni next year. I'm going to finish my degree."

"That's fantastic." Quinn beamed.

*   *   *

The ghost gums seem taller, watered so well earlier in the year. Inside the Pindarry, Chelsea waits on a group of elderly tourists from Victoria. They occupy two tables, drinking tap beer from glass jugs. A young couple strolls arm in arm along the fence line. They're from Tasmania, in their late twenties, and stop frequently to take photos on their phones.

In a few days, Andrea and Matt will be home with the children. It's going to be a squeeze, with a newborn baby and the equipment that comes with her, and so Matt has arranged for a caravan to be delivered. It will be air conditioned and heated, with beds at either end, and Quinn and Chelsea will move in there. Quinn thinks it's time to give Andrea's family their own space, although Andrea insisted she could keep her bedroom.

A new year is approaching, and Quinn wonders what's next. She could move down south and live with her mother, find another job in one of the many pubs or cellar doors. Ryan has invited her to join him in Canberra; he says there are plenty of junior administration jobs in Treasury and he would help with her written application. Quinn heard a weather forecast yesterday, warning that Canberra was set to experience freakish snow. She's never seen snow before. It could be fun.

Or Quinn could stay here at the Pindarry, more than a thousand kilometers from the city. She could reenroll in university online, studying between stints at the front bar, working toward a future that is as amorphous as it is somehow promising. She's been reading about an introduction to veterinary studies, and that's the option that appeals most.

Her shift begins in thirty minutes. She rests on a veran-dah bench and drinks in the vast horizon, blazing pink, ochre, and yellow. When the sun has gone down, the air will become crisp and visitors will retrieve jackets and bean-ies from their cars. This is her favorite time, this gateway between day and night, between hot and cold, the junction of change.

A rotund little shape comes trotting from behind one of the visitor cars. Bronte has been sniffing strange tires, deci-phering scents transported from far away. On light paws, she runs to Quinn, bumping her leg, demanding to be stroked.

Quinn slings an arm around the dog and pulls her close, buries her nose in her neck.

"I love you too," she says.

ACKNOWLEDGMENTS

THANK YOU, MELANIE Ostell. You made an extraordinary contribution to *The Rush* to get it into the best possible shape, and I'm very grateful to call you my agent.

Thank you, Cass Di Bello and the team at Simon & Schuster ANZ for believing in the manuscript. You connected to Quinn and Co. with a passion, and our meeting was the most exciting Zoom of my life. Thank you to Crooked Lane Books for taking on this Aussie thriller; it feels magical that it'll be available to more readers around the world!

Thank you, the Ladies Who Graze: Bianca, Bec, and Jane. Fellow booklovers, cheer squad, and comic relief.

Thank you, Aunty Angela, a ball of energy, an inspiration, the keenest reader I know. Honestly. Nobody else phones to chat about a book.

Thanks for your patience, Dad, I finally got there. And no, I'm not rich yet.

Thank you, Able and Kalyn, so adept at treading that fine line of being family champions and honest early readers. (Not to mention providing the Canadian backdrop for my author photographs.)

Thank you, Sam. Your presence makes the lonely work of manuscript writing easier, especially when you help me bounce around a phrase or find the right contemporary music reference.

Thank you, David, for making my writing possible and for not questioning my zigzag career choices—or at least, keeping your raised eyebrows to yourself.

Thank you to all the talented authors who took the time to read my thriller debut and provide a blurb; you're very busy people, and I truly appreciate it. Thank you, Writers SA, for the wonderful classes you provide and your manuscript assessment service: an incredible fillip for this story, my first indication I wasn't imagining that it could work.

Thank you, dear bookshops, booksellers, and libraries, the front line of reading recommendations. Thank you, book reviewers, bloggers, Bookstagrammers and BookTokers. Sadly, authors aren't as lauded as rock stars or sport stars are, so the love, attention, and spotlight you place on books can uplift and keep an author going.

Finally, thank you to the real Bronte, my little butternut pumpkin, heel nipper, lover of the chase. There's a lot of themes in this novel; I hope the unwavering devotion of a dog isn't lost among them.